P9-CSA-094

characters, humor, and understanding of what it means to be part of a family make each of her novels a treat to be savored."

—Jill Marie Landis, author of *Magnolia Creek*

"Delightful romances involving colorful and yet realistic characters make these two stories by Maureen Child a veritable feast for the eyes. The large Italian family of the Candellanos is very convincing and the characterizations are so mature and honest that the author is to be applauded for such skillful crafting and accurate portrayal . . . the heartfelt emotions leap from the pages, and the delicately blended humor and pathos render these stories memorable . . . after the exhilarating first story, readers will feel compelled to read the other one too, and neither disappoints. Maureen Child is an author to watch out for."

—*The Road to Romance*

"A fresh tale of family, conflict, and love . . . the characters are endearing."

—*Old Book Barn Gazette*

"Both of these novels are engaging contemporary romances with a warm ensemble that feels like the kitchen of many readers. The story lines will hook readers because the characters seem genuine and friendly."

—*Harriet's Book Review*

"Fall in love with this delightful family with these two tales, and prepare yourself for the next installment."

—TheRomanceReader.com

ST. MARTIN'S PAPERBACKS TITLES
BY MAUREEN CHILD

Finding You

Knowing You

Loving You

Some Kind of Wonderful

And Then Came You

$3.50

EXTRAORDINARY PRAISE FOR MAUREEN CHILD AND HER NOVELS

Some Kind of Wonderful

"The terrific Child introduces readers to some wonderful new characters and a very special town. Blending the power of love and forgiveness, Child will touch your heart."

—Romantic Times

"Child deftly invokes the full range of human emotion . . . thoroughly satisfying."

—Booklist

"A touching story of friendship, deep love and scorching passion . . . A very good read."

—Old Book Barn Gazette

"A heartwarming read filled with a terrific cast of characters."

—Rendezvous Review

"Romance and sexual tension . . . charming, emotional."

—RoadToRomance.com

BOOK RACK
1717 S. AIR DEPOT

MORE . . .

Loving You

"The boisterous Candellanos are back . . . in this latest heartwarmer."

—Romantic Times

"Packed with very strong characters and lots of emotion . . . an unforgettable story, and a romance to treasure."

—A Romance Review

"Maureen Child always writes a guaranteed winner, and this is no exception. Heartwarming, sexy, and impossible to put down."

—Susan Mallery, bestselling author of The Sparkling One

Finding You/Knowing You

"An absolutely wonderful contemporary romance. A delightful blend of humor and emotion, this sexy love story will definitely keep readers turning the pages."

—Kristin Hannah, author of Distant Shores

"The Candellano family is warm and wonderful . . . you'll get swept up in the lives and loves of these passionate and fascinating individuals."

—Romantic Times

"Maureen Child infuses her writing with the perfect blend of laughter, tears, and romance. Her well-crafted

A Crazy Kind of Love

Mike's Story

Maureen Child

St. Martin's Paperbacks

NOTE: If you purchased this book without a cover you should be aware that this book is stolen property. It was reported as "unsold and destroyed" to the publisher, and neither the author nor the publisher has received any payment for this "stripped book."

A CRAZY KIND OF LOVE: MIKE'S STORY

Copyright © 2005 by Maureen Child.

All rights reserved. No part of this book may be used or reproduced in any manner whatsoever without written permission except in the case of brief quotations embodied in critical articles or reviews. For information address St. Martin's Press, 175 Fifth Avenue, New York, NY 10010.

ISBN: 0-312-99753-1
EAN: 80312-99753-3

Printed in the United States of America

St. Martin's Paperbacks edition / January 2005

St. Martin's Paperbacks are published by St. Martin's Press, 175 Fifth Avenue, New York, NY 10010.

10 9 8 7 6 5 4 3 2 1

For Jeff and Amber Clausi
To celebrate their little miracle,
Reese
I hope your new little boy fills your
World with bugs and frogs and baseball
And sticky fingered hugs.
Oh! And tell Lucky and Bullseye
To watch their backs!

ACKNOWLEDGMENTS

My thanks to Jennifer Enderlin, Super Editor, who always knows how to bring out the best in a writer. Jen, thanks for asking for "more."

And to Susan Mallery—a great writer and an even better friend—for helping me define "more." You're the best, Susan.

1

Michaela "Mike" Marconi had never really planned on being a stalker.

It just worked out that way.

"You moved the balcony." A statement, more than a question, and he didn't sound happy about it. The deep male voice came from right behind her and Mike winced before she turned to face him.

"You're back early," she said, ignoring his accusation to throw one of her own. "Thought you were going to be gone until tomorrow."

"I came back early," Lucas Gallagher pointed out, biting off every single word, "because I knew *you'd* be here."

"Aw," Mike said, smiling in the face of the fury gripping the tall man looming over her. "You missed me."

His mouth opened and closed a few times as he sputtered and steam lifted off the top of his head. But Mike was used to this kind of reaction from him. And sure enough, he found his voice again a moment later.

"You are the most infuriating woman. Every time I turn around, there you are . . ." He was off and running, listing every way she'd been driving him insane for the

last couple of months. And since she'd heard it all before, she zoned out.

Instead of listening, she just watched him. And she
had to admit, Lucas made quite a picture. Tall, with
sharp-planed features, his face looked as though it had
been carved by a hasty yet talented sculptor. He had high
cheekbones, a square jaw, and chocolate-brown eyes behind wire-rimmed glasses. His too long light brown
hair was pulled into a ponytail at the back of his neck,
and his starched, dark blue dress shirt was tucked into
sharply creased black slacks. Tall and leanly muscled,
he was practically quivering with outrage.

Except, he was way too masculine to *quiver*. Maybe
just *vibrating*, she thought idly, enjoying the fact that
she was getting to him.

Mike was pretty much used to Lucas being mad.
The man had spent the last two months fighting her on
every little thing she'd "suggested" for his house. Even
when she was right.

Which she always was.

While he ranted, she let her gaze slide over the nearly
completed house and felt a small sigh of envy whisper
inside her. Tall trees surrounded the yard spreading out
in front of the two-story structure, and behind the house,
the lake's clear blue water rippled with every sigh of
wind. Shade dappled the yard and a soft breeze danced
through the trees, easing back the September heat.

By all rights, this should have been *her* house. She'd
been saving every stray dollar for years—had even
continued living at the family home with her father rather
than spend money on rent—all in the name of buying this
one piece of land and building her dream house. In her

mind, she knew every crack and corner of the place she would build. She knew where every window would go, what kind of cabinets to put in, and exactly the right front door.

It should have been perfect.

Until of course, that day earlier this summer, when she'd stopped to enjoy the peace and quiet and had, instead, found Lucas Gallagher telling her that she was on private property. Grace Van Horn, the very same woman who'd been driving the Marconi Construction firm nutso this summer, had sold the land out from under Mike. The fact that the older woman hadn't even known she was interested in the property was Mike's damn fault.

For which she'd been kicking her own ass all summer long.

So instead of building her dream home, she was here every week, trying to turn Lucas's house into the place she'd always wanted.

Did she feel a little bit guilty?

Sure.

But hey, being Catholic taught a person early not only how to live with guilt—but to be a master at it.

Besides, she'd been working in construction since she was old enough to hold a hammer. Who better to tell him what he was doing wrong with this house?

"—and who the hell told you that you could move the balcony?" Lucas demanded, finally pausing for breath.

"Of course I moved the balcony," Mike said, stepping past him to point up at the framework for the deck spearing off the second-story master bedroom. "If you'd left it where you wanted it, you would have had the sun blasting into your bedroom every afternoon around fourish. Does the word 'west' mean anything to you?"

He grabbed her arm, turned her around to face him, and leaned down to look her square in the eye. She felt the strength in his grip, but wasn't the least bit concerned. There was nothing violent about Lucas Gallagher. Sexy, though? Oh yeah. Despite the flash of fury in his gaze, something warm and liquid unspooled through her bloodstream. Mike ignored it—as she had been doing for the last two months. She wasn't interested in the nerd prince. She *was* interested in this house.

"I *wanted* to be able to watch the sunset," he said.

She laughed. For a smart man, he was really making some dumb decisions. "Hard to do when your retinas are burned out from too much sunlight. Not to mention it would have been hot enough in your bedroom come summer that you'd have been gasping for air and wishing you'd listened to me about the air-conditioning." She pulled free of his grasp. "Besides, you can still see the sunset. All you have to do is step out onto the balcony and look to the side. The way God intended."

He stared at her. "Are you *ever* wrong?"

Sarcasm colored every word, but she took the question seriously, tipped her head back, thought about it for a long minute, then said, "No . . . I don't think so."

"Why am I not surprised?"

Mike smiled. "Because, clearly, you're an intelligent man."

"Uh-huh." He let go of her and shook his head. "Well, I don't care if you *are* right. I want the balcony where it was supposed to go."

She frowned at him. "You're just being stubborn, now."

He folded his arms over his chest. "I wanted that balcony where *I* put it, damn it."

"You won't like it."

"Hell, I'll like it just because *you* won't."

"That's mature," she muttered.

"And even if I don't like it—I'll tear it down later with my bare hands. But *I'll* do it." He pointed over at the house just behind him and said, "You know, I had plans. Good plans. Designed by the top architect in San Francisco. And every damn time I turn around, you're changing something."

"For the better," she countered, just as hotly. "Your architect might be the shiznit in the city, but he doesn't know squat about Chandler. Or this property."

He barked out a laugh. "And you do?"

She leaned in farther, almost brushing her nose with his. "You're damn right I do," she snapped. "I know every inch of this property. I know the lake and where it crests during a rainy season. I know which way the land drains during the storms. I know everything there is to know about this place because it was supposed to be *mine*."

He ground his back teeth together, sucked in a gulp of air, and said, "But it's *not* yours, is it, Mike? It's *mine*."

Yes, damn it. It was his. All of it. Her special place. Her thinking spot. The one place in the world she'd always run to when she needed to get away from whatever was happening in her life.

And now she was a trespasser.

"You don't have to rub it in."

"Apparently, I *do*."

"Fine. Your house. Just tell the guys to go back to the original plans if you have to. But I'm warning you, you won't be happy."

"Hell," he shouted, "I just won an argument with *you*. I'm *already* happy!"

"Sure, until the solar flares in your bedroom kick in."

"You just never give up, do you?"

"Not when I'm right."

"Which you always are, of course," he said wryly.

"Usually," she agreed, then cocked a hip, tilted her head, and looked up at him. "What? Do you want me to apologize again for having an opinion?"

"*An* opinion?" He laughed shortly. "You have *an* opinion on *everything*." He blew out an exasperated breath. "What's the point? You've been coming out here at least once a week for the last two months. You've stuck your nose into every little detail of my house. You've 'apologized' before and then gone right on and done whatever the hell you wanted to anyway and something tells me you're not going to quit no matter what I say."

"True," she admitted, then squinted into the sunlight to stare up at him. "But admit it. You were glad to have me here."

"Glad?"

She shrugged. "Okay, maybe 'glad' is a little strong.

But I was right about the kitchen, wasn't I? The new layout's more efficient and the bay window overlooks the lake and you've *got* to admit the cabinets are way better now."

His jaw worked as if he were chewing on words he couldn't quite make himself say. In the distance, Mike heard the telltale crash and slam of hammers and the whine of a saw. She felt right at home. Of course, that was Lucas's point.

"Yes. Fine," he said. "You were right about the kitchen. About the window. About the cabinets. Oak was better than pine."

"And the arched doorways . . ."

He scrubbed one hand across his jaw and blew out a breath. "Them, too."

"And . . ."

"Never mind." He lifted both hands in surrender. "You were right. Right about all of it—*except* the balcony. Happy?"

Mike grinned at him. "What woman wouldn't be happy to hear a man say those three little words that mean so much . . . 'you were right'?"

He scowled at her, but the fury in his eyes was already dissipating. "Do you torture *everyone* building a house around here?"

"Nope," she said, "you're special."

"Lucky me."

"You know," she said, "I think you're beginning to like me." She felt another tiny ping of guilt. She really shouldn't enjoy these little "discussions" of theirs so much.

"Hey, Mike!"

They both turned to look at a workman standing beneath the shell of the balcony jutting out from the second-story master bedroom.

"What is it, Charlie?"

The older man hooked a thumb beneath his tool belt and jerked a nod toward the balcony over his head. "You decide whether you wanted iron or wood railings on the balcony?"

She opened her mouth to answer, but Lucas spoke up first.

"*My* house," he pointed out, but Charlie just shrugged as if he couldn't care less *who* gave the order, as long as *someone* did. "Wood."

"Iron," Mike shouted right over him, "it's already been ordered and the Donovans are bringing it around tomorrow." Then when Lucas turned to fix her with a furious glare, she reached out and patted his arm. "Wood rots. Iron might rust, but you can paint it with a sealant and it's good to go. It'll last as long as the house and, seriously, salt water is death on wood."

"Oh, for—"

"Whatever you say, Mike," Charlie shouted and headed back to work.

Lucas grabbed her again and Mike felt every one of his fingers digging into her skin right through the fabric of her MARCONI CONSTRUCTION T-shirt. He had long, narrow fingers that were, apparently, electric, since she felt the hum of singing warmth right down to her bones. He was so tall and wiry, a person wouldn't really expect him to be this strong. But Mike had always known. See? Just something else she'd been right about. In the last two months, she'd learned enough about Lucas Gallagher to know that he was some kind of scientist and knew diddly about building a house.

But this was the first time she'd seen the caveman side of him.

She kind of liked it.

But that was beside the point. "Gonna manhandle a woman because you can't talk your way out of something?" she taunted. "You know, they say 'violence is the refuge of the incompetent.' Actually, I forget who said it."

He released her instantly. "*Nobody* said it."

"I just did."

"That doesn't count."

"Of course it counts," she said. "But that's not what you're mad about anyway, you're just mad because I'm right about the house."

His dark eyes flashed behind the lenses of his glasses, and his jaw muscle twitched as if he were gritting his teeth. "Will you cut it out?"

He was still furious, but Mike could deal with fury. Anger to an Italian was like a week at a spa. Adrenaline rushed, senses cleared, and blood pumped.

"You know, I figure I've been a heck of a good sport about all of this."

"Is that right?" he demanded. "How's that?"

"You stole my land, you're building a house here that isn't *mine*, and to top it all off, you're doing it *wrong*."

"Your opinion."

"Heck, you're lucky I've only been coming around once a week!"

"Yeah, *lottery* lucky."

"Hey, if my sisters and I hadn't been off dealing with Grace Van Horn's place all summer, I'd have been here on site every damn day whether you liked it or not."

He stared at her, stupefied. "Where do you get off thinking you can just slam into someone's life and take over?"

"I'm not trying to take over your *life*."

"Just my *house*?"

"I'm trying to *save* your house. Big difference."

"Who asked you?"

"You didn't have to ask me, because I'm a fabulous human being."

He choked out a laugh.

"This whole fight started over that stupid balcony, so I can't even understand why you're so pissed," Mike said, trying for a calm she wasn't really feeling. "Because you don't know anything about balcony railings." She lifted one hand and pointed at him. "Oh, and off the subject for a second—just so you know—don't grab me again unless I *want* you to grab me. Which, by the way, isn't going to happen."

Muttering darkly, he dropped his chin to his chest and sucked in a breath rattled with frustration. Then he blew the breath out again. Lifting his head, he glared at her. "Sorry. Didn't mean to grab you."

" 'S'okay," Mike said, "I don't break that easy."

But he wasn't listening. Shaking his head, he grumbled, "Look what you're doing to me. I *never* lose my temper. Never. Ask anyone. I'm a *scientist*, for God's sake."

"What's that got to do with anything?" Mike wondered aloud.

"I'm a calm, rational man." His gaze slid back to her and narrowed again. "But for some reason, every time I get around you, I want to—"

"Punch something?"

He glared at her. "No."

She tipped her head to one side and stared at him. "Too bad. Sometimes it helps. Trust me."

"Why would I trust you?" he demanded. "You're taking over my *house*."

"Look, I know you didn't want the iron railing, but you'll like it. The Donovans are practically *artists* with wrought iron." Absently, she patted his arm again. "You'll thank me later."

He looked at her, wild-eyed—then glanced around the empty yard helplessly, as if searching for *someone* to help him deal with her. When he didn't find a soul, he looked back at her. "You keep saying that."

"And will keep right on until this house is finished."

"There's just no chance of getting you to go away, is there?"

She folded her arms over her chest, cocked her head to one side, and said, "Nope."

"I could call the cops. Have you removed." His face lit up at the thought. "Get a restraining order."

Mike smiled slowly. "The cops. Hmm. You mean the sheriff of Chandler?"

"Yeah." He folded his arms across his own chest and stared right back at her.

"You mean Sheriff Tony Candellano? The man who dated my sister Jo back when they were in high school?

The man who went fishing with my father last weekend? That sheriff?"

As slow, horrible realization crossed Lucas's face,
Mike started walking toward the side of the house, to
check on the back deck. "Just let me know when you
want to call him." She glanced over her shoulder at the
man standing silent behind her. "I've got his number
on speed dial."

"What's this about us doing a job for Cash Hunter?"

Samantha "Sam" Marconi looked up from the baseboard, paintbrush in hand. She scowled at her older sister and said, "I'm almost finished in here. Can this
wait?"

"Uh, *no*." Josefina, "Jo," stomped across the gleaming wood floor until she was alongside her sister, then
went down on one knee to look her square in the eye.
"Grace just told me that you agreed to do a rehab of
some old barn for Cash."

Sam blew a stray lock of red-brown hair out of her
eyes, rubbed the back of her hand under her nose, then
said, "Yeah, I did. It's a good job."

"For *him*?"

Sam had known this would be coming. She'd just
hoped to put off the confrontation for a couple of days.
Figured Grace would talk, though. The older woman
never met a pause in conversation that she didn't rush to
fill.

Jo's pale blue eyes were sparking with indignation
and her dark brown ponytail swung at the back of her
head like a pendulum during an earthquake.

"Look," Sam said, turning her attention back to the detail work she'd almost completed. "We both know, now that the summer's over and our work here at Grace's place is, thank God, almost done, we need to line up new jobs."

"But work for *him*?"

"We work for who pays us, remember?" She shot Jo a glance, but kept her paintbrush, loaded with soft-yellow semigloss, moving gently along the baseboard. "That's the whole point of running a business? Getting customers?"

Disgusted, Jo bounced up and started pacing, her heavy work boots pounding out a frantic rhythm. The big room had great acoustics, so in moments, the echo alone made it seem as if an army were marching through the place.

"It's just—" Jo stopped abruptly, stared out a window, and said, "He's dangerous. And a pain in the ass."

"He's only dangerous if you sleep with him," Sam pointed out with a grin.

Cash Hunter, mystery man. A carpenter, he'd been living in a house at the far edge of Grace Van Horn's property since he blew into town and pretty much kept to himself. Except, of course, for the women who were drawn to him like metal shavings to a magnet.

In the eight months Cash had been in Chandler, the man had built a reputation that was bordering on the scope of legendary. Every woman he'd taken to bed had awakened the following morning announcing that she'd seen the light or whatever and promptly gone off to do good works. One was now working for the Literacy Foundation, one was currently in Chechnya, working on foreign adoptions, and one had gone home to build houses for Habitat for Humanity.

Jo'd been keeping a wary eye on the guy for months—ever since their last secretary had been bitten by the Cash bug and gone off to save the world.

Although, Sam thought now, as she looked up at her sister again, maybe it wasn't so much wariness as *interest* that had Jo's radar bristling.

"You're not thinking about sleeping with him, are you?" she asked point-blank.

"Are you serious?" Jo gave her a look that said she suspected Sam was feverish. "The man's a walking cautionary tale. He's dangerous. He's sneaky. He's—"

"Apparently *very* good," Sam finished for her, then smiled wistfully. "Not that I need to find out about that personally, you understand. Not with Jeff and I so—"

"Yes, I know you're happily married," Jo said quickly, hoping to stave off another blissful round of listening to Sam sigh over the resurrection of her marriage. "And I'm glad for you, Sam. Honest. Glad the Weasel Dog made good and came through. Glad you found Emma and glad you've got the life you always wanted. It's just that—"

"Will you and Mike please stop calling my husband 'Weasel Dog'?" Sam interrupted.

"Old habits die hard?"

"Like the habit of taking jobs offered to us?"

"We don't have to take *every* job."

"This is a good-paying contract and the Marconis are not going to turn it down just because you're scared of Cash."

"Scared?" Jo snorted. "The day I'm scared of a guy

is the day you can pile the dirt on top of me, because I'll be dead."

"Fine. Then there's no problem."

"I don't like it," Jo muttered.

"You don't have to like it," Sam said, willing to give a little on this. "But you *do* have to suck it up and do the job."

Afternoon sunlight washed through the shining glass windowpanes and lay across Jo in a golden broadsword. Her eyes narrowed, jaw tight, she snapped, "What do Mike and Papa have to say about this?"

Finished with the baseboard, Sam picked up the small white bucket of paint and stood up. Stretching the kinks out of her back and legs, she shook her head. "Papa likes having jobs lined up. As for Mike . . ." She started across the room, knowing Jo would follow. "Haven't seen her to tell her. She left early again today."

"Did she go back over to the Gallagher place?"

"Think so."

"It's a wonder that poor guy hasn't shot her yet."

"Yeah, well, little miracles." Sam stopped at the doorway, turned around to look back at the now completed room. The new floor glistened under multiple layers of wax, new brass sconces adorned the freshly painted walls, and the pale green marble surrounding the fireplace was gorgeous. She smiled and sighed in satisfaction. "Damn. We do good work, don't we?"

Jo nodded and shoved both hands into her pockets. Now that the Van Horn job was nearly wrapped up, she was ready for a new challenge. She just didn't like the idea of having to work so closely with a man she didn't trust. A man who thought so much of himself that he walked into a room just *waiting* for women to fall at his feet. A man who was too gorgeous for his own good.

A man who made Jo way more nervous than she'd ever admit . . . even under threat of torture.

"Yes, we do *great* work," she finally muttered. "Too damn good for Cash Hunter."

"Has anyone ever told you you're like a broken record?"

"Broken CD," Jo corrected as they headed out into the yard. "And yes."

2

"You've got mail."

Lucas scowled at his computer. "Do they have to make that voice so damn cheerful?"

He yanked his desk chair back, sat down then scooted it forward again, the hard rubber wheels of the chair squeaking against the bare wood floors. Clicking the mouse button, he opened his e-mail account, still unfathomably annoyed.

It had been three days since Mike Marconi last "dropped by" and he felt like a man who knew there was a sniper out there somewhere, drawing a bead on him. He couldn't relax even when she was gone, because he never knew when the damn woman was going to pop up again.

But even worse than the sense of expectant dread was the knowledge that a part of him was actually looking forward to seeing her again. And how that had happened, Lucas had no idea.

For two months, Mike Marconi had been the bane of his existence. Ever since the afternoon he'd stumbled across her as she was talking to herself. If he'd known ahead of time that buying this land and building a house here would gain him an intrusive, opinionated, maddening, *gorgeous* female plumber . . . hell. He'd have done it anyway.

Afternoon sunlight streamed in through the brand-new windows in his second-story office. Outside that window lay the lake, with stands of trees thick enough to convince a man he was all alone on the planet. Unless of course, Lucas thought grimly, that man was listening to the staccato beat of hammers and the incessant whine of saws.

But to give the construction crews their due, they'd done amazing work in a short amount of time. Just two months ago, he'd had empty acreage, a set of blueprints, and enough money to pay for extra workmen so they could finish the job quickly. Now, he was only a few doors, a balcony, a bathtub, and some finishing touches away from having a completed house.

"If Mike Marconi stays the hell away." As soon as the words were muttered, though, he shook his head and pushed all thoughts of the irritating female out of his mind. Damn it, even when she *wasn't* there, she *was*.

Memories of her face, her voice, her eyes, danced through his brain with appalling regularity. Didn't seem to matter how many times he told himself he wasn't interested—she hovered at the edges of his mind. Just enough to irritate him.

And intrigue him, damn it.

His AOL account opened up and Lucas scrolled quickly down the list of letters in his in-box. Taking a sabbatical from the lab apparently didn't mean keeping out of contact. He'd been officially, if temporarily, unemployed for nearly three months and every day he had several letters stacked up demanding his attention. Today was no different. There were five letters marked "priority," a reminder about a fund-raiser, and . . .

"Shit."

Lucas leaned back in his desk chair and stared at the subject line of one particular letter.

DON'T DELETE THIS ONE

He had to get off AOL. Then the bastard wouldn't know if Lucas was reading his damn e-mails or not. Since last month, there'd been at least one letter a week from his twin brother. Letters Lucas didn't read. Letters he deleted without even thinking about it. There was nothing Justin could say that Lucas was interested in hearing.

God knew an apology would be too damn little and about four years too late. Besides, he didn't want an apology anyway. Wouldn't change anything. Wouldn't take them all back in time to set things right. Wouldn't mean anything but that Justin wanted forgiveness so he wouldn't be miserable.

"Too bad," Lucas muttered thickly. "I *like* your being miserable." A quick whip crack of temper spiked through him, then drained away again almost instantly. He wouldn't go back down that road. Not again. Justin wanted forgiveness? Then he should go see a priest. As for his e-mails . . . "Don't delete? Why the hell not?"

Deliberately, he sat forward again, moved the cursor to the box alongside the letter he had no intention of reading and clicked the mouse button. Then he deleted it before he could talk himself out of it. Pushing back from the desk, he left the other letters unanswered and stalked out of the office, as if distancing himself not only from the computer, but from the tenuous connection between him and his brother.

But it wasn't that easy. Images of Justin crowded his mind, forcing him to remember that it hadn't always been like this between them. Growing up, the two of them had been as close as anyone would expect a set of twins to be—despite their differences. Justin had always been the athletic one. The golden child whose room was stacked with trophies from Little League and Pop Warner football. Lucas's room, on the other hand, was filled with chemistry sets and books. It hadn't mattered then. They were still "the Gallagher twins"—the two of them against the world.

But all that ended a long time ago.

"What's so damn important that now, all of a sudden, Justin's trying to reach out and piss me off?"

Naturally, the only way he'd get that question answered was to read the damn e-mail—which he wasn't about to do. Lucas scraped his hair back from his face and headed out into the hall. The dark red tiles felt cool beneath his bare feet as he stalked along the hall and down the flight of stairs.

In fact, the whole house felt cool, despite the September heat outside. And he probably owed Mike Marconi for that, too, he thought in disgust. She was the one who'd insisted he insulate the thick stucco walls with straw. She'd cited a dozen different sources on environmental house construction, but she'd captured him with her last argument. That the early Spanish settlers in California had built their adobe homes with a layer of straw between the walls—keeping their houses cool in summer and warm in winter.

He ran the flat of his hand over the lightly textured, cream-colored wall on his right. The woman was a pain in the ass, but she knew her stuff. As he hit the bottom of the stairs, he paused to stare at the completed great room in front of him.

Wide and open, the area fed into the dining room and the kitchen beyond. But here, the walls soared and rough-hewn oak beams, which Mike had insisted on "distressing" with a propane torch, crisscrossed the ceiling. The effect gave the house the feel of its having stood here for centuries.

"Something else she was right about." Scowling, he wondered if the woman was *ever* wrong.

The window casements were arched and the glass panes leaded into diamond shapes that drew interesting patterns on the shining tile floor. A kiva-shaped fireplace stood in the corner, with built-in bookcases on either side.

Twin forest-green sofas sat facing each other in the middle of the room. Squatting between the sofas was the table Lucas had found in a furniture shop outside Chandler. A one-of-a-kind piece, it had been fashioned out of an old apothecary bench. Cut down and polished, it shone with a dark rich finish in the afternoon sunlight.

Heavy rugs dotted the cool tiles and tables and lamps were scattered throughout the room, giving the place warmth while still maintaining its open feel.

Amazing how much work could get accomplished if you were willing to pay extra to keep the construction firms working around the clock. Not for the first time in his life, Lucas was grateful to his father. If not for him,

Lucas would have been forced to live on the salary he made as a research scientist—which would never have afforded him this home.

The Gallagher money had been made years ago. When his dad invented a simple little device that was used in heart operations around the world. The patent and ensuing royalties brought in more money than anyone could spend in three lifetimes.

Though God knows, Justin had tried.

Nope, he told himself. His brother would *not* ruin this moment for him. Pushing thoughts of the bastard aside, he determinedly relaxed and went back to enjoying his new house.

He already felt at home here. With the woods surrounding him, the lake behind him, and the ocean just a mile or so away, he had the best of all possible worlds. Isolation that he'd need to work on the book that was due to his publisher in less than six months—and a small town close by for when he needed to see people. Hear voices other than his own—or Mike Marconi's.

And when the book was finished, and his year's sabbatical over, he'd go back to the lab and continue the research that he hoped would one day change the world.

He grinned at the thought. "No ego problems here," he murmured.

Still smiling, he opened the double front doors, stepped onto the wide front porch, and stopped dead. "How does she do it?" he wondered aloud. "How does she know to show up just when I'm relaxing my guard?"

But there she was.

Mike Marconi had parked her battered, dusty navy

blue truck at the end of the line of workmen's vehicles clogging his driveway. But instead of coming up to the house, the woman was bent over his mailbox, peering inside as if looking for buried treasure.

Annoyance rattled through him and was quickly followed by a different emotion—one Lucas was in no hurry to explore. His gaze locked on her, he noticed how her thick blond braid swung down off her shoulders. He watched as she tucked a large brown paper bag beneath her arm, then reached in to pull out his mail before snapping the mailbox closed again. He shook his head as she started across the yard, thumbing through the letters and circulars as she walked.

For years, Lucas had lived a secluded life. So wrapped up in his research, his work, that he hadn't had to worry about letting his emotions run amok. A couple of months with Mike Marconi was changing all that. All of a sudden, he was experiencing a *flood* of emotions. Everything from anger to a soul-stirring lust. And he wasn't happy about it.

All around him, construction noise sounded. Men shouted to each other, hammers crashed, and beneath it all lay the steady, rhythmic hush of the ocean whispering from a distance. But all he could see, all he could focus on, was the woman who'd wormed her way into his world and now showed no signs of leaving.

One shoulder pressed to a porch post, he crossed his feet at the ankle, folded his arms over his chest and watched her. Hell. He couldn't take his eyes *off* her.

Her worn, faded jeans clung to her legs and her red T-shirt with the peeling MARCONI CONSTRUCTION logo looked as if it had been washed a thousand times. She wore heavy work boots and the dark red baseball cap she was never without. And yet somehow she managed to look more completely *female* than any woman he'd ever known.

Damn it.

"Anything interesting?" he called out when she was close enough.

She stopped, looked up at him and grinned. "Actually, yeah," she said, picking out one long business-sized envelope and waving it over her head. "What's 'Pacific Scientific Laboratories'?"

Lucas pushed away from the porch, took the steps in a couple of long strides, then stalked across the grass to meet her. Snatching the mail from her, he said, "It's where I work. Anything else?"

She shook her head and blew out a whistled breath. "A whole building full of science geeks? Sounds boring."

"Completely. So why are you collecting my mail?" He looked through everything quickly, then stuffed the letters into his back jeans pocket. "The mailman doing something wrong, too? Or maybe you want to tear the mailbox down and rebuild it to your specifications?"

"Well, you're not a happy camper today, are you?" She grinned and a flash of one dimple in her right cheek caught his attention. Her pale blue eyes danced with humor and he really wished he could stop noticing these things.

"I *was*," he pointed out. "Until about ten seconds ago."

"Gee," Mike said, still smiling. "Just when I got here. What a coincidence."

"Amazing. So. You going to tell me what you were looking for in my mailbox?"

"Just checking for any stray cash," she said, tipping her head back to stare up at him.

"Cash?" He glanced out at the mailbox, then back to her. Dappled shade from the surrounding trees waved across her in lazy sweeps. "Why would I keep money in a mailbox?"

"Didn't you hear?" she asked, stepping past him and heading for the house. "There's a mailbox fairy at work in Chandler."

He watched her go and couldn't help the fact that his gaze landed on her nicely rounded backside. But he shook himself out of it and followed her. He'd learned a couple of months ago not to give Mike Marconi any time alone in his house.

She was already halfway through the living room when he caught up to her. Her boots clicked musically against the tiles and a slight fall of dust marked her every footstep.

"What are you talking about?"

She turned left into the kitchen, then set down the paper bag onto the black granite counter. Looking at him, she said, "A few months ago, somebody was leaving money in library books in town."

He frowned. "Why would they do that?"

"Who knows?" She shrugged, then opened the bag and plunged one hand inside. "Anyway, the crowds at the library were getting so bad that old Mrs. Rogan, the librarian, who at her last birthday was judged to be about a hundred and ten, was going nuts. Chasing people around with her yardstick—and she's no spring chicken, so she had to keep stopping for breath."

"A hundred and ten. It's a wonder she *has* breath."

"Yeah, well, only the good die young," Mike quipped. "Mean goes on forever." She stared into the bag, threw a quick look at Lucas, then started digging around again. "Anyway . . . it got so crowded and ugly over at the library, with people going through books that hadn't been opened in centuries, that Mrs. Rogan put an ad in the paper, asking whoever was putting money in there to cut it out."

"Did it work?"

"Yep." Mike glanced at him. "The money fairy took out an ad the next week, saying there would be no more money left in the library."

"So Mrs. Rogan was happy." Lucas leaned back against the refrigerator and folded his arms over his chest. Intrigued, he watched her and waited for the rest of the story.

"Oh yeah. She was happy and everyone else was miserable," Mike said, forgetting about the contents of the bag for a minute to enjoy herself. "Which just made Mrs. Rogan *more* happy. The woman lives to see people suffer."

He smiled, too, and told himself he had to get into town to get a look at this librarian. "So how'd the mailboxes come into play?"

"That's the best part." Mike braced both hands on the counter behind her, jumped up and plopped onto the counter to sit in a splash of sunshine streaming through one of the windows overlooking the back deck. Folding her hands between her knees, she locked her ankles and swung them lazily. "A week or so ago, people started finding money—some twenties, but mostly fifties—in with their mail."

"Everybody?" Lucas asked, his mind clicking along as if picking up clues. This was what he did best. Unlocking mysteries.

"Nope." She unclasped her hands and pointed an index finger at him. "That's the interesting part. See . . . the only people who are getting money *now* are the ones who really need it. Like for example, last week, Mr. Parsons. He lives out past Mama Candellano just off the coast road—he got slapped with a tax assessment for a shed he put up behind the house, and bingo!"

"Bingo what?"

"He found the exact amount he needed in his mailbox. Went into town the next day, told everyone who'd stand still long enough to listen, and then paid off his bill."

"Interesting." Lucas frowned thoughtfully. So not only was the good fairy generous, he or she obviously had an inside source, telling him or her exactly who needed what, when.

"Oh yeah. But as far as anyone knows, nobody else knew about Mr. Parson's debt. So how'd the mailbox fairy find out?" Mike jumped off the counter, landing with a solid thump. "*And*, it's not just big stuff, either." She glanced at him again as she opened the brown bag and reached one hand in. "Elinor Hyatt's ten-year-old daughter wanted to take ballet lessons, but Elinor couldn't afford it. Told Hayley she'd have to wait till next year. Guess who's taking ballet lessons?"

"Hayley?"

"You win a year's supply of Turtle Wax. Got signed up this morning. Apparently, Elinor found the money for the lessons in her mailbox yesterday and Hayley's all set to be a diva." She took a small brass object from the bag and grinned at it. "Won't be hard for her to pull off, either. Hayley's always pretty much acted like a star. Elinor's gonna have big trouble with that kid one of these days."

Lucas was hardly listening. Instead, he watched as Mike snatched a screwdriver out of a kitchen drawer—how'd she know it was in there?—and started taking off one of the kitchen-cabinet pulls. "What're you doing?"

"Oh," she said, looking at him over her shoulder. "The ones you have are all wrong. I brought these from home. Bought them about a year ago when I saw them at this little place in the city. And as soon as I remembered 'em, I knew they'd look perfect in here. Figured you'd be out today and I'd surprise you."

"The latches I have are not wrong," Lucas said, pushing away from the fridge to walk across the room. He slapped one hand on the cabinet to stop her. "I picked them out myself."

"I know," Mike said and patted the hand he'd dropped onto the cabinet before pulling it off. "But really. Could they be more boring?"

"Cabinet handles *are* boring. That's their function," he argued.

"Don't have to be," she said, and held up the brass

object she'd brought with her, and grinned at it proudly. "Now see, *these* are fun."

Lucas just stared at her. "A *parrot*? You want me to have *parrots* on my cabinets?"

Mike looked from him to the small, perfectly detailed brass parrot in her hand. She'd found them more than a year ago at an outlet place in San Francisco. She'd bought every one they had and tucked them away, for the house she was planning to build.

For *this* house.

They were whimsical, charming, and just quirky enough to brighten up a kitchen. And she'd been waiting a solid year to see them as they'd been meant to be seen. They were *perfect.* "They're cute."

"They're *stupid.*"

Mike swallowed hard and folded her fingers around the little parrot protectively. "You haven't seen them up."

"Don't want to."

"You could give them a try."

"Why would I want parrots in my kitchen?"

A surprising sting of tears rushed to her eyes and Mike thought for one horrifying moment that she might actually *cry.* She *never* cried. Much less here. In front of *him.*

She swallowed back the knot of emotion that was suddenly, completely, filling her throat and reached down deep inside to find her inner indignation. Looking around the sun-washed room, she took note of the cozy nook nestled in front of a bay window, the strategically placed cooking island in the center of the kitchen, the miles of gleaming black granite and the rich blue tiles beneath their feet. She glanced at the small pass-through fireplace she'd insisted Lucas add on the wall separating the kitchen from the dining room and knew she'd done her part to make this house special.

Which was why, really, she'd brought the parrots here. There was no point in holding on to them for the dream house that was now not going to be built. Besides, she'd bought them for *this* house.

"You know," she said, sliding her gaze back to the ungrateful geek in front of her. "If it wasn't for me, you wouldn't have a fireplace in here, or a cooking island or the extra counters or cabinets."

He glared down at her. "None of those things were on the blueprints, remember? They weren't *supposed* to be here."

"Yeah, but they look great, don't they?"

His jaw worked as if he was biting back words trying to spill from his mouth. At last, though, he grudgingly admitted, "Yes. The kitchen is great. Just the way it *is*."

She looked down at the brass parrot in her hand and thought for one brief shining moment about throwing it at him. But she might nick the brass. Lifting her gaze, she said, "Fine, then. You don't want the parrots, you can keep your boring, plain cabinet pulls."

"You're surrendering?" He sounded amazed.

"Hah!" It cost her, but she put enough emphasis into that laugh that she was pretty sure he believed her. "Marconis never give up. I'm just not going to waste my parrots on a man who can't appreciate them."

She tightened up the old cabinet pull, slammed the

door shut, then, still clutching the cold brass parrot, turned around and stomped across the gleaming blue tiles. Grabbing the paper bag she'd left on the counter, she swung around to face him again and winced as she heard the soft *clink* of the parrots crashing against each other. "I'll see ya. Gotta go meet my sisters."

He frowned at her but didn't speak, and Mike figured it was just as well. If he said anything right now, she couldn't be held responsible for her actions. She was just so damn mad. She'd planned this house. This life. For herself. All of the little touches that had become a part of the dream she'd built in her head were being wasted on a man who probably wouldn't even notice them anymore after a while.

She'd put her heart into this house and it wasn't hers.

She had no place here.

Pain, sharp and sweet, slapped at her and she rocked on her heels with the impact. God, she felt like an idiot.

"Mike, wait."

She didn't.

Couldn't.

In fact, her steps quickened. Everything inside her was clamoring to be gone. To be away from him. She was the dummy here, not the nerd prince. It was *his* house. Didn't matter how many times she came over. How many changes she made. How many things she tried to fix.

It wasn't hers.

And it never would be.

"Damn it, wait." Lucas grabbed her forearm and tugged her to a stop in the middle of the great room.

"Let go," she warned, giving him a look that would have terrified a lesser man. He didn't even blink.

"In a minute."

He blew out a breath, then shoved his free hand through thick brown hair that hung down to his shoulders. *Very* thick, she thought. And a soft honey brown that looked rich and sleek and—oh man, she needed a date. Soon.

If she was starting to hyperventilate over a geek, then obviously she was *not* getting out enough.

"Let me see the parrot," he muttered.

"Why?"

"Do you have to argue about *everything*?"

"Of course I do," she snapped. "I'm Italian."

He choked out a short laugh. "And I'm Irish. It's a wonder we *ever* have a conversation without arguing."

"I don't think we have."

"Good point." He let her go and took a step back. "Can I just see the damn parrot?"

Her arm felt warm where his fingers had been and since she *so* didn't want to think about *that*, she said, "Fine. Here."

He took the little parrot and studied it, rubbing his thumb across the cool metal while shaking his head. "Kitchen parrots."

"Do you have this problem with *all* birds?" she asked. "Or just parrots in particular?"

His gaze lifted and collided with hers. Dark brown eyes locked on her and Mike ridiculously felt as though she couldn't have looked away even if she'd tried. Which she didn't.

"I'd like to keep them," he said, his gaze still holding hers.

"Why?"

"I changed my mind?"

"Why?"

"God. Does there have to be a reason for everything?" he demanded, throwing both hands high.

"You're the scientist," Mike said. "You tell me."

"You're not an easy woman, are you, Mike Marconi?"

"Just picking up on that?"

His lips twitched briefly. "Can I have the parrots for the kitchen or not?"

She tipped her head to one side and stared at him. The fist of emotion in her throat was looser now, but no less there. Okay, maybe she'd come on a little strong with him about this house, but damn it, it wasn't easy giving up something you'd been dreaming about for years. And maybe she could have cut him some slack now and then, but that just wasn't her style.

The question was, why was he being so . . . *nice*? Something was going on here and she wasn't sure what, exactly. But if he was doing this because he felt sorry for her, because he thought he'd hurt her feelings—which he hadn't, not really, and even if he had, she'd never admit it to him—then he could just cut it out.

"You don't have to do me any favors, you know."

"Why would I do you any favors?" he asked tightly. "You've been driving me nuts for two months."

"True."

"I just," he said softly, "*like* the parrots. Okay?"

She curled her fingers into the brown bag and squeezed tight. Her gaze locked with his, he smiled, and something warm and luscious and just a little overpowering slithered through her. Mike took a deep breath and felt the tiled floor beneath her feet shift a little.

Earthquake?

But he wasn't reacting.

So maybe only *her* world was getting rocked.

Oh boy.

3

Cash Hunter was making Jo nuts.

"Do you have to stand right there?"

"Where should I stand?" he asked, a small smile tugging at the corner of his mouth.

"How about Saturn?"

"Touchy today, aren't you?"

Not just today. Jo grimaced tightly, spun the measuring tape back into its metallic shell, and kept her gaze fixed on the battered wood floor. Maybe, like the boogeyman, if she ignored him, he'd just go away. Although, she had the distinct impression that boogeymen could take lessons from Cash Hunter. His old "barn" was really no bigger than Grace's goat shed. And he wanted it turned into a little guesthouse. Sort of a studio-apartment thing with a Murphy bed, a bathroom, and a kitchenette. Sam was right. It would be a good job for them and wouldn't take much more than six weeks or so, once they got going. Unless of course, Cash insisted on hanging around every damn minute.

She'd been taking measurements for the last hour and she felt as if every nerve in her body were stretched as tightly as a string of Christmas lights around the edge of a house. It wasn't *all* Cash's fault, but damn it, he wasn't helping any.

"Yeah, I guess I am touchy. But I'm almost finished here."

"Don't hurry on my account."

She turned her head to look up at him. Big mistake. His thick black hair was just long enough to be sexily rumpled. His dark eyes shone with a kind of inner light she could only assume was the porch light to hell, and his long, rangy body looked both lazy and coiled for action. How in the hell did he do that? Then instantly she told herself not to wonder about Cash.

He was *so* not on her radar.

The man was a walking hormone. And judging by her own body's reaction to him, even women who weren't interested in him weren't immune.

Irritated both by her own reaction to him and his easy acceptance of the effect he had on her, she asked, "You're still doing it."

"What?"

"Turning every question into a sexual innuendo."

"Am I?" That half-smile curved his mouth once more.

Amazed, she said, "You just did it again."

"Wow. I'm good."

His smile widened and Jo's temper spiked. "So the rumor mill says."

He laughed and went down on one knee, bracing his forearm across his thigh. Too close, she thought. The man had absolutely no respect for personal space. His eyes flashed and his scent was sawdust and man. A dangerous combination.

"You intrigue me, Josefina."

"Lucky me."

"So what's bugging you besides me."

She didn't really care for the fact that he seemed to know something else was bugging her. What she ought to do was jump up and stalk out. But then he'd think he'd chased her away—which he would have, but she didn't want *him* to know it, so she stayed put.

Annoying man.

"What makes you think it's not just you?"

"You've made it clear many times that *I* don't worry you—so there's gotta be something else going on."

"Even if there is," she hedged, "what do you care?" She shot him a look, then took out her pad and wrote down the last measurement she'd taken before it rushed out of her mind.

"Let's say I'm curious."

"Great." She stood up and muttered, "You're curious and I'm drowning."

He stood, too, and looked down at her. "Okay, now I *have* to know."

Jo rubbed her eyes with the tips of her fingers— more to avoid looking at Cash than in any hope of easing the headache that had been pounding in her skull for hours. Heck, *weeks.*

He was waiting. Standing there as patient as a statue. Hardly breathing, just watching her. Waiting.

She never should have said anything. Didn't know why she had. Stupid. She shouldn't tell him. But she'd been thinking about this for two weeks and had to tell *somebody.* She couldn't tell the family. She didn't want them to know what she was up to until she'd succeeded.

Which was beginning to look a little iffy at the moment.

"Fine," she blurted, speaking up fast before she could change her mind. "I'm— Oh God." She slapped one hand to her abdomen to try to still the butterflies suddenly swarming inside. It didn't help. Still felt as though each of those cute little butterflies was carrying a power drill, using them to bore holes in her stomach lining.

"I can't believe I'm going to tell you this." Jo paused to glare at him. "And if you *ever* repeat it, I'll have to kill you . . ."

"Understood."

Clutching her tape measure and notepad tightly, Jo stalked around the perimeter of the small barn. Her brain raced and her nerves jumped. She glanced at him as he stood in one spot, turning to follow her progress around the room.

"Jesus, Josefina, what's wrong?"

"I'm getting to it."

He intercepted her and dropped both hands onto her shoulders. "What is it? Are you a contract killer? Married to a felon? Pregnant with quintuplets?"

"Nothing that easy," she said. "I've been . . ." She took a breath and blurted out the truth. "I've been going to school. College. At night. A couple times a week."

She expelled a breath and felt . . . better. Weird.

"Interesting, but hardly worth all this drama."

"There's more."

"Can't wait."

She stepped out from under his grasp, and admitted, "I'm flunking my science class."

"You're kidding."

She snapped him a look designed to age him ten years. "Do I *look* like I'm kidding? I needed a stupid science credit and I didn't want to dissect anything and God knows I suck at chemistry—an incident in high school we won't go into at the moment—so I picked astronomy. I mean, how hard could it be? Look at stars through a telescope, for God's sake."

"And . . ."

She shot him another stony look. "Turns out there's just a touch more to it than that."

He grinned. "How bad is it?"

"Did you miss the part about me flunking?"

"So you study harder."

Jo gave him a long dismissive look up and down, then pushed past him, saying, "Gee, why didn't I think of that?"

"Jo—"

"Just forget it. Can't believe I told you about this anyway." She kept walking, faster now, headed for her truck. She was parked at the back edge of Cash's property. What would be the little guesthouse was separated from the main house by a patch of woods so thick not even sunlight could punch through the leafy cover. She'd wondered when she arrived what Cash's house looked like; now, all she could think about was getting out of there.

How humiliating was *this*? Now, not only was she flunking a stupid college course that some idiot eighteen-year-old could probably pass in his sleep, but Cash Hunter knew all about it. *Smooth move, Jo*. Damn it. Why was it genetically impossible for a Marconi to keep her damn mouth shut?

She heard his footsteps right behind her, so naturally, she sped up and managed to yank her truck door open just as he caught up to her. She climbed in fast, but he grabbed the edge of the door and held it when she would have slammed it closed, sealing herself inside. "Go away."

"You don't have to run off," he said, his voice a low rumble of sound that seemed to be pitched at precisely the right note to skim along a woman's nerve endings. He probably practiced it.

"Yeah, I do. Got a meeting with my sisters and Papa."

"Okay," he said and closed the door, as she fired up the engine. But he didn't let go. Leaning his forearms on the window frame, he stared in at her. "But we could talk about this another time . . ."

She snorted. "Sure. Another time."

"When?"

He was way too close. Jo leaned back as she looked at him. Snapping her seat belt on, she shook her head and said, "When you're strapping on ice skates in hell?"

He smiled and, damn it, something inside her lit up before it was quickly snuffed out by memories and instinctive caution.

"I really like you, Josefina," he mused, and sounded as surprised as she felt.

"Well," she said, dropping the gear shift into drive, "now I can die happy. And I told you, I don't like that name."

"Too bad. *I* do."

She growled and stepped on the gas. He leaped back out of the way as the truck jumped forward. The spinning tires spit up a tail of dirt and gravel as she bulleted away from the scene of her latest humiliation.

Deliberately, she reached out and flipped the rearview mirror up so she wouldn't have to look at him as she left.

Change just really sucked.

Oh, not that anything about the Marconi family house *ever* changed. Here, in the comfortable kitchen, time had stood still. They'd been holding the construction company meetings around the old kitchen table *forever.* Hank Marconi, better known as Papa, had never minded having daughters instead of sons. In fact, he'd treated his daughters as he would have sons. At least as far as construction work went.

When they were little, it had been an adventure, going to work with Papa. By the time the sisters were teenagers, they were working construction regularly—Jo's expertise lay in roofing, Sam was the painter/refinisher/*artiste*, and Mike had never met a pipe she couldn't undo and put back together better than new. They each had their specialties, although all three of them could do just about anything in construction. The girls and their father ran the business, and business was good.

That didn't change, either.

It was the family itself that was spinning in new directions all over the place.

Take what had been happening around here in the last couple of months, for example.

Mike's gaze landed on her middle sister, Samantha. Sam had done more smiling in the last few weeks than she had in the last nine years. Not surprising, really, since she'd not only managed to reunite with Emma, the daughter she'd given up for adoption, but with the little girl's daddy, Jeff "Weasel Dog" Hendricks. Although, Mike admitted silently, he was turning out to be less of a weasel dog than she'd thought.

So maybe *some* changes weren't all bad.

Then her gaze shifted to Josefina. As the oldest, Jo had pretty much stepped into the breach as mom/sister/warden when Sylvia Marconi, their mother, died nine years ago. Jo'd given up on college, come home and taken over. The fact that she thought she was *still* in charge led to some pretty spectacular fights, but that was all in a day's work for an Italian family. Yelling just meant you were breathing.

But even Jo was changing. Mike stared at her older sister and frowned thoughtfully. Something was going on with her. She disappeared two nights a week and wouldn't tell anyone what that was about—and judging from her attitude lately, Mike was fairly certain Jo wasn't out meeting some guy for sex. Anybody getting laid regularly would be in a better mood.

One thing she could count on, though, to always remain the same was this house where they'd all grown up. Mike let her gaze sweep the kitchen quickly, taking in the butter-yellow walls, the white cabinets, and the damn near antique appliances. The refrigerator hummed like a forgetful old aunt and Papa's huge golden retriever, Bear, snored under the table like an elephant.

It was . . . comforting.

Even if she *was* still living at home at the ripe old age of twenty-six. Which was really sort of embarrassing to admit.

"Will you quit that?" Jo snapped the words out, shooting Mike a glare that should have curled her long blond braid.

"What'm *I* doing?"

"You're rocking on that damn chair and it's squeaking and making me insane."

Mike stopped, leaned forward, and let the kitchen chair slap down off its rear legs to thud onto the linoleum. "I'm not making you nuts, Jo. You were *born* that way."

"I was born," she retorted, "an only child. Would that it had stayed that way."

"Thanks very much," Sam piped up.

"See? Now you're insulting the sister who likes you," Mike said.

Jo smirked at her. "Clever. Just"—she shook her head—"shut up."

"God, take a pill, will ya?" Mike should have known better than to race home to get to this meeting. After all, when Karma started going bad on you, things usually just went right to hell.

And hadn't Karma been kicking her ass for months now? Ever since Lucas Gallagher strolled into town and snatched her dreams away?

"If you guys are through . . ." Sam held up both hands and stepped into her traditional role of peacemaker. No matter how many times Mike had warned her that it was usually the innocent bystander who took one between the eyes, Sam just couldn't seem to help herself. "I want to get this stuff done—Jeff and I are taking Emma out to Rosie's tonight."

Rosie's Café. A great little place, sitting right on the coast road, overlooking the rocky cliffs leading down to the ocean. And right now, a night at Rosie's sounded much better than the frozen dinner Mike had planned on. "Great idea," she said quickly, "I'll join you."

"You're not invited," Sam said and reached out to pat her hand.

"Fine." Mike sniffed, pretending to be insulted. "I'll call Terrino's and order pizza."

"Now that the menu's settled . . ." Jo said, and picked up one of her gazillion file folders.

Mike leaned back on the kitchen chair again, pushing it until it rested on its two rear legs, then she rocked idly and watched Jo scowl at her. But quickly enough, she pretended to ignore Mike and the squeaky chair and get right down to business.

The woman could give God an ulcer when it came to organization. Seriously, Mike mused, if the universe ever got too much for the Big Guy to handle, he could just turn the whole mess over to Jo—who would have the world whipped into shape in no time.

She had a file folder for every job and every estimate they'd ever made tucked away in the Marconi family vault—a big steel file cabinet they kept stored in the workshop out back.

"Aren't we going to wait for Papa?" Sam asked.

"Oh, crap." Mike let the chair slap down hard again and then leaned her forearms on the table. "Forgot to tell you. Papa went to San Francisco for the weekend. With *Grace*."

Jo's hands stilled on the sheaf of papers. She shifted her pale blue eyes to Mike. "What do you mean, *with*?"

"I think I mean just what you think I mean."

"Well, that was clear," Jo muttered, "thanks."

"I think she's right," Sam said.

"She's almost never right," Jo argued.

"Feel the love," Mike quipped and reached for the bowl of fall apples in the center of the table. Grabbing one, she took a huge bite, then talked around it. "I know what I saw, and I'm telling you, something's up over there."

Jo snorted. "Please."

"Papa and Grace have been seeing each other."

Mike and Jo both turned to stare at Sam, who shifted uneasily in her chair, then cupped both hands around a cardboard cup of coffee from the Leaf and Bean. That latte had to be ice-cold by now, but Sam's fingertips danced up and down the sides of the cup as if it were boiling hot.

Outside the cozy kitchen, wind screamed in off the ocean and slapped at the house as if trying to find a way to sneak inside. Under the table, Bear snorted, grumbled, then shifted until his heavy bulk was stretched out across the toes of Mike's boots. She sighed and got used to the pain because Bear was just too damn old to be nudged off. Besides, she had bigger things on her mind at the moment.

"You know something." Mike narrowed her gaze.

"Spill it." Jo folded her arms on the table and waited.

"It's just something Emma said on the Fourth of July."

"Two months ago?" Amazed, and just a little offended that Sam had kept the news to herself, Mike stared at her sister. She never would have believed a Marconi could be quiet for so long.

Sam winced a little. "Hey, I wasn't sure. Still not. But anyway, Emma went home with Papa after the carnival and apparently they went to Grace's. Where they watched movies and played games until Emma fell asleep."

"Well," Mike said dryly, not sure if she was disappointed or relieved at the innocuous disclosure. "Hire a minister and buy me a dress. I'm convinced."

Sam withered her with a quick look. "That's not the best part. Emma said that after she fell asleep 'Grace and Papa played games all night and that Grace said Papa knows *lots* of fun games.' "

"Oh God." Jo dropped the file folder and didn't even cringe when several of the papers inside slithered loose. A sure sign that she was upset. "Games? What kind of games?"

"Don't ask," Sam said.

Mike knew just how she felt. "You know, there are just *some* images of her father a daughter shouldn't have in her mind."

"I'm with you on that one." Jo cleared her throat, gathered up the scattered papers, and carefully aligned each one of them with the other. "That's . . . interesting. But it's still not proof."

"Proof?" Mike laughed at her. "Who're you? The

prosecuting attorney? Who said we have to have proof?"

"Atta girl," Jo said with a slow shake of her head. "Grab the rumor first, look for facts after."

"Both of you cut it out," Sam said shortly. "It's none of our business if Papa has a girlfriend."

"Oh, jeez . . ." Mike practically moaned. "Could you not call her that?"

Sam smiled, clearly enjoying this. "*And*, if the two of them want to go to San Francisco and 'play games,' that's up to them. God knows they're old enough."

"Stop," Jo said tightly, covering her ears with both hands. "Too much information. Disk full."

"Fine," Sam said. "I was a little freaked out, too. But I've had a couple months to get used to the idea and now I think it's kind of cute. Besides, I like Grace."

"Me, too," Mike said, and slid a glance at Jo, just uncovering her ears. "But what if he marries her or something? We could be redoing that damn house of hers for the next thirty years."

Jo slapped her hands back into place and started humming.

Mike grinned.

Sam slapped her arm. "Just for saying that, you can go to church and light a candle."

"Just one?" Jo muttered.

Then as her sisters settled down to tackle the business end of Marconi Construction, Mike's brain wandered. Something was going on with Jo, Papa was out getting *laid*—God help her—and Lucas Gallagher was ensconced in *her* dream house.

Yep.

No doubt about it.
Change sucked.

Change was a good thing, Lucas told himself as he stepped out onto the front porch to watch a storm blow in off the ocean. A line of tall pine trees stood at the edge of his yard, waving frantically in the rush of wind sweeping in from the Pacific, more than a mile away. Overhead, the sky was being blanketed by clouds racing in from the horizon and the deep-throated rumble of thunder grumbled in the air.

Only a few months ago, he'd been tucked away in a sterile lab outside San Jose. His days had been filled with equations, experiments, and too many disappointments to count. He went to work before sunrise and left long after sunset. The only time he ever got outside was walking from his condo to his car.

Not much time for a social life, which was fine by him. The few dates he had were generally with coworkers. Women who understood what he was trying to do and appreciated the fact that sometimes he just didn't have *time* to call.

Four years ago, he'd dived into his work and submerged himself. Cutting himself off from memories that tore at him, he'd forced himself to stop looking back. To look only at the future that would, if he and a few other dedicated scientists could pull this off, be changed forever.

"Change is good," he muttered and sat down on the top step. Leaning back on his elbows, he stretched his long, jean-clad legs out in front of him and crossed his feet at the ankles. The wind battered him, fast and cold, tugging at his hair, pushing at him, as if trying to get him to go back inside.

But as clouds rushed toward him and the last rosy streaks of color faded into black, Lucas stayed where he was. Thinking. Always thinking.

Three months ago, he'd been a solitary man with a mission.

Now, he still had the mission, but he was far from solitary. Mike Marconi had pushed her way into his world and then left her boot prints stamped all over the damn place.

Hell, he even had brass parrots in his kitchen because he'd looked into her sky-blue eyes and seen hurt there. Hurt he'd caused by laughing at her stupid parrots. Scowling into the wind, he told himself that it didn't mean anything. That of course he wouldn't want to deliberately hurt her.

He didn't want to deliberately hurt anyone.

Except for Justin. He wouldn't mind planting his fist in his twin's face—although for that to happen, he'd have to actually *see* Justin again and Lucas wasn't interested in that happening anytime soon.

But he didn't want to think about his twin at the moment. Hell, even thinking about Mike was preferable. And she was making him insane.

He hated like hell to admit that the plain truth was, the only person he'd have taken brass parrots from was Mike.

And for the first time in his scientifically inclined life, he didn't much care for the truth.

4

There was just nothing better than a whole Saturday off. Sure, they didn't work on Sundays but that didn't really count.

Not that Mike went to mass on Sundays, but she was still Catholic enough to feel guilt about choosing sleeping in over a sermon—and that sort of ruined the feel of a day off.

Today, though, was a gift. A gorgeous Saturday—deep blue sky, lots of white clouds muting the heat of the sun, and a great sea breeze whipping in off the ocean. A perfect September day, just warm enough to remind you of summer, but cool enough to convince you that fall was headed right at you.

By rights, the Marconis should have been working, or at least getting started, over at Cash Hunter's place. But yesterday at the family meeting, Jo had brushed right over the suggestion of getting a jump on things over there. In fact, she hadn't wanted to talk about Cash at all. No big surprise there, since the man had a talent for pushing every one of Jo's buttons. And God knew, she had plenty of 'em.

"Seriously," Mike muttered as she parked her truck

at the end of Main Street and unlatched her seat belt. "Jo so needs a man." A second later, though, she was whispering, "But there's a lot of that going on."

She herself hadn't had a date in so long that Frank Pezzini was starting to look good to her. Which just went to show that a lack of sex killed brain cells. Because Fabulous Frank, as Carla Candellano Wyatt liked to call him, was forty, with a comb-over he'd been perfecting for the last ten years, a potbelly, and a propensity for shiny white shoes.

She shuddered, shook her head, and climbed out of the truck. A freshening wind rushed at her, lifting her long blond hair, freed from its usual braid, until the thick, wavy mass danced around her head. Smiling to herself, she slung her black purse over her shoulder, slammed the truck door, and hit the sidewalk.

Up and down Main Street, shop doors were propped open in silent invitation. Old-fashioned globe streetlights stood in splendor, with wildly blooming chrysanthemums planted at their feet in bright splotches of color. Tourists wandered, neighbors stopped to chat, and traffic crawled from stoplight to stoplight while drivers looked for parking spaces.

And under it all, the constant murmur of the sea rose and fell as if it were the heartbeat of Chandler itself.

Still smiling, Mike headed down the sidewalk, passing Jackson Wyatt's law office on the corner, the candle shop, Wicks and Wax, and, God help her, Terrino's pizzeria. But it was too early for pizza, despite how good that sauce smelled as the scent of it poured through the open door in tantalizing waves.

She hurried past, listening to the soft click of her

heels against the pavement. It felt good to be out of her work clothes. God knew, she loved being a plumber—and she was good at it—but she also loved being a girl. And wearing soft blue linen slacks with a pale cream silk blouse and strappy, bone-colored sandals made her feel . . . like shopping.

Mike glanced in the window of the Spirit Shop as she passed and almost paused to drool over a new set of Celtic-design tarot cards. Inside the shop, Trish Donovan was busily waiting on a stream of tourists. But Trish would keep her talking for an hour. Not that there was anything wrong with that, but "first things first."

She followed her nose toward the Leaf and Bean, two doors down.

In Chandler, the one place to get an outstanding cup of coffee was the Leaf and Bean. Stevie Ryan Candellano was a wizard with an espresso machine, and even if you didn't like coffee—and Mike didn't want to know someone who couldn't appreciate liquid caffeine—the biscotti and other pastries Stevie made fresh every day were well worth the stop.

Mike pushed the door open and took a deep breath, enjoying the rush through her system as nerves danced and blood pumped in anticipation. Cinnamon hung heavy on the still air and the low growl of dozens of conversations sounded like the hum of a white-noise machine.

The cream-colored walls and ceiling were accented by thick, dark wood beams and the polished wood floor gleamed in the sunlight streaming in through the front window overlooking Main Street. Copper planters and baskets, filled with ivy, ferns, and all kinds of flowers that always seemed to bloom for Stevie, no matter the season, hung from heavy silver chains. A long glass case on the far wall displayed the amazing baked goods made fresh every day, and the rich scent of coffee pulled customers in the moment the door was opened.

Mike paused on the threshold and looked around, spotting familiar faces in among the tourists. Summer season was almost over, but the autumn crowd was just beginning to trickle into town.

In another week or two, the Autumn Festival would set up shop in the meadow just outside town, giving the local artisans a chance to showcase their stuff. Then, when that was over, the day-trippers would start filtering in, coming for a look at the fall foliage. In December, there'd be the Victorian Christmas Festival, with wandering carolers and street stalls selling everything from hot apple cider to roasted chestnuts. By the time winter was over, everyone looked forward to the Flower Fantasy in April, when the farmers sold cut flowers, bulbs, and seeds. And then summer was back and the whole cycle started over again.

Mike grinned at the thought. People in the city thought small-town life was boring. Nope. There was always something new going on and a dozen people who could tell you all about it.

"Hey, Mike," someone called out, "need you to stop by the house sometime this week. The pipes in the house are groaning like an old woman in heat."

Mike laughed. "Right, Mr. Santos. I'll call and set up a time."

"Old woman in heat." The woman sitting beside the

older man swatted his arm. "What would you know about that?"

Mike left the Santoses to their bickering and walked across the room, nodding absently to everyone she passed. By the time she made it to the counter, she was more than ready for her coffee. Leaning both arms on the cool, shining glass, she smiled and said, "Latte, Stevie. Fast."

Stevie Candellano laughed and turned toward the espresso machine, a silver pitcher already filled with fresh milk. Slipping it under the steamer, she glanced over her shoulder while the machine hissed and did its magic. "Haven't seen you in a couple of days. You trying to kick the coffee habit?"

Appalled, Mike shook her head. "Hell no. That'd be like trying to quit breathing."

"Glad to hear it." Stevie turned and grabbed a cardboard cup. Turning off the steamer, she wiped down the twin blades, then poured the hot milk into the cup before spooning on a light layer of foam, just the way Mike liked it. Slipping the lid on the cup, she handed it over. "So, you find any money in your mailbox yet?"

Mike laughed, took the cup and swallowed a careful sip of her drink. "Nope. And I've been checking." She glanced around behind her at the crowd, then met Stevie's cool blue gaze again. "Anybody else find some?"

"Oh yeah." Stevie leaned forward and tilted her head in the direction of the back of the store. "Mr. Bozeman over there? His TV broke a few days ago."

"Not surprising." The old man was Sam's neighbor and to hear her tell it Mr. Bozeman had the damn thing running twenty-four hours a day.

"What's interesting, though," Stevie pointed out, "is that the very next day, he found five hundred bucks in his mailbox."

"No shit?" Mike turned to look at the older man, who was so deaf he had to get nose to nose with his friends just to hear what they were saying.

"Yep. So naturally, he went right out and bought himself a better, *bigger* TV."

"Oh," Mike said, laughing, "Sam'll be happy to hear that."

"My guess is she already has. He got surround sound this time."

"Good God." She took another sip and shifted a look across the pastries behind the glass. Considering blowing her diet all to hell, she thought about it while she asked, "No one's got a clue about who the good fairy is yet?"

"Nope." Stevie shook her head, then wiped a clean, soft towel across an already immaculate counter. "But the Stevenson kids have hooked up a motion-sensor camera to their mailbox—"

"Those kids are scary," Mike put in, remembering the time the twins had set fire to their parents' garage by trying to launch a homemade missile *inside*.

"Too true. And they're offering their services to anyone else who wants to try to catch the money fairy."

"Great." She laughed as she imagined mailboxes all over town bursting into flames or something.

"Oh yeah. Things're getting interesting."

"Things're *always* interesting around here."

"Uh-huh," Stevie said slyly, "and speaking of

interesting, how's the cutie in the new house on the lake doing?"

Mike stiffened. "Cutie? Lucas?"

"Hello?" Stevie looked at her as if she were insane. "You do have eyes, right?"

Oh, nothing wrong with her eyes and, yes, she'd noticed Lucas's a time or two, which she really didn't want to think about at the moment. "Well, yeah. And I suppose he's not too bad, but *cute*?"

"Hey, I'm *married* and I noticed. What's your excuse?"

"Sanity?" She shifted position uneasily and told herself that there was no reason to get defensive. Heck, there was nothing going on between her and Lucas. Just some minor irritation and a little . . . okay, a *lot* of humming attraction, but hey. She was human.

"Very funny. But not only is he cute," Stevie said, "Paul says he's brilliant."

"He would know, I guess." Paul Candellano, Stevie's husband, was pretty damn smart himself. A computer genius of some sort or other, he did lots of work for the government and designed programs for all kinds of things, which just baffled Mike, since the only computer stuff she was qualified for was pushing the ON button.

So the nerd prince was brilliant. Was she surprised by this? No. A little intimidated? Maybe. But why should she be? she thought defensively. She could have stayed in college. She could have gotten a degree—if she hadn't been bored to tears.

All right, maybe not bored. But she did remember at

the time being too anxious to get on with living to sit in a series of classrooms. Papa hadn't been happy about it, but he'd learned to live with Mike's decision.

So Lucas was brilliant. Could he install a Jacuzzi tub or do a full copper repipe? She didn't think so.

"Hey, Stevie," a man called out from across the room. "How about a refill?"

"Coming up, Joe," she answered, already reaching for the coffeepot. "I gotta run. But hey, Mike, tell Jo I need to talk to her about a new roof."

"For here?"

"Yeah." She stopped and smiled. "There's a leak over the bedroom in the loft apartment. I hardly go up there anymore since I got married. So didn't notice it until yesterday when I went up to clean out the last closet."

"Sure," Mike said as she walked away, "I'll tell her."

Hmm. The loft apartment over the shop was empty now that Stevie had moved into Paul's house. She'd been in that apartment. It was big, roomy, and God knew, it was close to coffee.

There was no reason now for Mike to keep living at home. Not now that she wasn't saving up for her dream house. Why shouldn't she think about renting Stevie's old apartment? It'd be good to get out of the family home. Especially, she thought with an inner cringe, if Papa started bringing Grace home. No *way* did she want to be around to see the two of them cuddling and cooing.

Something to think about, she told herself, and happily sipping the world's best coffee, she left the shop to enjoy her day off.

. . .

Lucas sat in his car and seriously considered throwing it into reverse and just backing the hell out.

All he'd wanted was a cup of coffee to go, and now he not only had no coffee, but wasn't going. Because of *her*.

Mike Marconi and a dark-haired woman were standing directly outside the Leaf and Bean. Beside the brunette, a small, blond girl and a big golden retriever waited impatiently to get moving again.

Lucas's gaze locked on Mike Marconi and, despite his better instincts, he looked her up and down in slow approval. For once, she wasn't wearing her uniform of battered jeans and faded T-shirt. Instead, she wore tailored slacks and a silk shirt that clung lovingly to every curve. Her long blond hair hung loose to the middle of her back in a fall of sunlit waves. She swayed slightly as she talked and his gaze locked on the curve of her hip. Damn it, he'd thought her a distraction in the jeans and T-shirts. The way she looked now took the word *distraction* to a whole new level.

Then he noticed her tense smile.

Why tense?

Her body language was tightening up even as he watched her. She folded her arms across her chest, took a step back from the pretty, dark-haired woman she was talking to, and shook her head while she pointed vaguely across the street. Trying for an escape?

Grumbling, Lucas climbed out of his car and stalked the few steps separating him from the two women. Mike turned at his approach and gave him a smile usually reserved by kids for the arrival of the ice cream truck on a hot summer day.

"Lucas! Hi. Sorry I made you wait," Mike said, threading her arm through his.

He felt one eyebrow lift, but then he saw something in Mike's eyes that had him going along with her. "No problem," he said easily. "Haven't been here long."

"New friend?" The dark-haired woman winked at Mike, then smiled up at Lucas. "Hi. I'm Carla Wyatt. This is my daughter Reese and, well, the furry beast currently leaning against you is Abbey."

"Nice to meet you," he said and petted the dog before glancing at Reese when she tugged at his pants leg. "Yes?"

"Abbey's gonna have a baby, just like Mommy."

"Really?" He felt Mike's fingers tighten on his arm just a little, so he straightened up and added, "Congratulations. To you and your dog."

Carla laughed. "Thanks. It's pretty exciting." She laughed again. "Abbey's probably not excited, but I am. Just left my husband in his office mumbling something about college funds and high quarterly yields or whatever." She grabbed the little girl's hand and started for the door of the coffee shop. "Now I'm going in to tell Stevie I win the baby bet. We were sure she was going to be the one pregnant first, because, you know, Paul's working at home most of the time now and, well, Jackson's been out of town a lot and—" She caught herself, laughed again and shrugged. "Sorry. Didn't mean to give you the whole story. Just excited. You know?"

"Sure," he said, though he didn't have a clue. Lucas

had never really been the "fatherhood" type. He'd always been too focused on his work to think about spending any time with diapers and baby puke. But anyone with half an eye could see that Carla was excited enough for four people. So why wasn't her good friend Mike happy for her?

He shifted a look at her, but she was watching Carla.

"Tell Jackson I said happy baby, okay?"

"You bet," Carla said, still grinning. "And tell Sam I'll call her tomorrow."

"Right," Mike said and backed away, drawing Lucas with her.

When they reached his car, Mike let him go, and then walked around to the passenger side and got in. Lucas stood there, looking at her through the windshield. Until she waved her fingers at him in a "come on" motion.

Once in the car, he glanced at her. "Why are you in my car?"

"Hello?" She blinked at him in stunned amazement. "Because I just told Carla Candellano that I was meeting you and you went along with it, so I had to get into the car or she'd think I lied to her."

"You did lie to her."

"Well, I don't want *her* to know that."

"I thought her name was Wyatt."

"Is now, but she'll always be a Candellano." Mike tossed her purse onto the floor. "Italians may get married, but they never leave the family."

"Like the Mafia family, you mean?"

"Stereotypes. I'm panicking and he's talking sterotypes." She sighed. "Not *the Family*. The family. Her family. The Candellanos."

"Ah . . ."

"Are you going to fire up the engine any day soon?"

"Where are we going?"

"I'm not picky." She propped her elbow on the window ledge and speared her fingers through her hair. "Let's just get gone, okay?"

"*You* not picky?" He stared at her, dumbfounded. "The woman who changes every line and drawing on my damn blueprints *isn't* picky? The woman who put *parrots* in my kitchen *isn't* picky?"

"Funny." She looked around furtively. "Should I drive?"

"Then do I get to know what's going on?"

"Sure. Whatever. Later."

Muttering things under his breath that his mother would have slapped him for, if she were still alive, Lucas started the car, put it in reverse, and backed out. As he steered the car down Main Street, he spared another quick look at her. Her eyes looked a little . . . *haunted.* He snorted. When the hell had he gotten so sensitive? Why was he noticing Mike's eyes at all? And why the hell had he ridden in to her rescue like some modern-day knight on a two-door red charger?

Screw that.

He didn't need this.

Scraping one hand across his jaw, he asked tightly, "Where do you want me to drop you?"

"My truck's back in town."

"Naturally. I'll take you back."

"No." She shifted in her seat, turning her back on the ocean on her right, to look at him. "I'll just go where you were going."

"Not a good idea." He shot her a quick glance and tried not to notice that her long blond hair flew about her head like a distorted halo. Which, considering her temperament, was a joke and a half.

Hell, he didn't want her along. He'd left his house early this morning in an apparently futile attempt to keep her from "dropping by." So what does he do instead? Pick her the hell up in town?

Was there a conspiracy of some sort going on around here? Some twisted sense of fate that kept throwing this woman at him, like darts at a target?

"Why? Robbing a bank?"

"Nothing so interesting. I'm buying furniture. You'd be bored."

"Bored?" she repeated and gave him a grin that zapped something deep inside him. Something he was going to ignore completely. "How could I possibly be bored, shopping with someone else's money?"

He sighed, threw the gear shift into fourth, and stepped on the gas as they took the coast road. "What was I thinking?"

The furniture salesmen followed Mike around the store like kids scrambling to be the first one into a carnival. They jockeyed for her attention, and when she smiled at one of them, they acted as though someone had handed them a fistful of cash.

Lucas couldn't blame them. Even he was impressed. She knew furniture. She knew fabrics. And damned if she didn't have an opinion about everything in the place.

Not that he cared. He knew what he wanted.

"I'll take this one," he said, and was forced to grab the arm of the salesman closest to him because the man was so focused on Mike he was hardly breathing.

"What? Yes. Oh sure." The guy looked from Lucas to Mike and back again. "This one?"

"Yeah." Lucas looked at it again. Mission style, the big bed would go along with the Spanish-style house. Plus, it was huge. Simplicity itself, the head and footboard were made of wide, polished oak slats and at each corner stood sturdy oak posts. Perfect.

"You've got to be kidding."

He looked at Mike. She stared at the bed for a long minute and then looked up at him again and shook her head. "That's all wrong."

"How can a bed *I* want be the wrong bed for me?" He folded his arms across his chest and loomed over her. Not too difficult since the top of her head hit his chin. But the woman was nothing if not sure of herself.

She glared right back at him. "Just because the house is Spanish style doesn't mean everything inside it has to be. Expand your horizon a little."

The salesmen standing around her in a half-circle all nodded sagely as if she'd just stepped down from the Mount with two tablets in her arms.

"My bed. My house."

"Your house," she agreed. "Please, not that bed."

"What the hell difference can it possibly make to you?"

"Oh please." She waved one hand at her own face. "It would upset anyone with a sense of style. Could there be a more boring bed? It looks like a high-school wood-shop project."

One of the salesmen sniffed.

Mike ignored him.

"Why are you here again?" Lucas muttered.

"To save you from yourself apparently." Mike smiled, took his arm, then parted the sea of salesmen with the wave of one hand. Steering him across the showroom, she slipped behind a set of leather sofas and a plaid recliner that looked damn comfortable and came to a stop in front of the bed *she* preferred.

"This is the one."

Lucas was determined not to like it. Damn it, she'd stuck her nose into everything in his life in the last two months and the only thing he'd stood his ground on was his damn balcony in his own damn bedroom. Well, Mike Marconi was in for another disappointment. No way was he going to like the damn bed. No way was he caving in. He wanted the big, plain, sturdy bed and that's just the one he was going to . . .

He looked at the one she'd chosen.

Bigger than the Mission style, the sleigh bed was solid mahogany and richly beautiful. "One of a kind," the salesman closest to him muttered and Lucas believed him. The dark wood was burled on the head- and footboard and deeply carved into the grain was a twining spiral of ivy. The mattress was high and thick and damned if it didn't look inviting.

"You like it."

Yeah, he did. But he hated like hell to admit that to her. He glanced at Mike and the satisfaction on her face made him grit his teeth. "It's all right."

"Lie down, sir," one of the salesmen prompted. "You'll see. Your wife has selected one of our finest pieces. I'm sure you'll be swayed. She seems to have excellent taste."

"My—" He flashed her a look and Mike smiled and shrugged.

"They assumed—"

"Since you're the one doing all the talking."

"—that we're married." She finished with another shrug and he tried not to notice how the silk of her shirt pulled across her chest with every movement.

"Try it out," the salesman urged again and Lucas, grumbling all the way, did just that. He walked to the side of the bed, sat down, then stretched out atop the quilted mattress. Hell, anything to get this expedition finished and his day back on track.

He nearly groaned. The mattress felt plush and soft and welcoming. Long enough for a tall man to stretch out comfortably, the bed was, damn it, *perfect.*

"You, too, ma'am," the slightly built man with horn-rimmed glasses insisted. "Both of you should lie down as you always do, to get the feel for the furniture."

"Oh," Mike said and backed up a step. "I don't think that's—"

"Sure, *honey,*" Lucas said, and patted the mattress beside him in invitation. "Come on. Park it."

She sneered at him. "Thanks for the invite, but I'll pass . . ."

"Well," Lucas said, enjoying the fact that he'd put her on edge. "Sorry, gentlemen, but if my wife doesn't try out the bed, we won't be able to get it today, after all."

"Oh, please, madam, I assure you, you won't be sorry." The salesman talked fast, already seeing a hefty commission flying out the nearest window.

"Fine." Mike muttered the single word, walked to the opposite side of the bed, and lay down, keeping plenty of distance between her and Lucas.

No way was he letting her get away with that. She'd driven him crazy all morning, now it was payback time.

"Now, don't be shy, honey," he crooned and reached out for her. Scooping one arm under her shoulders, he pulled her in close. "Just snuggle in close like you do every night. I'm sure these gentlemen won't mind."

"You idiot," she grumbled into his shoulder.

"There, see? I knew you'd like it," the salesman crowed and looked around at his friends, happily counting the sale already.

"Well, I'm not sure yet," Lucas said, and reared back so that he could look into pale blue eyes glinting with everything *but* amusement. "I think we need one last test."

"If you're thinking what I think you're thinking, just start thinking something else, bucko," Mike said, and tried to wriggle away.

"I'll give you a moment," the salesman said instantly and scuttled away to write up the sale before anyone could change their minds.

"Hey," Lucas said quietly, for Mike alone to hear. "You want me to get this bed, then prove to me that it's going to be comfortable in *all* situations."

"Oh please." She snorted. "The nerd prince is worried about that once-a-year special night with a lady friend?"

"Once a year?"

One blond eyebrow rose high on her forehead. "You haven't exactly been swimming in babes for the last two months," she pointed out.

"By choice."

"Sure. That's what they all say."

"Could you just shut up for ten seconds?"

"My sister Jo's always asking me that."

He stared down into her eyes. "And does it work?"

"Never."

"Then let's try this."

He kissed her.

His mouth brushed across hers once, twice, and then fastened on in a hunger he hadn't been expecting. Hadn't counted on. His tongue dipped into her warmth, swirled with hers, danced and dipped and tasted and explored. Her breath shot into his throat, his lungs, and he felt her slide all too deep inside him.

Oh no.

This he hadn't counted on at all.

Neither, apparently, had she.

Mike broke first, pulled back and stared at him.

"What?" he asked.

"Do that again."

"Finally. An order I'm happy to take."

5

It was like grabbing hold of a live electrical wire.

Her mouth was buzzing, her skin sizzling, and her blood was steaming.

Oh boy.

One part of her still realized that, hey, they were lying in the middle of a furniture store. But another, more insistent part of her was screeching, *Who cares? Go for it!* And that was just crazy enough to douse the blistering heat engulfing her.

Mike broke the kiss and rolled away from Lucas in one incredibly awkward move. But she wasn't thinking graceful, she was thinking, *move.* When she hit the edge of the bed, she kept right on rolling until she landed on her feet, stumbled, then backed up another step or two, just for good measure.

Lifting one hand, she pointed at him and squeaked, "What the hell was *that*?"

He was lying there like a man who'd just been hit in the head with a monkey wrench—and hey, not a bad idea, when you come down to it. Slowly, he turned his head toward her and he looked as dumbfounded as she felt.

Small consolation.

She didn't like surprises. Didn't like to be caught off guard. She needed her defenses up and running—especially when some guy was making a move.

Damn it, *guys* didn't surprise Mike.

She'd always been able to read the signs. Though to be fair, most guys weren't that hard to read. She could tell when a move was coming and knew just how to deflect it or welcome it, depending on her outlook at the time.

But the nerd prince had just sneaked under her radar and landed a Stinger missile on her unprotected . . . *ass*ets.

"That . . . was a *kiss*," he muttered, and rubbed both hands across his face briskly before shaking his head like a man stepping out from under a shower.

"That was no simple kiss. I've been kissed before," Mike said, still pointing at him and now reduced to shaking her index finger at him in accusation. "And they were nothing like that. Hello? You're carrying a secret weapon around with you or something."

"Me?" He rolled off the bed on his side and glared at her from the safety of about seven feet of distance. The look in his eyes wasn't exactly flattering. "You weren't exactly resisting, you know. Actually, *you're* the one who said 'do it again.' "

She snorted. "And you always take orders from women."

"Lately? Just one," he grumbled, and glanced over his shoulder at the showroom behind him as if expecting her trained herd of salesmen to come flooding back into the bedroom setup. When he was sure that it was all clear, he blew out a deep breath, held up both hands and said, "Anyway. No big deal. We tried out the bed. We kissed. Now I buy the damn bed and we get the hell out of here."

"Right. No big deal." What had she been thinking, letting him know that he'd gotten to her? *Never* give a man the advantage, for crying out loud. She knew that. Hell, she insisted on it. She'd learned early on to stay in control of any situation. And she'd learned it the hard way. No way in hell was she going to forget those lessons *now*.

Mike nodded at him and dropped her accusatory finger back to her side. Good plan. Out of here. Away from the surprising geek and his electric lips. "Good. Okay. Let's go."

He stepped back and let her walk in front of him, and even as she passed him, Mike was wishing they could change positions. Right now, she felt as though she ought to be keeping a wary eye on him. Having him behind her just meant she couldn't see his face. She couldn't read what he was thinking in his eyes.

Then again, she thought as she wended through the arranged tableaus on the showroom floor, maybe that was a good thing. Because if *he* was thinking what *she* was thinking right at the moment, things were going to get a lot more complicated.

Fast.

Jo hunched over her kitchen table, and glared at the open astronomy textbook in front of her. "For God's sake," she muttered as she threw her pencil at the wall opposite. "How hard can this be? Stars? Planets? And why the *hell* do I have to know how far away they are? Isn't it enough to know that they're in the sky?"

She pushed her chair back and jumped up, stalking across the blue-flecked cream-colored linoleum. The kitchen of her rented condo was as small as every other room in the place, but it had never bothered her before.

It was temporary. One of these days, she'd find the perfect house to buy and redo. Until then, the condo was as good a place as anywhere else and substantially better than an apartment. At least here she had a yard, small as it was, and the sense of privacy that having someone live above and below her wouldn't afford.

Although today she was feeling just a little bit . . . *trapped.*

Hitting the open doorway, she left the kitchen, stomped into her tiny living room and flopped onto the sofa. Propping her feet up on the coffee table in front of her, she shoved a stack of mail order catalogues and magazines to the floor in a heap. Snatching the remote from the cushion beside her, she turned on the TV and pretended interest in a home makeover show.

Ordinarily, Jo loved these programs. This was right up her alley. Breathing new life into old homes. But today her mind was too fixed on her failures to enjoy the thought of new projects.

She'd made a solemn promise to herself years ago— to complete the education she'd run from and to prove to herself that she was stronger than she'd once been.

And it fried her ass to have to admit defeat.

The hum of voices from the television faded into the background as her mind kicked into high gear. And it wasn't just flunking that was bugging her. She never should have told Cash about this. What in the hell had she been thinking? Her head dropped to the back of the sofa and she stared up at the sunlight streaking across the ceiling.

Dust motes drifted in the breeze slipping beneath the open window. The McKenna kids next door were out tossing a football and the accompanying shouts and laughter sounded like a song heralding the end of summer.

Cash.

A man she didn't trust and didn't like.

And as soon as the Marconis started work on his place, she'd have to see him every damn day, knowing that *he* knew she was flunking a stupid college course that eighteen-year-old kids passed in a walk.

"Perfect," she muttered and lifted her head to flip through the channels. "Just perfect."

A knock on the door interrupted her black thoughts and she gratefully leaped up off the couch. She slipped on the stupid magazines, caught her balance again, and glared at the mess on the floor as if it had deliberately set out to trip her up.

Grumbling viciously, she stalked across the room. The beige generic no-style carpet muffled her footsteps, and when she yanked the door open, the guy standing on the porch jumped a foot.

"Crap, lady. Scared me to death." His brown uniform was rumpled and way too big on him. He was short and skinny with bright red hair, big blue eyes, and an Adam's apple that was bobbing up and down like a cork tossed into the rapids.

Jo chuckled and tossed her dark brown hair over her shoulder. "Sorry. Bad day."

"Yeah, well, mine's not getting any better." He checked the clipboard he carried. "You Jo Marconi?"

"Yeah?"

"Never met a girl named Joe."

"Wow," she said, sighing, "never heard that one before."

"Right. Got a delivery." He bent down, picked up a thin brown box, and held out the clipboard. "Sign there. At the bottom."

She stared at the box in his hand. "What is it?"

"Do I look psychic?"

"No," she said wryly, cocking a hip and leaning against the doorjamb. "You look like a guy who's not trying for a tip."

He laughed. "Hey, the guy who ordered this already included a tip for me. Big."

Intrigued, Jo signed her name, then took the package. She shut the door on the kid and leaned back against it. Holding the package carefully in both hands, she studied it warily and told herself she ought to just throw it out.

Cash Hunter.

"What the hell is he sending me?" she asked the empty room. "And *why?*"

She lifted the box and listened for a second or two just to make sure it wasn't ticking. Then she laughed. Of course it wasn't a bomb. "Cash doesn't blow women up. He breaks 'em down."

She pushed away from the door and carried the package to the couch. Dropping the box on the coffee table, she sat down and flipped the TV on, deliberately ignoring the box. "Not me, though. He's not getting to me."

On the TV, a husband gave his wife a new dishwasher with a bright red ribbon on it. "Gifts. Hah! If a man gave me a dishwasher, I'd stuff his lifeless body inside it and shove it off a cliff."

Okay, maybe she needed to calm down a little.

On the other hand, how the hell could she calm down when her archnemesis was invading her space via UPS?

She glanced at the package again. It might as well have been ticking. Its very presence in the room was disturbing. Annoying. Irritating. She'd never been able to stand against an unopened box. As a kid, she'd hunted down her Christmas presents way ahead of time and opened them all before rewrapping them. She just didn't like surprises. She wanted to *know*.

Like now.

The box was taunting her.

And damn it, she couldn't stand it.

Tossing the remote, she grabbed the box and ripped the package open, cursing at the strapping tape until she managed to wrest it free. "The only reason I'm opening this," she muttered, as if apologizing to the universe at large, "is I can't *not* open it. Fine. I'm weak. Shoot me."

When she had one end open, she tipped the box onto its side. A thick yellow and black book fell onto her lap. She took one look at the title and a spurt of fury shot through her like water from a fire hose.

She dropped the damn thing when she jumped to her

feet and, wouldn't you know it, the book landed faceup, so she could still see the title, in thick white and yellow letters.

"You bastard." She kicked it and watched as it slid across the carpet.

Cash Hunter thought he could take something she'd told him in private and turn it into a *joke*? He thought it was *funny*? She's drowning and he's enjoying the show?

"You self-serving, sanctimonious tower of testosterone," Jo grumbled as she crossed the room to pick up the blasted book. "I'll get you for this. Seriously."

Still scowling, she looked down at the book and thought about driving over to his place and launching the thick volume at his head. But it probably wasn't heavy enough to make a dent. A hammer then. She'd throw a hammer.

"But not my good one," she said, disgusted, as she dropped onto the couch. "My *old* one. You're not worthy of a brand-new hammer."

Imagining Cash flat on his back with a huge knot rising on his forehead calmed her down long enough to allow her to snatch up the book, open it, and flip through the pages quickly. Okay, maybe she should at least *look* at it. But she was still mad and, damn it, he was going to hear about this. Soon.

For now though, she checked the table of contents on *Astronomy for Dummies*.

Lucas concentrated on the road.

It was much better than thinking about the woman

sitting next to him in the car. She was being too quiet. In the two months he'd known her, he'd seen Mike furious, amused, thoughtful, and, God knew, intrusive. But he'd yet to see her so damn silent.

Unsettling.

But then, that kiss had been pretty damn unsettling, too. His body stirred, but he ruthlessly quashed the hot ball of lust bouncing around inside him. Wasn't easy, but the last thing he needed was to let Mike even further into his life. Although at the moment, all he could think about was laying her down on the big bed they'd just picked out and—

Conversation.

Talking would keep him too busy to think about what might have happened if they hadn't been in a damn showroom full of unctuous salesmen. Hell, even having her irritate him was better than this quiet that gave his mind too much room to wander.

He had to say something—anything. Otherwise, he'd be admitting that the kiss had taken on a life of its own in his mind.

"So."

She jumped, startled, and looked at him as if she'd forgotten he was there. Pushing her hair back out of her eyes, she held it down at her nape with one hand and snarled, "What?"

Lucas ignored her battle attitude—in fact, he was grateful for it. An angry Mike he knew how to deal with. "You never said. Earlier. When you were talking to your friend. You never said why you were so anxious to get away."

"Not anxious," she argued. "Ready."

"Fine. Ready. Why?"

She blew out a breath and shifted her gaze past him to stare at the ocean, stretching out to the horizon. He spared a quick look, too, and saw the wide, golden path lying across the dark blue surface of the water as the sun slowly slipped from the sky.

"No biggie, really," she said after a long minute or two. "It's just— Carla's sister-in-law Tasha just had a baby girl, her other sister-in-law Beth had a boy a couple months ago, now Carla's pregnant. Hell, even *Abbey's* pregnant again."

Confusion reigned, but then he'd started this conversation. "So?"

"So, nothing. It was just hormone overload, okay?" She turned and fixed her gaze on the road in front of them. "I'm tired of hearing about babies. It's like everyone in Chandler is baby nuts. That's all Sam can talk about as she and the Weasel Dog try to make another one—"

"Weasel Dog?" he asked.

"Long story," Mike said, brushing that aside. Then she added, "And hey, I love Emma. My niece," she added by way of explanation. "Sam's daughter, and it's great that she's back in the family—"

"Back in?" Lucas asked. "Your niece left the family?"

"Long story," Mike said again, and Lucas had the feeling that everything about this woman would eventually be a long story. There was nothing simple about her. Nothing understated. Everything about Mike Marconi was over the top. Her hair, her eyes, her laugh, her sexy, rough, low-pitched voice.

She threw both hands up and her hair flew out around

her face in the rushing wind. "But God, does *everyone* have to get pregnant at once? Is there something in the water?"

He squinted into the sunlight. "Remind me to keep bottled water at my house."

"Oh yeah. You're in real danger." She laughed suddenly and he was amazed again at her changeability. Mike's moods could shift so quickly, a man had to be wearing a seat belt just to avoid whiplash. "All those women coming and going from your place must really worry you."

Insulted, he cocked an eyebrow and glanced at her. "I'm not as big a loser as you seem to think I am."

"Yeah?" she asked, turning in her seat again to smile at him. "You're a scientist, aren't you?"

"And that's spelled *l-o-s-e-r*?"

"Please. Have you *seen* a picture of Einstein?"

A short bark of laughter shot from his throat. "He was married *and* had affairs."

"A prince of a guy."

"Not a prince. But hardly a virgin."

She lifted one index finger. "Didn't say you were a virgin."

"Gee, thanks for that."

She nodded regally, like a queen briefly recognizing a peasant who just happened to stumble across her path. "I figure you must have gotten lucky at *some* point in your life."

The knot of lust that had held him in its grip since the furniture store eased back and irritation simmered to life again. Damn if the woman didn't provoke all manner of emotions in him. "Thanks very much."

She waved a hand. "I'm just sayin'—"

"Saying exactly what?"

She sighed. "Looks like we're gonna talk about that kiss after all."

Crap.

"I figure if you kiss that well, you've got to get some action sometime. So," she said before he could prepare himself for whatever else might be coming, "how come no girlfriend? For the lack of women around your place, you could be a priest—you're not a priest, are you?"

He scowled. "No."

"That's good." She blew out a breath and smiled. "I don't go to mass or anything, but I draw the line at de-frocking a priest." She frowned to herself. "Not sure I know *how* to defrock somebody. Do you actually have to be *frocked*, first?"

Lucas shook his head and hit the turn signal on the steering column. He passed the beat-up camper-shell truck in front of them, then cruised back over to the slow lane. "Are you insane?"

"Not technically, but as I might have mentioned, I am Italian, so . . ."

"Okay, never mind."

"So if you're not a priest, what exactly are you?"

His hands tightened on the steering wheel. "Scientist."

"Yeah, I get that. Forget who told me, though. What kind? Rocket? Mad? Which?"

"There's that humor again," he muttered.

"Oh, I'm a laugh riot. Just ask my sisters."

"No, thanks, one Marconi is more than enough for me."

"That's what they all say."

"You've got a response for everything, don't you?"

"Usually," she admitted, and propped her elbow on the window frame. "But you didn't answer my question and I rarely forget to drag a conversation back to the subject I was interested in. So what kind of scientist?"

"Research."

"Well, that's vague enough. Researching what?"

Fine . . . He'd tell her. But damn, he hated to. Invariably, someone heard what he was working on and it set off a long train of questions designed more for Arthur C. Clarke than Lucas Gallagher.

"I work with nanotechnology."

Her eyes widened. "Nanites? Hey, I saw them on *Stargate* once." She scooted around in her seat until she was facing him again. "They had these tiny nano-whatevers and they were in Colonel O'Neill's bloodstream and they made him like a hundred years old in two weeks. It was really weird, and you know, for a completely cute man, he's not going to age well at all."

Her words came so fast, it was hard to keep up, but Lucas caught the gist, and wasn't surprised. "It's not like that. That's science fiction. What I do—what *we* do—is research nanotechnology for medical uses."

"Okay. Like . . . ?"

He sighed, stepped on the gas, and wished it weren't such a long drive back to Chandler. "Like, maybe, one day, nanotechnology can be used to fight cancer cells. Inject them into the bloodstream and they attack only the diseased cells. Right now, they're looking at ways to use the technology to devise better ways to administer medicine. There are researchers in every conceivable field, looking for ways to incorporate tomorrow's science today."

She applauded.

He frowned at her. "What's that for?"

"You sounded like a commercial."

"Hey, you asked."

"True. So these nanothings . . . are used in what?"

He sighed, but gave her points. Most people he talked to about his work would glaze over and slip into a coma about now. She, at least, was pretending interest.

"You use sunscreen?"

"Hello? Italian. Years of pasta sauce and olive oil have built up an internal sunscreen to beat anything on the market today."

"You should still use—"

"Geez. Kidding. Yeah, I use it. Why?"

"Nanotechnology is used in that, for one thing. Tiny nanoparticles that make zinc oxide clear instead of snow white."

"Seriously?" She grinned and Lucas couldn't help smiling along with her. He glanced at her. She had an amazing mouth. Wide and mobile and . . . way too tasty.

"Nanobots right there on your nose?"

"They're not nanobots," he said with a patient sigh. "There's no such thing."

"Maybe not, but who can keep saying nanotechnology all the time?"

The exit for Chandler was just a mile ahead and Lucas spared her another quick look. She was still smiling and damn if she didn't look good. Too damn good.

"So are you working on nano stuff here? At your place?"

"No," he said, pointing the car toward the exit. The curve in the freeway exit was bordered on both sides by towering trees with leaves just beginning to change color. "I'm on a leave of absence. I'm writing a book about the research being done and——"

"Sure to be a best seller," she murmured, lifting both eyebrows.

At the end of the curve, he stopped at the traffic light and looked at her. "Some people are actually interested in what the future's going to be made of, you know. In what we can do to make that future better."

She just stared at him, and for some reason, Lucas felt compelled to go on. As usual, when talking about the work that had fascinated him for so long, his excitement colored his voice. "Think about it, Mike. In ten years, twenty, we could wipe out cancer. *All* cancers. This could be a cure for the modern plague. And it's not just medicine that nanotechnology will affect. This science will be used in everything from plastics to making better, cleaner engines for cars . . ."

A slow smile spread across her face. "You really think you could cure cancer?"

He eased back into his seat. Adrenaline still pumped inside him and Lucas reminded himself to dial it down. No one ever got it. No one ever understood what the research meant to him. "Maybe not me. But someone like me will. One day, people will get anticancer shots as easily as they get tetanus boosters today."

She nodded slowly, pushed her hair back from her face, and said, "You know something, I believe you."

He looked at her and took off his sunglasses to get a better view of her clear, summer-sky blue eyes. "Yeah?"

"Yeah," she admitted quietly. "I just wish it had been around nine years ago."

"You lost someone?"

"My mom." Mike took a deep breath and blew it out again. When she spoke, her voice was low, soft, and hinted of pain that still had the power to tear at her. "She died of cancer nine years ago. Still feels like yesterday sometimes." She dipped her head, then looked up at him again. "You know?"

"Yeah, I do." He put the car in gear and turned right, heading for downtown Chandler. "I lost my folks five years ago. Car accident."

"I'm sorry."

"So was I." His own pain reared up and reminded him of the emptiness he carried around inside him. He was alone now. Alone, except for Justin—so, *alone*.

"It's hard," Mike said, letting her fingers play with the rubber stripping along the edge of the car window as she added, "If I hadn't had my sisters, and Papa, I don't know what I would have done. As it was, I—" She broke off and looked at him. "Do you have brothers? Sisters?"

Everything in him tightened up. "No sisters. One brother."

"Where's he live?"

He lifted one shoulder in a careless shrug. "I don't know."

"What's that mean?" Mike looked at him and saw that his jaw was clenched and his hands were fisted around the steering wheel tight enough to make his knuckles white. Probably not a good sign, but hell, if they were going to talk, then he couldn't just shut up whenever the hell he felt like it. "You have a brother and you don't know where he lives?"

"Yes." He shot her a sidelong glance then slipped his sunglasses back on—but even from behind those dark lenses, Mike felt the chill in his gaze. So she backed off. For now. Lifting both hands, she said, "Hey, no problem. Not my brother, although in my family, if everyone doesn't know where everyone else is at any given moment, the earth shakes and the skies thunder."

"Not all families are like yours," he said, and there was as much regret as anger in his voice now. Mike wondered what the rest of the story was, but then reminded herself that she had plenty of her own secrets. Who was she to go digging his up to air them out?

To ease them both back from the edginess suddenly spiraling around them, Mike changed the subject. "You know, I've been thinking about that kiss."

He snorted. "When? We've been talking for the last fifteen minutes."

"You can't talk and think at the same time?" She shook her head. "And you call yourself a scientist."

He muttered something under his breath and Mike was pretty sure she was glad she hadn't heard what he said. Still, his reluctance to talk about this wouldn't stop her. "You need to get out more. That's why the kiss happened. You need a woman."

He stiffened, clearly offended. Okay, maybe that had come out wrong.

Before he could speak, she interrupted quickly. "I didn't mean anything by that, so chill out. It's just that you haven't met many people and—"

"I've been busy," he reminded her and made a left turn onto Main Street. "Protecting my house. From you."

"Cute. My point is, that kiss—and okay, it was a beauty—just tells me that maybe you've been concentrating on nano stuff too long instead of the *fun* stuff."

"You're amazing."

"Thank you."

"Not sure it was a compliment."

"That's how I'm taking it."

He shook his head and steered the car into a parking space right alongside her battered truck. He pulled up the brake but didn't turn off the engine. "Whatever helps."

"So," Mike said, as he just sat there, watching her, "I'm thinking maybe Trish Donovan. She's really nice. How do you feel about redheads?"

"They should be shot."

"Huh?"

His chin hit his chest. "I don't feel anything about them."

"See?" she said. "Not out enough."

"I'm out *now*."

"With *me*."

He lifted his head, pulled off his sunglasses, and hooked them through the neck of his dark green T-shirt. "Look. You want to help? Fine. You can help. I have to go to a fund-raiser for the lab next weekend. It's at an old estate just outside San Francisco. Come with me."

"Huh?" Mike wanted to thunk the heel of her hand against her ear, but that probably would look weird. Instead, she repeated, "Huh?"

He scrubbed one hand across his face—something she'd noticed he usually did when she was showing him one of her improvements on his house. A clear sign he was walking a ragged edge. But he was talking again and Mike told herself she'd better listen up.

"It'd be easier on me if I took a . . ."

"Date?" she asked. "Jesus, it *has* been too long. You can't even say the word."

"—*date* to this thing." Frowning, he continued as if she hadn't spoken. "I go up Saturday morning, come back Sunday afternoon. What do you say?"

What was she supposed to say? She'd planned on fixing him up with someone else. Not herself.

Mike didn't date fixer-uppers.

But damn it, he was kind of cute.

In a nerd-prince sort of way.

Then she thought about that kiss, damn it. And it had been a long time since she'd been out with anyone who could stir her up like that—even if he was a *Weird Science* guy.

"Separate rooms?" she asked, because hey, you should always check these things out in advance, and if she changed her mind later, well then, she could change her mind. But she'd been out with guys before who figured that springing for a fifty-dollar dinner also entitled them to Mike as dessert.

He frowned at her. "I said a date—not sex."

There was that insulted look again.

"Fine. Take it easy. Just asking." She tipped her head

to one side to study him for a long minute. His dark brown eyes met hers steadily and she wished for one moment that she could actually know what he was thinking. Then she remembered he was some sort of genius and she probably wouldn't understand anything she read in his mind anyway, so what would be the point?

He muttered something else, then said louder, "Do you want to go or not?"

"Sure," she said before she could say no. "Why not?"

"Okay, then." He nodded, revved the engine, then glanced at her again. "So. Thanks, I think, for all the 'help' today."

"You're welcome." He gunned the engine again and the sleek little convertible roared like a mini Tiger. Apparently, he was expecting her to bail out and get gone. She stayed put and enjoyed the sizzle of frustration on his face. The nerd prince was turning out to be even more surprising than she'd thought.

"Are you just going to sit here the rest of the day?"

She grinned. "I was thinking about it."

He sighed. "You want some coffee?"

"You buying?" She perked right up at the offer of coffee, and seriously, what red-blooded female wouldn't?

"Why not?" he grumbled as he shut off the engine. "I bought everything else today."

"Rocket man, I like your style."

Both dark eyebrows lifted. "Rocket man?"

"Yeah." She opened her car door, but paused to smile at him. "Rocket scientist, rocket man, get it?"

He laughed, and God, when his mouth curved, it did some pretty spectacular things to her belly.

"I told you. I'm not a rocket scientist."

"Yeah, I know," Mike teased, still smiling at him, "but 'nano man' sounds so lame."

He thought about it and nodded. "True."

"So, you up for one of Stevie's cinnamon rolls, too?"

"Are they good?" he asked as he stepped up onto the sidewalk and waited for her.

"Good?" Mike laughed, threaded her arm through his, and promised, "Your mouth is about to get a helluva treat."

"Another one?"

Her stomach jittered, but her steps didn't falter and neither did her smile.

Ohboyohboyohboy.

Going away for the weekend with Rocket Man just might be a little more dangerous than she'd figured.

6

"Your father is the most stubborn man on the face of the planet."

"Yow!" Startled, Mike jumped, then thunked her head on the elbow joint beneath the sink in the second kitchen at Grace Van Horn's house. Scooting out from under, she rubbed at the throbbing spot, looked at the woman pacing, and said, "Hi, Grace. What's new?"

The tiny woman in designer slacks and shirt, not to mention enough gold jewelry to sink a rowboat, huffed out a breath then sucked in another one before speaking again. While she talked, she walked, briskly paced little steps, the heels of her shoes clacking noisily on the Italian tile floor. "It's your father."

"I got that much." Mike pulled her hand away from the knot on her skull and checked for blood. Not that she wasn't interested in what was going on with Papa, but if she was bleeding, she wanted to know about it in time to keep from dying or something. Nope. No blood. Just mind-numbing pain.

Grumbling a little, she squinted into the afternoon sunlight streaming through the kitchen window. Grace Van Horn, somewhere around the age of sixty, looked like a white-haired pixie. Her hair was short and stylish, her dark eyes were usually sparkling with good humor, and she pretty much *flitted* from one place to another. But at the moment, she looked like she wanted to slam the toe of her elegant, sling-back heel into someone's backside.

"It's at least ninety out there in the sun today."

Mike stood up and raked a quick look across the compound. Most of the crew had left for the day, but there were a few guys left, tidying up some last-minute jobs.

Last weekend, the weather had been autumnish.

Last weekend.

Saturday.

She'd spent the whole day with Lucas, shopping, talking, *kissing*. Mike blinked and shook the thought away, like a big dog coming out of a lake. Naturally, the thought came skittering right back.

Insidious, really.

She'd been working herself half to death for the last few days, trying to keep her mind off Lucas and The Kiss, which she'd now started thinking of in capital letters—and, God help her, The Date.

Why in the hell had she agreed to go away for the weekend with him? And more importantly, why wasn't she backing out?

Well, she knew the answer to that one. Mike Marconi never backed down. She'd done all the running she'd ever do back when she was sixteen. And hadn't *that* ended well?

Nope. She'd go through with the date, suffer through boring speeches and even more boring scientist talk, then maybe she'd kiss Lucas again and then she'd come home.

No.

Wait a minute.

There would be *no* more kissing.

None whatsoever.

Probably.

"Mike!"

Grace's voice, set at a pitch designed to make dogs deaf, rattled Mike enough to get her attention.

"The heat?" Grace demanded, staring up into Mike's eyes impatiently. "Your father? Sunstroke?"

"Right." Damn. Even when he wasn't around, Lucas was making life harder.

Grace was right. Last weekend, the weather was nice. Today, summer had apparently decided to charbroil Chandler one last time.

All summer the Marconis had been here, working at Grace's. She always paid well, but most of the extra money went to buy aspirin. Working with Grace was like working with a millionaire child. She just couldn't make up her mind—there was always something new that she'd heard of. Or something she wanted to try.

Every year, the construction firms in the area took turns working for Grace; this time the Marconis had been up to bat. But now that the summer of hell was winding down, Mike was feeling relaxed enough— except for her throbbing skull—to actually wonder what the latest fuss was about.

"Yeah, it's hot, but—"

Grace stepped up closer to her, lifted one hand and pointed through the window. "Everyone with an ounce of common sense is in the shade. Or inside."

"Sure, but—"

"But not your father." Grace stamped one foot against the ground and a tiny cloud of dust rose up from the floor and settled over the toe of her brown leather shoe. Mike winced, glad she wasn't going to be in charge of cleaning the mess construction left behind.

"The man has a head like rock, Mike."

She had to smile. How often had she heard her own mother make the same complaint? Until, of course, the ugly year. The year when Mama had gotten sick then slowly withered away until the only thing recognizable about her was her smile.

Mike lifted one shoulder, easing that memory away, and looked through the window toward her father. Hank Marconi wasn't a tall man. But his short body was muscular, even for a man of sixty-five. His shoulders were broad, his hands huge and work worn, and his full, gray beard neatly trimmed. Some of the kids in Chandler were absolutely convinced that Papa Marconi was actually Santa Claus. Which delighted Papa no end.

But as Mike watched him now, she noticed that his features were bright red, sweat ran down his face, and he seemed to be breathing heavily.

"I told him to come inside and have some tea, but he refuses to quit until he's finished that ridiculous gate for the goat shed." Grace was furious, but Mike caught the undercurrent of concern in her voice.

Shifting position uncomfortably, Mike winced as the memory of what Sam had said about Grace and

Papa reared to life in her brain. Oh, man. She so didn't want to think about that.

"Don't worry, Grace," she said quickly, before a vision of Grace and Papa caught in a lip-lock could invade her mind. "Papa knows what he's doing."

Though even as she said it, she wondered.

"A man his age, standing around in the afternoon sun, working himself half to death over a ridiculous goat gate," Grace muttered.

It *was* ridiculous. But Mike hesitated to point out that the stupid gate was Grace's fault. It had been one of the older woman's many "changes" to the plans. Scrolled woodwork lined the top of the gate and had to be fastened to the solid oak doors with dozens of finishing screws. Why Grace's cashmere and angora goats needed a decorative gate in the first place was beyond Mike.

But she knew her father was stubborn enough to stand in the sun until he dropped rather than admit that he was uncomfortable.

"I'll talk to him."

"Good luck to you."

Grace marched off and Mike shrugged as she dropped her wrench into the toolbox and left the kitchen through the side door. "Trouble in paradise, I guess," she murmured as she stepped into the blast of afternoon heat.

Waving to a couple of the guys as they packed up the equipment, Mike felt concern spike inside her. The closer she walked to her father, the more worried she was. He really didn't look well at all. His blue eyes were glassy and his hands shook as he wielded the power drill.

"Papa—"

Instantly, he shut off the tool, let his arms drop to his sides, and looked around at her. Forcing a smile that didn't reach his eyes, he said, "Almost finished."

That about covered it, Mike thought guiltily. She should have been paying more attention to him. He wasn't a young man anymore and it had been unusually hot today. Hardly a breath of air stirred the trees around them—and standing directly in the sun made it seem even hotter. "Papa, why don't you let me finish that?"

"What?" His gaze snapped to hers. "Since when do you do my work?"

"Since I'm finished and it's really hot and you look—"

"What?" he argued, throwing his shoulders back and lifting his chin. "I look what?"

"Tired?"

He scowled at her, and just for a moment, Mike was sixteen again. That niggling curl of dread settled in the pit of her stomach just as it used to when he gave her a look that said he was both furious and disappointed.

"Grace sent you out here, didn't she?"

Mike nodded and reminded herself she wasn't sixteen anymore and Papa knew it. "She's worried."

"She doesn't have to be. I'm fine."

"Yeah," Mike said dryly, "I can see that."

"Don't you be smart, Michaela." He shook the electric drill at her as if it were a pointer. "I'm still the papa around here."

Male egos. Touchy. In this situation, Sam would back down, tell Papa that he was worrying *her*. Jo would work Papa with a few wisely chosen words, figuring out a way to make him think that quitting was *his* idea.

Mike, though, worked differently. Always had. For better or worse, she just jumped in with both feet, and to hell with the consequences. "Yes, you're the papa and you should know better than to stand in the hot sun without even wearing a hat, for God's sake. You'd never let *us* get away with that."

He scowled at her and she was glad of the beard. It hid the fact that his lips were no doubt thinned into a razor slash of disapproval.

"Papa," she said, "you look crappy and it's really hot out here. Would it kill you to go sit in the shade for a few minutes and cool down?"

"This is how you talk to your papa?" he demanded, his face getting, if possible, even redder than it had been a moment or two before.

"My papa has a hard head," she countered, lifting her own chin in a mirror of his stance. "Like *me*. You always said that sometimes you had to shout at me just to get my attention. So . . ."

Heartbeats ticked by.

Somewhere a bird called and was answered by a dozen friends. A blessed breeze danced through the tops of the trees and tossed dappled shade across the dusty yard.

Mike held her breath and waited. Her head pounded, her mouth was dry, and a curl of worry kept trying to spread through her as she watched her father. Damn it. When had Papa gotten *old*? Sure, he wasn't *elderly* or anything. Yet. But when had his hair gone completely gray? When had the lines around his eyes etched so deeply into his skin? And why the hell hadn't she noticed?

He'd always been just *Papa.*

Unchanging.

There.

Her rock in the wildly swirling river that was her life.

It terrified her a little to see that rock wearing down. It horrified her to think of that rock one day not being there at all.

"Papa?" she said, her voice softer, less antagonistic. "Please?"

He frowned, then grabbed a handkerchief from his back pocket to wipe the sweat from his forehead. Shoving the cloth back into his work pants, he nodded. "It *is* hot. Maybe me and my girl should go sit in the shade and take a rest."

Now that he'd given in, she felt better, and wanting to get them both back on their usual track, Mike winked, slung her arm over his shoulders, and steered him for the shade. "Your girl, huh? So, Papa, does that mean *me*? Or Grace?"

He stopped dead, turned his head and looked at her. Narrowing his eyes, he studied her for a long minute before his lips twitched. "Michaela," he said, lifting one index finger to wave at her. "That smart mouth of yours is going to give you trouble one day."

She kissed him and laughed. Everything was okay again. He'd never been able to stay mad at his daughters. The man had a heart as soft as his head was hard. "Then

I'll just run home to my papa. *He'll* protect me."

"Yes, he will," Papa said, wrapping his thick, beefy arm around her waist and giving her a squeeze. "Your sisters? They know, too? About Grace?"

Mike laughed. "Please. We're Marconis. Of *course* we know everything."

He sighed and dropped into a lawn chair as Mike poured him some iced tea from the jug in the cooler. The deeply shaded spot was as welcoming as a sweet dip into a chilly pond. Papa accepted a glass, took a long drink, then winked up at her and said, "Girls are so bossy. I should have had boys."

Grinning at the old complaint that meant absolutely nothing, Mike plopped down on the dirt at his feet and leaned her head against his knee. "You'd have missed us."

"You're right," he said softly, one hand playing with Mike's long blond braid. "I need my girls—and I wouldn't change a thing."

"Me, either, Papa." Mike closed her eyes and concentrated on the moment, etching this one tiny piece of time into her brain. "Me, either."

Three days since the last time he'd seen her and Lucas still felt the residual effect of kissing Michaela Marconi. It helped him to think of her as Michaela, while remembering the incredible sensations she'd aroused in him. After all, a lover named Mike wasn't something he'd ever considered.

He laughed at the thought. Hell, there was absolutely

nothing about Mike that wasn't completely feminine. She smiled and her eyes lit up. She laughed and everyone around her lit up.

Rocket Man.

He grinned and caught himself. Damn it, he didn't have time for this.

Shoving thoughts of Mike to one side, he focused on the computer screen and told himself to concentrate. His desk faced the window, most likely a big mistake. He'd probably spend too much time staring out at the pretty spectacular view.

From the second-story office at the back of the house, he could watch the wind dance across the surface of the lake. From his bedroom at the front of the house, he could almost catch a glimpse of a strip of ocean. When the wind hit the trees just right, they parted long enough for him to see that line of blue water where it met the blue sky and land and air dissolved into each other.

His yard was green and even now being filled with plants by a team of gardeners who spoke such rapid-fire Spanish that he missed most of the conversation, even though he spoke the language. The trees surrounding the house gave it a sense of peace and isolation that he'd been looking for when he left the lab.

A man more used to his own solitary company than to that of hordes of people needed quiet to work. Not that he was getting a hell of a lot of work done.

Scowling, he turned his gaze back to the computer screen, ignoring the near siren call of the wind battering the leaves and the birds singing and the soft sigh of the reeds dancing at the lake's edge.

At long last, most of the work on the house was complete—so though he still heard the occasional hammer ringing, there was enough quiet to at least *look* at his research. He adjusted his glasses, then studied the lines of figures and notations scrolling past as he kept his finger on the mouse button. It had taken years of work to get this far—to know so much—and still nanotechnology was nowhere near being ready for general use.

But if they could keep donations coming in, keep increasing the money for research, then maybe, within the next ten years or so, nanotechnology would really be the miracle Lucas thought it could be.

Fund-raising.

The party.

He sat back, forgetting about the book, the work, his dreams, lost in the memory of looking at Mike and hearing her agree to go to the damn fund-raiser with him. Still wasn't sure why he'd asked her. But it had felt . . . *right.* He'd rather not go alone. And Mike was entertaining, if nothing else.

A shout from downstairs had him jumping up from his desk chair and walking into the hall. Leaning over the wrought-iron railing, he stared down at a burly man in coveralls, standing in the middle of the foyer.

The man tipped his head back and squinted up at Lucas. "Just wanted to let you know, we finished up in the guest bathroom and we're headed out now."

"Great. Thanks."

"No problem." The man let his gaze wander around the foyer before looking back up. "You sure got a nice place here, Lucas."

"Yeah." He nodded and smiled. "Thanks to you guys. You do good work."

" 'Preciate it." The man waved and headed out the front door.

Alone in his house, Lucas forgot about going back to work and instead headed for the guest bathroom, to check out the finished job. He walked through the big, airy room that overlooked the backyard and had its own balcony and set of French doors. Smiling to himself, he kept going, into the adjoining bath. It was the last piece to his house. Once that tub was in, then the job was complete and . . .

He looked down for a long minute, grinding his back teeth together. Then he snatched his cell phone from his jeans pocket, flipped it open and punched in a set of numbers. He'd dialed the damn numbers so often in the last two months, they were branded into his brain.

She answered on the first ring.

"This is not the tub I ordered," he snarled.

She laughed. "Who is this?"

"Damn it, Mike—" His fingers tightened on the cell phone until he almost expected it to snap in his hand. "This was supposed to be a dark blue tub. Nothing fancy. Just dark blue."

"Yeah, I know," she said, "but—"

"*This* tub is green," he pointed out tightly, waving one hand at it like a cheap magician trying to make too many rabbits go back into a hat. "And it's got Jacuzzi jets in it."

"Geez, Rocket Man," Mike said, "chill out, will ya? The green is much better with the wallpaper."

Lucas wondered if she'd dropped the tone of her

voice to *raw sex* on purpose. And knew it didn't matter. She'd done it again. Stepped all over his plans, waltzed through his house in her size 7 combat boots, and left muddy footprints all over the damn place. She hadn't even had to *be* here to do it!

His chin hit his chest, he felt his eyeballs roll in his head and his blood pressure spike. "Mike," he said slowly, silently congratulating himself on his forbearance, "there *is* no wallpaper."

"There will be tomorrow morning. Sam Chaney will be there around nineish—can't be more specific than that, his wife has line dancing lessons and he has to drop her off at the community center first." She paused for breath, but not long enough to let him get a word in. "Sam's great. He'll do a good job."

Lucas muffled a snort of what he was really afraid might be hysterical laughter. Dropping down onto the edge of the tub, he sighed. "I'll thank you later, I suppose?"

"See? You really *are* a genius, aren't you?"

"Right." He shook his head and threw one hand high, signifying surrender. He was only glad she wasn't there to see it. "If I'm so smart, why do I have a Jacuzzi tub I didn't order?"

There was a long, heartfelt pause before Mike spoke again and this time her voice was even lower, skimming along his nerve endings. Making him think of hot nights and silk sheets and cool breezes drifting across naked bodies. "Rocket Man," she said, purring out each word softly, breathlessly, "if you don't know what those jets can do—you really *do* need to get out more."

Then she hung up.

Lucas's blood turned to steam and heated him through from the inside out.

"She did that on purpose," he said and glared at the phone. "She knew damn well what that voice does to a man and she used it to steamroll me."

He ought to be furious.

What he was, was hard and horny.

"Damn it."

Alone, Lucas sat on the edge of a damn tub he hadn't ordered, and didn't want. The woman had shifted his world completely off its axis and he wasn't sure how to get it back on again. "I thought life in the country— hell, small-town life—was supposed to be *easier*."

He turned to get a good look at the thing and damn if he didn't instantly imagine Mike there. He could see her, wearing nothing but a layer of bubbles and that smile that did some very unexpected things to his blood pressure.

And he could see himself, joining her, and showing her that he knew *exactly* what a Jacuzzi could be good for.

He stood up and let that image dissolve as quickly as popping soap bubbles. Groaning, he left the room and headed for his own bathroom. So he could stand under the stinging spray of an icy cold shower.

For all the good it'd do him.

7

A few hours at Castle's Day Spa was enough to improve *anyone*'s attitude.

Nothing quite like being pampered by people who knew what they were doing. Mike sighed and rolled her shoulders on a soft groan of satisfaction. A massage, a facial, and now, a manicure/pedicure. "God, does it get any better than this?"

The question was rhetorical but naturally Jo couldn't leave it at that. "Why is it when we have a sisters' day, we end up here?"

Mike opened one eye and looked at her sister. "Because God loves us?"

Sam laughed from her chair on the other side of Jo. "Put a sock in it, you two. You're ruining the atmosphere."

True. Mike leaned her head back against the spa chair and let herself relax into the damn near blissful sensations of a foot rub.

Castle's had started out life as a three-chair beauty parlor. But once Tasha Flynn married Nick Candellano, they'd redone the old Victorian—well, actually, the Marconis had done all the work, and a damn fine job of it too, if she did say so herself. With Nick's money and Tasha's sense of style—not to mention the Marconis' excellent work—they'd turned the old house into the most plush spa in the county.

On the main floor, there were manicure/pedicures, and a row of hair-styling stations facing large, ornate mirrors. The walls were a soft butter yellow with cream-colored crown molding along the edge of the ceiling. Strains of classical music pumped through speakers discreetly hidden behind copper planters from which ferns and brightly colored flowers tumbled in abandon.

Upstairs were several different massage rooms, each painted in soft, soothing colors, boasting comfy beds and piped-in New Age music designed to slip into every cell of your body and induce relaxation.

And back on the ground floor, muted conversations from contented women whispered through the open spaces. In the far corner of the room, the Leaf and Bean concession boasted plushly cushioned chairs and impossible-to-resist pastries.

In short, Mike thought, a half-smile on her face, it was a little slice of heaven.

"We just did this last month," Jo complained and jerked her ticklish foot out of the pedicurist's hands.

But, Mike told herself, even paradise had had a snake.

She glared at her older sister. "I'm amazed that you're willing to admit you haven't had a pedicure in a month."

"I've got a few more important things going on."

"*Nothing*'s more important," Mike said. "For God's

sake, Jo, you're a girl. Try to keep that in mind occasionally, huh?"

"You think of it often enough for all of us." Jo winced when the manicurist snipped at her cuticle. "Isn't it enough that I agreed to *you* taking the day off to get ready for your weekend of sin in the sun? Did you have to drag *us* along for the ride?"

Mike straightened in her chair, despite the muttered warnings of her manicurist. "Nobody said anything about *sin*," she pointed out, and scowled as the woman polishing her toes smirked. "Besides, if I'm gonna sin, I sure as hell don't have to apologize for it."

"Who asked you to?" Jo demanded, then added to the girl still happily snipping away, "Hey, I'd like to *keep* that finger, okay?" before turning her gaze back on Mike. "All I'm saying is that just because you wanted to spend a day here—"

"Would it physically *kill* you to enjoy yourself?"

One of Jo's dark brown eyebrows lifted. "Possibly."

"Well, I for one am enjoying myself," Sam muttered thickly.

"See? *She*'s my sister," Mike said.

"What'm I?" Jo demanded.

"Still working that out," Mike countered, grinning.

Jo sighed and gave her foot back into the care of the woman glaring at her. "Fine. We'll do the girly thing, so you can run off and play . . . whatever, with your latest conquest."

"He is *so* not a conquest."

"Then why the weekend getaway?" Sam asked on another sigh.

Good question. Mike had been asking herself that

very question for days. The best she'd been able to come up with was pretty pitiful. But she tried it out on her sisters anyway. "Lucas doesn't know anybody around here. He's got some big-deal fund-raiser to go to and he doesn't want to go alone."

Jo gave her a wry, sidelong glance. "So this is a pity date."

She stiffened. "Who said anything about pity?"

"So why, then?" Sam asked, stepping into the middle of a blossoming argument, just as she always had. Sam, the peacemaker. Sam, the middle child. Sam, the sister waiting for an answer.

"He's . . ." Mike's voice trailed off and she would have waved her hands but they were held in a tight grip by the manicurists stationed on either side of her. She searched wildly for what to say, but a good Italian required her hands to have a decent conversation, so she came up empty.

"You like him." Sam sounded pleased.

"I don't hate him anymore," Mike allowed.

Jo looked at her. "Decent of you to forgive him for building his own house."

"On my land."

"Which he bought," Jo pointed out.

"After going behind my back," Mike countered, feeling the old resentment spring to life inside her again.

"Which he didn't even know was there," Jo said amiably.

Hell, Mike thought grimly, Jo was always amiable when she thought she was winning an argument.

"*Back* to the point of this," Sam said, winning a glare

from both of her sisters. "Which is, you're going away with a guy you've only known two months."

"Hah!" Mike snorted. "Excuse me? Aren't you the one who *married* the Weasel Dog after three hot weeks of sex and giggles?"

"Yeah," Sam agreed. "And remember how well that turned out."

"Worked out now," Mike reminded her.

"Sure, nine years later."

"Got you there," Jo chortled.

"Are you almost finished?" Mike asked the manicurist on her left. "I'd like to punch my sister as soon as possible."

"Nails are wet." The girl laughed.

"Damn it." Mike inhaled sharply and huffed it out again. "Look, I'm going away for the weekend. It's a . . . *favor*."

"*That*'s a new one," Jo said, chuckling.

Mike snapped her a killing look that bounced right off her, like bullets off Superman's chest. "Is it so hard to believe that I could do a nice thing?"

"No," Sam said quickly, as Jo was just opening her mouth to comment. "It's just that, while you're doing this nice thing . . . I hope you're careful."

"Yes, mom," Mike muttered. Sam's warnings were *so* unnecessary. Mike had been giving herself this same speech for *days*. Actually, since right after agreeing to go with Lucas in the first place. She'd thought about The Kiss every night in her dreams. Well, not really *thought* about it. More like relived it. In glorious Technicolor with Dolby digital-enhanced detail.

The man might be a scientist, but he had some really

interesting *layers*. The question was, did she want to *peel* him?

Always before, the men in Mike's life had been temporary. Deliberately chosen to be temporary. She didn't want to fall in love. Actually, tried hard not to fall in *like*. She preferred keeping things on a strictly hormonal level. *Want* was okay. *Need* was not. *Lust,* yes. *Love,* no.

Not that she had anything against the whole "happily ever after" thing. Hey, she'd listened to as many fairy tales as the next woman. It was just that Mike would never be able to have the *whole* fairy tale.

And half a "castle" worked for nobody.

"Fine. We're supporting our sister during her charitable mission," Jo said grimly, with a glance at Sam. "But while we're here, could we at least—I don't know . . . talk about *work*?"

"You really need a life," Mike muttered.

"Like yours? No, thanks." Then Jo ignored her. "We signed on to do Stevie's new roof, so I'll be handling that while you guys start working on Cash's place next week."

"Us? Not you?" Sam asked.

"It'll be easier this way," Jo insisted, taking her now freed right hand and inspecting the clear polish with a nod of approval.

"Easier on who?" Mike asked. "If we all do Stevie's roof we can have it done in three or four days. You working alone will take nearly two weeks."

"Your point?"

Mike blinked and looked at Sam.

"Her point"—Sam picked up the thread and ran with it—"is that we work together, Jo. You know that."

"Not all the time."

"*Most* of the time," Sam insisted.

"I just thought it would be easier to get both jobs going at once." Jo frowned at the pink polish on her toes.

Curious, Mike leaned closer to her oldest sister. "What's going on with you and Cash?"

Jo's blue eyes snapped up to meet Mike's. "Absolutely *nothing*. The man is a pig. A self-satisfied, arrogant, know-it-all pig."

"Whoa," Mike said, laughing, "don't hold back, Jo. Tell me what you really think."

"Cute."

"Are you sure you're not—"

"What?" she snarled.

Mike looked at Sam, smiled, then shifted her gaze back to Jo. "You know what. Worried about maybe spending so much time with drop-dead gorgeous Cash and then sleeping with him only to discover your hidden altruistic side? Marching off to do good works?"

Jo scowled at her. "Do you *ever* get tired of talking?"

"Nope."

"Any woman who sleeps with Cash needs her head examined," Jo grumbled and waved both hands, hurrying up the nail polish drying.

"He's hot."

"So's nuclear waste."

"He's also living like a priest."

"*Huh?*" Both Jo and Mike said the word at the same time and turned astonished gazes on Sam, who was thanking the pedicurist and admiring her dark-coral-painted toes. Slowly, she lifted her gaze to her sisters and smiled. "Didn't you hear? Women all over Chandler are pining away, apparently."

"Since when?"

"By all reports, our secretary Tina was the last one to fall to Cash's charms."

"But that was like two months ago," Mike said, remembering that Tina had spent one night with Cash and then gone home to Georgia to work for Habitat for Humanity. The man was a sexual hypnotist or something.

"Yep," Sam said. "Two months. It seems Cash has taken a vow of celibacy."

Jo snorted. "A vow. His dick probably wore out and fell off."

Mike laughed. "You volunteering to find out?"

"You *are* insane."

"Hi, you guys, how's everything?"

All three of them turned to look at Tasha Candellano. She'd just had a baby a couple of weeks ago and already her figure had snapped back into shape—she was as tiny as ever. Her dark auburn hair was streaked with blond and paler shades of red and her green eyes sparkled.

"You look way too good," Sam said to her. "Seriously, there are women here who would kill to look like that so soon after giving birth."

"Trust me," Tasha said, giving her almost flat stomach a pat. "There's still plenty there. I just hide it well under clothes." Then she looked around, nodding at the girls who were packing up the manicure/pedicure kits, and asked, "You guys having fun?"

"Oh, a blast," Jo grumbled.

"Pay no attention to her," Mike piped up. "She's obviously deranged. So how's the baby?"

"She's gorgeous," Tasha said, grinning. "Two weeks old and Angie has taken over the household. Jonas is nuts about her—he and Nick are always fighting to hold her."

Tasha's foster son, Jonas, had been adopted by Nick and Tasha the minute they got married and the boy was a sweetheart, even if he was closing in on being a teenager.

"I swear," Tasha continued, "if I wasn't breast-feeding, I'd never get any time with my daughter." She caught herself, stopped and smiled even wider. "Can't believe I can say that. My daughter. Wow."

"Yeah, it's pretty great," Sam said.

Mike smiled, too, knowing her sister was happy at last, with her husband, the "Weasel Dog," and her daughter, Emma, back in her life. And she really was happy for Sam. Really. It was only that—

"Ah good, the Marconis." Another voice, older, warmer, and carrying the flavor of Italy.

Angela Candellano, known universally as Mama, stepped up next to Tasha and gave her a quick hug as she sent a welcoming smile to the Marconi girls. Mama was short, a little round, and a woman who had her finger on the pulse of everyone—not only in her own family, but in all of Chandler. And the woman never seemed to change. Her long gray-streaked black hair was always piled in a knot on top of her head and her sharp dark eyes missed *nothing*.

"Is a long time since I've seen you three," she said, propping one hand on her hip. "What? I have to have you come work on my house to make you stop by for a hello?"

Mike glanced at her sisters, then shrugged and provided an excuse for all of them. "Sorry, Mama. It's been a busy summer."

"Oh yes. A happy summer, too, eh? New babies—a boy and a girl"—she hugged Tasha again—"now my Carla's going to make me a nana again. Sam's little girl has come home, and Jackson is the new mayor." She frowned. "But Mayor Vickers wants a—" She turned to Tasha. "What did Jackson say it was?"

"A recount, Mama," Tasha provided.

"You're kidding," Jo said.

"No. He says chads work in Florida, they should work here." She shook her head grimly. "I think is Rachel, his wife, who is the problem."

"Not surprising," Sam muttered. "Rachel really likes being the mayor's wife. Not surprising she wouldn't want to give it up."

"Jackson won, that should be it," Jo snapped.

Mike agreed. Jackson Wyatt, Carla Candellano's husband and the father of the little girl Carla had adopted as her own, had run for mayor and won in a damn landslide. Everyone in town had been ready for a change. And maybe, she considered, the fact that Rachel Vickers was always foisting her poisonous attempts at cooking on everyone was one of the reasons.

"He'll win in the recount, too," Tasha said loyally.

"Of course he will," Mama agreed, nodding hard enough to loosen a few strands of hair from her topknot. "And this Christmas, my Tony's brother's son Alex is coming from Omaha for a visit. His wife died and he should get away for a while. Is not good to be alone."

"Another Candellano coming to town?" Mike asked.

Mama smiled benevolently. "We'll try to make him stay here. With family." Then she inhaled sharply and said, "Molly is going to fix my hair, so I have to hurry. You girls say hello to your papa for me, all right? And Grace, too."

"Grace?" Mike blurted. Hell. Had *everyone* but his daughters known about Grace and Papa?

Mama bent down and patted Mike's hand. "He missed your mother so much, God rest her soul." She paused to quickly cross herself and bob her head. "It's good Hank and Grace found each other. Is not good to be alone."

As Mama and Tasha said goodbye and wandered off together, Mike thought about what she'd said. No, it wasn't good to be alone. But sometimes, it was much *easier.*

Lucas snatched the phone up, eager for a distraction. He'd been working on his book for the last three hours and had managed to type one whole page. Nanotechnology research was a hell of a lot easier than writing.

"Hello?"

"Lucas."

His hand tightened on the receiver and his features went hard and stiff. Lucas actually *felt* ice move through his veins, despite the unexpectedly sharp burst of fury that slammed through him.

"How the hell did you get this number?" he demanded.

"I called the lab," Justin said, "your secretary gave it to me." His voice sounded faint, far away.

Not far enough.

"I'll fire her tomorrow." Not really, but damn if he didn't want to. Sharon shouldn't be giving out personal information to anyone. Least of all to brothers who should have stayed the hell away.

"Damn it, Lucas, I have to talk to you and you won't even read my e-mails."

Lucas fixed his gaze on the lake. Keep staring at the cool, clear surface of the water, he told himself. Feel the calm settle. Feel the tension drain away.

Fuck that.

"In case you didn't get it," Lucas said, and every word had to be *pushed* past the knot of anger nearly strangling him. "I don't *want* to talk to you, Justin. It's been four years. Nothing you can say to me now will mean a damn thing."

"Damn it, Lucas—"

"Get the hell out of my life, Justin." His fingers tightened around the phone. His breath labored in his lungs. His vision suddenly clouded with a red haze of pure rage and he whipped his glasses off, tossing them onto his desktop.

"I'm about to."

"Don't wait," he snarled. "Do it *now.*"

Lucas stabbed the TALK button, hanging up and ending the conversation before Justin could manage to say another word. "Does he think I want an *apology*?" Shaking his head, he threw the phone onto the chair and glared at it when it rang again. "Does he think that there's *anything* he can say to make this all right?"

The phone rang again and Lucas took two steps back and away from the chair where the phone lay, its red light blinking frantically with each ring. Gritting his teeth, he reached up with both hands and scraped his hair back from his head. He dragged one uneven breath into his lungs, then another, then another. His heartbeat slowed down, the inferno of rage faded into a few hotly smoldering coals, and the haze around the edges of his vision slowly cleared.

"You're not doing this again, damn it," he said, as the answering machine kicked on, inviting Justin to leave a message. He took two long strides to the desk, and punched the OFF button on the black and chrome machine. "You're not leaving me any damn messages, and you're not sneaking back into my life just so you can screw with it some more. Stay the hell away, damn it."

Wherever Justin went, destruction wasn't far behind. The Golden Boy, Justin had skated through life on charm and a winning smile. He built skyscrapers of cards, and when they eventually tumbled down, Justin was never around to get crushed. It was the people surrounding him who were left battered and bleeding and wondering what the hell had happened.

But it wasn't going to happen to Lucas

Not again, anyway.

As the phone started ringing again, Lucas turned his back on his office and headed out into the hall. The shrill sound of the phone chased him as he went, but he kept moving, determined to put at least *emotional* distance between him and his twin.

He took the cold tile steps at a dead run and kept right on going when he hit the foyer. Ignoring the phone in the living room, as well, he opened the front door, stepped outside into the cool afternoon, and slammed the door behind him.

An icy wind off the ocean slapped at him, and wrapped itself around him as he stalked down the front steps, marched across the yard, and rounded the corner of the house, headed for the lake.

At the water's edge, he dropped to the sun-warmed grass, yanked up a fistful of the stuff and shredded it between his fingers. Then he tossed the remnants into the wind and watched as they floated out to the lake and rippled away, carried on currents created by the wind.

A pair of ducks swept in from somewhere and settled on the water, oblivious to the man sitting on shore watching them.

Lucas took a deep, cleansing breath and told himself that fury wasn't the answer. He'd tried that once, and had lost a year of his life, buried in pain and regrets and an anger that had kept him from seeing the truth.

Well, he'd finally accepted reality.

He had his home.

His work.

Hell, he even had Mike Marconi to think about now. *Mike.*

A part of him wondered . . . *again* . . . if she wasn't the reason his emotions were all churned up and too damn near the surface. He'd kept everything bottled up for so long—and now, he was feeling again. She tapped into something inside him that hadn't seen the light of day in years.

And worse—he was starting to enjoy it.

Not the rage part, of course.

But the fact that he was starting to feel something for Mike pleased him almost as much as it terrified him.

He wiped one hand across his face and blew out a breath. Whatever the hell was going on between him and Mike, his brother had no part in this world.

He'd be damned if he'd let Justin get anywhere near the new life he'd built. And damned if he'd allow himself to get sucked back into the funnel cloud that was Justin Gallagher.

8

The Barrington Estate was a splashy blend of old Hollywood and old Italy. The perfect place for Lucas's fund-raiser.

Perched on a hill overlooking the ocean, the grounds raced to the edge of a cliff in manicured splendor. Cypress trees stood like crippled soldiers, twisted and bent from the wind but still holding their guard positions around the vast, manicured gardens.

The stately mansion's cream-colored walls had been aged by sun and sea until it looked as if it had stood in that spot for centuries. Wide, thick columns lined the front of the estate and a circular drive adorned by chrysanthemums in bright, jewel colors welcomed guests.

A hundred years ago, the estate was a family home, built by one of the lucky few forty-niners who hit a thick vein of gold. That first Barrington had spared nothing in furnishing his home by the sea. Marble tiles from Italy, Tiffany lamps and windows, tables from England. For years, the palace by the sea had sheltered the Barrington family until the last surviving descendant,

Selena, decided that penthouses in the city were more fun to live in than a mansion.

Selena Barrington turned the place into a corporate rental and charged companies small fortunes to experience a lifestyle that had disappeared into the same past that had swallowed the forty-niners.

Mike stepped out onto her balcony and took a deep breath of the sea-scented air whipping past her and into the huge bedroom behind her. Her view stretched out over the wide expanse of lawn to the sea beyond—out to where sea met sky and both dissolved into each other until eternity was born.

Turning her back on the ocean, sparkling with silver glints of moonlight, she stared into her room and hugged herself. Oh, she'd seen fabulous places before. Hearst castle, for one. But she'd never been able to sleep over in a damn palace before.

The room was a dream in soft blues and greens. A king-sized bed covered in a lacy duvet and a mountain of decorative pillows was the main attraction. Original oil paintings of misty lakes and gardens dotted the walls. The pale blue carpet was thick enough to take a nap on and the adjoining bath was damn near decadent. An orgy-sized peach-colored tub dominated the pale white-and-peach-tiled room and boasted a bay window with enough hanging ferns to qualify as a rain forest.

Chuckling, she stopped in front of an old-fashioned dressing table and stared into the mirror. She pulled two strands of blond hair free of the nest of curls at the back of her head. The long, spiraling curls lay against her cheeks and the small diamond studs in her ears winked in the light. Leaning forward, she applied a layer of deep rose lipstick, then stood back and admired her reflection for a minute or two.

"I think I can hold my own with the wheelers and dealers."

A knock on the door made her smile. Walking across the room, she snagged her black silk bag off the edge of the bed and opened her door to face Lucas.

"Wow."

Mike looked him up and down and said, "I was just about to say the same thing."

Tall and lean, he wore a tuxedo as if he were born to it. His dark brown hair was pulled straight back and gathered neatly at the nape of his neck. Behind those wire-rimmed glasses, his brown eyes flashed with something that started a small fire in the pit of her stomach. Her fingers curled into the fabric of her evening bag and squeezed as if she were holding on to a lifeline.

Lucas couldn't take his gaze off her. Who would have guessed that a *plumber* could look like *this*? His eyes widened, his jaw dropped, and every ounce of blood in his system sizzled and popped.

The black dress was sexy and elegant and displayed just enough honey-colored flesh to tantalize a man into wanting to see more. Not that he needed any urging.

She stood in the open doorway and smiled at him and Lucas had to remind himself to breathe. The sleek black gown had narrow straps in a halter style and a deep vee neckline that showcased the tops of her full breasts. The fabric clung to her every curve, making her already narrow waist look as though he could span it with his two hands. The skirt of the dress fell straight to the floor in a long, elegant column. Dark rose polish decorated the toes peeking out from beneath her hemline and all Lucas wanted to do was lift that hem and slide it up, up, up, along the length of her legs, until he could see every hidden inch of her.

"You look," he said, shaking his head, stalling in an attempt to find just the right word. *"Amazing."*

"Thanks." She grinned up at him and what was left of his brain dissolved. That smile of hers was as infectious as laughter.

"Are we ready to go downstairs?" she asked.

"Yeah." He swallowed hard and told himself to get a grip. Hell, he hadn't been so tongue-tied around a woman since his first date. Justin had coached him on what to say, how to act, because even then, Lucas's twin had been more at ease with people than Lucas himself would ever be.

But as soon as thoughts of his brother intruded, Lucas shut them down again. He wasn't going to waste a minute of this evening thinking about the man who'd made a mess of everything he'd ever touched. "Let's go," he said firmly.

She stepped into the hallway and turned around to pull the door closed behind her.

"Holy—" Her back was bare. Absolutely, completely bare, right down to the bottom of her spine, just above the sweet curve of her behind.

She glanced at him over her shoulder and her knowing smile rocked him back on his heels. "So, you like the dress."

The dress wasn't bad. But the woman *in* the dress had him salivating.

"Yeah," he said, exhaling slowly as he tried to get a grip on those runaway emotions she'd stirred up inside him. "You could say that."

"Good." She straightened up, threaded her arm through his, and started walking down the long, carpeted hallway. "That's just the reaction I was hoping for."

She looked like a damn queen, Lucas thought. She lifted her chin and a riot of blond curls danced around her shoulders down to the middle of her bare back. Her steps were slow, measured, as if she was completely aware of the beautiful picture she made and wanted to make sure everyone else was, too. And damned if it wasn't working.

As they started down the wide marble staircase, he saw people—men—stop and stare at her in appreciation. And a part of him wanted to hurry ahead of her and punch them all out so they couldn't see her as he did. For two months, he'd known Mike. Watched her. Listened to her. Hell, wanted to kill her from time to time.

But under it all, there'd been a sense of attraction.

A sense of . . . hunger, just pulsing beneath the surface of their "relationship."

Tonight, with her hand on his arm, her hip brushing against his, he felt flames leaping to life inside him. And he wanted more than anything to blow off this damn fund-raiser, take her upstairs, get her out of that dress, and spend the rest of the night learning his way around her curves.

That thought brought him up short as he realized just how close to the ragged edge he really was. Somehow

Mike had gotten under his skin. And now she was there so deep, he had to fight to keep thoughts of her at bay. Even though he wasn't really sure he wanted to.

A waiter in black slacks, crisp white shirt, and bow tie met them at the foot of the stairs and offered a silver tray crowded with champagne flutes.

Lucas took two, handed one to Mike, and lifted his own glass in a silent salute.

In moments, they were swept into the crowd and the hundreds of faces blended into a surreal blur. After a couple of hours, Mike stopped trying to remember names. She just kept a smile on her face and a glass of champagne in her hand.

The men were in tuxes and the women were draped in diamonds. If they really wanted to raise funds, she thought, they ought to consider just turning the women upside down and shaking them. Heck, just cashing in the necklaces and earrings could keep their research budgets going for years.

But it wasn't the fabulousness of the moneyed people surrounding her that was so fascinating. It wasn't even the place itself, though the Barrington estate was breath-taking.

It was Lucas.

Though he kept her close beside him all night, she couldn't help noticing that she might as well have been invisible. The women in the crowd didn't even spare her a glance as they fluttered and fawned over Lucas. He was like Justin Timberlake in a room full of teenybop-pers. During an interminable dinner, Lucas's speech on the benefits of nanotechnology had even Mike ready to write a check. He made the future sound so close, so immediate, so—*magical.*

His passion for his work colored his voice and made his eyes dance with visions only he could see. The crowd went with him willingly, believing him, trusting him. She watched him work the crowd and Mike felt . . . okay, a little intimidated. He was brilliant, damn it. He might not know jack about plumbing, but she was willing to bet he could single-handedly put a man on Mars.

She smiled to herself.

Rocket Man.

"Lucas," a tall, curvy blonde said as she swept up to greet him with a quick, familiar kiss. She gave Mike an absent smile, then focused on Lucas again. "Wonderful speech."

Mike watched the woman as she slipped back into the crowd again, then she shifted her gaze up to Lucas. "You slept with her, didn't you?"

He shrugged and said, "Long time ago. Big mistake."

"Uh-huh." Mike caught another woman sending him a little finger wave and one more blowing him a discreet kiss, and asked quietly, "And just how many 'mistakes' are in this crowd?"

He snatched another glass of champagne off a passing tray and handed it to her. Smiling, he admitted, "A few."

"Rocket Man," Mike said with a slow shake of her head, "you're just full of surprises, aren't you?"

"So then," he asked, "even scientists aren't completely boring?"

"Not completely," she allowed and slanted a look at him. She looked up into his eyes and felt a curl of something warm and delicious spiral through her insides, rippling and spreading as it went.

"Then since we've decided I'm fascinating, after all," he said, still smiling, "how about a dance?"

The small group of musicians in the corner were playing something soft and fluid. The notes drifted on the still air and settled over the softly murmuring crowd like a gift.

"You dance?"

"On occasion."

He led her toward the empty space in front of the small string orchestra and then turned her into his arms. He moved to the music and held her so close that not moving wasn't an option. His legs shifted, hers went along for the ride. His hand on her bare back felt warm and strong. His chest, pressed to hers, felt broad and muscled. He led her around the floor, moving in and out of the other dancers with the ease of a man who knew just what he was doing.

Champagne bubbles frothed in her brain and something just as delicious pumped through the rest of her body. The lights in the ballroom were soft, subtle, making for shadowed corners and quiet conversation. Couples swayed on the dance floor while others slipped through the French doors onto the stone balcony overlooking the gardens.

Mike pulled her head back to look up at Lucas and found him already watching her. A half-smile tugged at one corner of his mouth.

"What?"

"Nothing," he said and the smile slowly spread. "Just wondering how many other men ever get the chance to dance with their plumber."

Her own mouth twitched. "A select few."

"So I should be honored."

"Oh yeah," Mike assured him as he swept her into a turn that had her head spinning. "Whoa," she said, her left hand clutching at his shoulder, "you're good at this."

He grinned down at her. "I'm good at a lot of things."

"Such as?"

"You want a list?"

"A short one," she quipped, her gaze holding his. "Don't have my memo pad on me."

"Short, then," he agreed, his grin slowly fading as his gaze drifted from her eyes, to her mouth to her breasts and then back up again.

Fire.

Fire leaped to life inside her and Mike felt every flicker of every flame dancing along her nerve endings.

His grip on her right hand tightened, his arm around her waist squeezed.

"I'm a scientist," he said softly, "so I'm good with the details."

"Uh-huh." Breathless now, she simply stared into his brown eyes and watched as reflections of the light in the room glanced off the lenses of his glasses.

"I like to take my time," he said, his voice dropping another notch or two. "Start off slow and build to the major discoveries."

"Good idea," she said and stumbled slightly in his grasp.

"I focus on the task at hand," he said and dropped his head so that his voice hummed in her ear, his breath brushed her skin in a warm caress. His hand at the small of her back dipped down, lower and lower, until his fingertips were just above her behind—so close . . . and yet still so far.

"Mmm . . ."

"Explore *every* nuance," he was saying, and she barely heard him over the roaring in her ears.

"Exploring's good," Mike murmured, and silently congratulated herself on making her voice work at all. A knot of something hot and hard was lodged in her throat and it wasn't helping the situation any to feel something hard and hot pressing into her abdomen, the closer he held her.

She was damp and ready and so damn eager, she could hardly believe it herself. She'd thought she was doing him a favor. The poor scientist, without a date. She'd thought him a little cute, but a little awkward.

Now, Mike knew if she didn't get him upstairs within the next few minutes, she was going to dissolve into a really messy little puddle of want, right in the middle of the dance floor.

"Oh yeah," Lucas said, and nibbled at her earlobe as he carefully led her through another turn. "Exploring, finding your way through new territory, is always the best part."

"Oh boy," she said on a sigh of breath that started at her toes and worked its way up. "And you're good with the details."

"Oh yeah."

"How good?"

He lifted his head and looked down at her, eyes narrowed. In his gaze, she read the same level of greed and hunger she knew was shining in her own eyes.

"Damn good."

Mike sucked in a breath and held it. Every inch of her body was trembling, waiting, filled with a sense of expectation she hadn't known in a long time.

She felt as though ever since the moment she and Lucas had met, they'd been heading toward this moment. Before she'd come away on this weekend, she'd known this would happen. And a part of her had been counting on it.

Swallowing hard, she accepted the inevitability of it all as she said, "Prove it."

It wasn't easy getting away from the crowd.

But Lucas had never been more motivated.

Keeping a firm grip on her hand, he made his way through the crowded main floor, nodding and smiling at people he passed, but keeping his attention focused on the goal.

Upstairs.

A bed.

Mike.

The party was winding down anyway, he told himself. The invited guests would soon be making their way out to their cars and heading home. The few board members present would stay up late, have a few more drinks, then retire to their own rooms.

He was just beating them to it.

Mike lifted the hem of her dress and took the stairs

at a dead run, keeping pace with him. Her laughter bubbled up around them, as intoxicating as the champagne. Grinning like a fool, he charged down the dimly lit hall, dragging her in his wake.

Outside her room, Mike fumbled with the key until Lucas muttered a frustrated oath, took it from her, shoved it home and turned the knob. Ushering her inside, he was right behind her, closing the door and flipping the lock again. When he turned to face her, she was in the center of the shadowy room, standing in a spill of moonlight cascading through the open French doors. Sheer white curtains lifted and danced in the ocean breeze.

As he watched, she reached up and pulled three long pins out of her hair, releasing the blond curls to tumble about her shoulders.

She tossed the pins at a nearby dresser as Lucas reached for his tie and tore it off, opening his collar button just so he could breathe. Then he forgot about breathing, forgot about everything in his need to touch her.

Three long strides brought him to her side and he caught her in a viselike embrace, pulling her tight against him. Spearing his fingers through the curls he'd wanted to touch all night, he cupped the back of her head in his palm and held her for his kiss.

He took her mouth with a desperation that had been building all night. He'd watched her socialize in his world, and though she hadn't known a damn soul, she'd made herself at home. She'd smiled and laughed and chatted and had charmed some of those stuffed shirts into enjoying themselves at a fund-raiser.

He'd met her gaze many times during his speech, and though he knew she must have been bored senseless, she'd watched him with eager anticipation. He'd sensed her gaze on his while he was working the room, and every time he turned around, his gaze met hers and he felt the slam of something hot and powerful.

She was like no one he'd ever met.

She reached him in places no one ever had.

And he wanted her more than he wanted to see his precious research come to fruition.

At the first touch of his mouth to hers, an instant, damn near electrical surge pulsed inside him. Her lips parted for his tongue and she sighed into him. He took her breath then gave it back. His tongue entwined with hers, tasting, exploring, defining. Heat spilled through him and Lucas held her tighter, closer, sweeping one hand down to her behind and pressing her tightly to him, easing the pain in his own throbbing body.

She groaned and fed his hunger. She held him, stroking her hands up and down his back, and all he could think was, he wanted her skin on his. Flesh to flesh, heat to heat, hard to soft.

He needed.

Damn it, he didn't *want* to need, but there it was, clamoring inside him.

He tore his mouth from hers and ran his lips along her jaw, then down the column of her throat. She shivered and he felt it. She sighed and he echoed it. She was everything.

She was the center.

He tasted the pulse beat at the base of her neck and

smiled at the ragged beating of her heart. He tasted her, nipping her flesh, sweeping his tongue across her skin.

"Oh God . . ."

Her whispered, broken words fed the flames within and Lucas straightened up, moving his hands to the back of her neck. He found the hook-and-eye closure of her gown and, with a quick flick of his fingertips, released the silky black fabric. He stepped back to admire the view as the bodice of her dress dropped away, freeing her breasts.

Her nipples peaked and he smiled hungrily, already wanting to taste her, to suckle her.

He cupped her breasts in his hands, rolling her nipples between his thumbs and forefingers, tweaking, teasing, tugging until she rocked on her feet unsteadily.

"Okay, that's . . . *good*. Really *good*."

"Glad you approve."

"So far? Oh yeah." She opened her eyes and looked up at him blearily. "But I think you're wearing too many clothes."

"I think you're right." He reluctantly let her go and stepped back. Then he held up one finger. "Don't move."

"Don't think I can," she quipped, "so, not a problem."

Lucas tore off his jacket and shirt, feeling her gaze linger over his body. She heated him through.

He stepped back close, pulled her up against him, and, just for a minute, enjoyed the feel of her breasts pressed against him. "You feel even better than you look."

"Same goes," she murmured, dipping her head to

kiss his shoulder, his neck, his throat. Her teeth nibbled at his skin and every cell in Lucas's body tightened.

"I want you bad," he admitted. "Didn't expect to."

"Gee, thanks," she said, chuckling softly.

"You know what I mean."

"Yeah, I do." She pulled back and looked up at him. With the moonlight behind her, her eyes were in shadow, but Lucas didn't need to read them to know what she meant when she said, "I feel the same way. You kind of sneaked up on me, Rocket Man. Not sure how I feel about that."

"Me, neither."

She nodded and slid her palms slowly up his chest, defining every muscle, testing the feel of his skin against her own. Until finally, she hooked her hands behind his neck and pushed herself closer, tighter, to him. "But we can talk about that another time, right?"

"Oh yeah," he agreed, releasing a shaky breath. "No talk right now."

"My kind of man," she said and squeaked when he bent and picked her up, swinging her into his arms. "So, you gonna show off those exploratory moves you were bragging about?"

"Every damn one," he promised.

9

Mike inhaled slowly, deeply, and Lucas couldn't help but watch her truly exceptional breasts rise and fall as she did.

"Way to go, Rocket Man."

He grinned, carried her to the wide, king-sized bed, then dropped her onto the mattress from such a height she bounced once or twice before settling. When she had, she propped herself up on her elbows and unabashedly let him look his fill.

"I've been thinking about getting you out of that dress since the moment you opened the door tonight."

"Then get busy."

"Good point."

He joined her on the bed and lowered his head immediately to take first one of her nipples then the other into his mouth. He tasted her thoroughly, swiping his tongue across each pebbled surface until she moaned and writhed beneath him. He ran the edge of his teeth over her skin, tormenting her, torturing them both. His hands swept the hem of her gown up and up the length of her legs. No stockings. Just bare, warm, smooth flesh. Higher, higher, as he tasted her, his hands explored her. Up her calves and along the inside of her thighs, higher, higher, to the center of her.

And when he cupped her, his heart stopped.

He lifted his head and stared down into her glassy pale blue eyes. "No underwear?"

She licked her lips, breathed heavily, and managed a shrug. "Dress was too clingy. Would've seen lines."

"God help me," he whispered as he pushed first one finger, then another into her depths and watched her eyes widen. "If I'd known that, I never would have made it through my speech."

She groaned and lifted her hips into his invading touch. "Surprise."

His thumb caressed the small, sensitive bud of flesh at her center and she moaned.

"I never used to like surprises," he murmured, moving, pulling his hand free of her body despite her groan of disappointment. He shifted position until he was kneeling between her legs. "Do you?"

"Huh?" She lifted her head off the mattress and watched him as he lifted her legs and laid them across his shoulders.

The hem of her dress pooled at her hips as he slipped his hands beneath her bottom and scooped her high off the bed.

"Oh yeah," she whispered, swallowing hard, "I love 'em."

"Good. Surprise," he said and covered her with his mouth. Her scent filled him. Her taste flooded him. He sucked at her core, running his tongue over her sensitive flesh until she twisted in his grasp, grabbing fistfuls of the lacy spread beneath her.

Again and again, he licked her, exploring her with his mouth, discovering what made her shiver, finding the secrets to her body. His hands squeezed the soft flesh of her behind and held her steady when she continued to rock her hips helplessly under his tender assault.

Mouth, tongue, teeth, he sent her to the edge again and again, only to pull her back and leave her dangling helplessly on the cusp of completion.

"Lucas," she finally cried brokenly, "you son of a bitch, if you don't finish me, I'm going to have to hurt you."

"You'll just have to hurt me, then," he teased, pausing just long enough to look up at her. Her eyes were wild, her breath frantic. "Because we won't be finished for a long time."

"You're killing me here," she whispered and reached for him.

"I'm just getting started."

"Lucas, I want—"

"I know just what you want," he said softly, then dipped his head to send her back to the edge of oblivion. He knew now just where to devote his attention. Knew when to move faster, slower, knew when to lick, when to nip, and this time when she climbed to the peak, he gave her that final nudge she wanted so desperately. He felt her body quiver in his hands as she whimpered with the release quaking within. And as the last tremor rocked through her, he eased her back down onto the bed, then reached for her dress and pulled it down and off, tossing it to the floor behind him.

He stared, looking his fill, and in the moonlight, the

diamond-topped gold bar in her navel glinted. His mouth watered and his breathing hitched.

Sex.

Sex in the moonlight.

She was all that and more.

So much more, he didn't want to think about it.

Instead, he kept his tone light as he asked, "You pierced your belly button?"

She lifted one shoulder in a shrug. "I tried to pretty things up a little down there."

Then he saw what she was talking about.

Her skin shone like fine porcelain in the glow of the moon—except for the smattering of tiny scars stretching across her belly like a gossamer spiderweb.

Her breath shuddered from her lungs and she smiled lazily, satisfaction glittering in her eyes as she watched him.

Lucas reached out and gently ran his fingertips across the fine, fragile-looking scars. Hunger reared back as an unexpected sense of tenderness caught him by the throat and squeezed.

"Hey," she said quietly, "I know they're ugly, but fascinating?"

"Not ugly," he said, meeting her gaze. "What happened?"

Mike sucked in air, then stretched languidly, despite the sudden pounding in her head. Briefly, she wished they could have avoided this, but only a blind man could miss the tangle of fading, silvery scars that stretched across her skin. Reaching down, she caught his hand in hers and spread his palm flat against her belly.

"Don't look so serious," she said, regretting again that she had to have this talk. Anytime she got close with a man, she was forced to relive a memory she preferred to keep buried. Normally, she gave a guy a song and dance story that wouldn't have the power to touch her. Because anything else would just bring back a night she'd rather forget.

God knows she hated reliving the past, hated remembering that a stupid decision made by a foolish teenage girl had so affected her future. Most times, she was able to put it out of her mind, tell herself it didn't matter.

But it did, of course it did.

Hell, it was the reason she avoided landing herself in a serious relationship. It was the reason she kept away from anything that went deeper than lust and dated only guys who were looking for the "right now" instead of "forever." The reason she couldn't have the complete Fairy Tale. The reason that a marriage and kids would never be a part of her life.

Lucas was still watching her, waiting. And for some reason she really didn't want to explore at the moment, she heard herself tell him the truth. If an abbreviated version.

"It happened a long time ago. A car I was riding in crashed. I got hurt."

He pulled his hand free of hers and once again lightly traced the pattern of scars with the tips of his fingers. "Pretty bad, was it?"

Oh God, yes, she almost said, but pushed that response away in favor of a smile. She wasn't here to share her feelings and learn and grow. And she was pretty sure Lucas wasn't interested in hearing the sad story of her misspent youth.

So instead, she said, "Yeah, it was. And the scars will always be there—hence the whole piercing-my-belly-button. I know it's like planting roses in the middle of a parking lot—but hey. Who doesn't love gold and diamonds?"

"The scars aren't ugly, Mike," he said, his voice a low rumble of compassion. Tenderness. She felt the sting of unwanted tears behind her eyes and determinedly kept them at bay with sheer force of will.

"Right. But they play hell with a tan, let me tell you."

He wasn't listening.

He bent his head and slowly, carefully, gingerly, kissed her scars, tracing the frail outlines with his tongue until she felt herself melting into the mattress.

Oh God, no one had ever done that.

Most guys, once they'd remarked on the scars, would ignore them or try not to look at them. Mike knew all too well just how ugly they were. And it was always a difficult moment when a man first saw them.

Wouldn't you know Lucas would be different about this, too?

He kissed her again and she felt his breath against those scars that had been a part of her for so many years. And an aching sweetness built up within her.

No one had ever touched her so deeply with such a feather-light caress.

"You don't have to—"

"What?" he murmured. "I don't have to admire your badge of courage?"

"Stupidity, more like," she said and looked wildly around the room. She hadn't counted on this. Hadn't counted on him being so . . . *nice*.

He lifted his head to look at her. "You survived. Isn't that what counts?"

"I guess," she said, tearing her gaze from his. There were too many emotions in his dark eyes. Too many things she didn't want to face. Didn't want to think about, much less talk about. "But look," she said and winced at the overly cheerful note in her voice. "There's an upside to carrying those scars."

He leaned on one elbow and propped his head on his hand. "What's that?"

She blew out a breath and once again shifted her gaze to the ceiling, away from his. Her fingers plucked at the lacy spread beneath her and a part of her brain thought that maybe, hey, they should pull the duvet back before they ruined it, but then she was just stalling. She caught her runaway train of a brain, took a deep breath, and said, "Um, I don't know if you're carrying condoms on you . . ."

He slapped his naked hip and felt around as if looking for pockets. Then he grinned. "Not on me, but—"

She laughed. "Right. Right. Well, the thing is, I've never really said this to anyone before, but—" She shifted her gaze to his and stared at him. "If you can swear to me that you're healthy, then we don't have to worry about condoms."

"What?"

"Weird conversation, I know, and usually, I'm like the poster girl for condoms and safe sex and, hey, get away from me with that thing if it's not wearing a hat—" She took another breath and held up one hand when he started to speak. "Sorry. Babbling. I do that. Anyway, the deal is, with *you*, tonight, I'd like to try it without the condom—I'd like to feel you inside me and—"

"Whoa," he said, shaking his head.

"See." She lifted her voice to interrupt and shout him down all at once. "That upside I mentioned?"

"Yeah?"

Upside.

Pain stabbed at her and Mike winced slightly at the familiarity of it. She had to treat this as an upside. Otherwise, she'd drive herself insane with regrets and misery.

Forcing a smile she didn't quite feel, she said softly, "I can't have kids." A tremor of old pain rocked through her like a lazy tide slapping onto shore. She'd grieved so long ago for the family she'd never have, that the pain now was more of an echo than a sharp jolt. Yet still, it had the power to stun her with sorrow.

She took a breath. "The accident and the surgery and all, and well—you don't need to hear the details, do you? I mean, who would want to? I sure didn't—" She took a breath. "Babbling again. Anyway, what I'm trying to say is, I'm totally safe."

"You're sure?"

Unfortunately.

"Yep." She swallowed hard against the personal hurt and disappointment that had been a part of her life since she was sixteen and woke up in a hospital to see a doctor's long face and empathetic eyes. "My shop's permanently closed."

Lucas looked at her for a long minute and Mike held her breath, hoping to hell he didn't ask any more questions. If he realized that *this* was the reason she'd tried to escape Carla when the woman was so excited about being pregnant, she hoped to God he wouldn't bring it up. And oh yeah, please, God, don't let him say he was sorry.

Having some guy look at her like she was a little less than female was always a big turn-on. If Lucas gave her that look, she wasn't sure she'd be able to stand it.

She stared up at him in the moonlight and watched as he pulled away from her and stood up. Mike braced herself, and tried to read his eyes. But the silvery moonlight filling the room created shadows, not clarity.

He pulled off his glasses, then undid his belt and stepped out of the rest of his clothes. Mike's stomach jittered and her mouth went dry. His body was long and leanly muscled and more tanned than she would have guessed. Apparently this scientist didn't spend *all* his time in the lab.

Tossing his shoes and socks, he came back to the bed, kneeled beside her and looked down directly into her eyes.

"Lucas?" She murmured his name and stared up at him.

"Not interested in making babies," he finally said, that half-smile tugging at his mouth again. "Just in making love."

She released the pent-up breath she hadn't realized she'd been holding. He cupped one of her breasts and

Mike sighed. "You wanna reach down and take my heels off for me?"

He glanced down at the black sandals with the three-inch-high heels. Looking back at her, he winked. "Leave 'em on."

"Rocket Man, you are full of surprises."

"You ain't seen nothing yet."

She cupped his face in her hands and smoothed her thumbs across his sharp cheekbones. "Then show me what you've got."

Jo stared down at the stupid textbook and wished she were anywhere but where she was.

"It's your own damn fault," she muttered with a shake of her head. "If you'd had the guts to stick it out ten years ago, you wouldn't be in this mess now."

But she hadn't been able to stay at school.

Not after . . .

She jumped to her feet and stalked barefoot into her kitchen. She thought about pulling down the dusty bottle of tequila and blending up a batch of margaritas. But instead, she set up the coffeepot. If she started heading for a drink whenever old memories got too bad—then she'd have a whole new set of problems.

"And *that* you *don't* need."

The coffeemaker sizzled and popped and the hot water drained through the filter, sending the scent of freshly ground beans through the room. Outside, the night crouched at the windows and the wind slapped at the panes, rattling them in their frames. Rain spit from the sky in fitful bursts, as if it couldn't decide whether to become a real storm or not.

Jo hardly noticed. Arms folded across her chest, she leaned back against the kitchen counter and crossed her feet at the ankles.

The house was too quiet.

For a woman who'd grown up with two sisters and loud parents, silence could be an enemy.

It made you concentrate on the little noises.

The house settling.

The tick of the clock.

The groan of the wind.

When the phone shrieked, Jo shot away from the counter, slapping one hand to her chest as if to hold her heart in place.

Then, laughing at herself, she snatched up the receiver. "Hello?"

"Jo, oh, thank God."

Instantly alert at the sound of her sister's frantic voice, Jo's fingers squeezed the receiver. "Sam, what's wrong?"

Minutes passed, drifting one into the other as Lucas took Mike on the most amazing ride of her life.

Boy howdy.

Never challenge a scientist.

Although, she thought as he slid his palms along her body with the assurance of a master pianist stroking the keys, maybe a challenge could be a good thing.

She tipped her head back into the mattress and stared

up blindly at the shifting, moonlit shadows on the ceiling. Lucas's hands were everywhere, his fingertips exploring every curve, every inch of her body.

He touched her and she lit up inside.

He tasted her and the fire within became an inferno. Lips, tongue, and teeth assailed her body and she gave as good as she got.

She scraped her fingernails down his torso, flicking her thumbnail across his flat nipples until he groaned and flipped her over, pulling her body atop his. Then hands at her hips, he slid her up and down his length, meshing their bodies until the friction alone was soul-shattering.

She kissed him, taking his tongue into her mouth and delving his with her own, tangling them together in an erotic dance of temptation. Of expectation. Anticipation.

His mouth was fabulous.

And talented.

And . . .

He broke the kiss and trailed his tongue down the length of her throat, sliding his hands between their bodies to tweak her nipples.

"You've got some moves on you, Rocket Man."

"I keep telling you . . ." He grinned up at her.

"But I've got a few of my own," she countered and pushed herself up until she was straddling him.

"Show me what you've got," he murmured, grinning up at her.

Mike laughed, hearing her own words thrown back at her. "Buckle your seat belt, buster, I'm about to give you a ride like you've never had."

She went up on her knees and looked down at him. His brown eyes were glassy, hazy with need, with hunger, and she loved it. Loved seeing his desire for her.

Straddling him, she swayed, as if to music only she could hear, and let the moonlight spotlight her. She ran her hands along her own body, up and over her belly, past the twinkling diamond in her navel and up her rib cage.

He ran his hands over her thighs, all he could touch, and watched her hungrily.

She took that hunger and fed it. Sliding her hands higher, higher, she cupped her own breasts, let her head fall back while she played with her nipples, squeezing, touching, tweaking.

His grip on her thighs tightened reflexively and she felt the imprint of each of his fingers like tiny candle flames pressed to her skin.

Her body quivered, tingled, and hungered.

She kept swaying over him, lowering herself just enough to skim her center over the very tip of his hardened length.

He gasped each time she dusted past him, leaving him wanting more. But still she teased him, pushing him as high as he'd taken her moments before. Her hands on her breasts, her fingers at her nipples, she slowly, slowly, slid her hands higher, up her chest, along her neck and into her hair.

She lifted the curly blond mass off her neck and writhed above him, rocking her hips in silent invitation.

"Damn it, that's enough," he growled, and reached for her, slamming his hands onto her waist.

"Not nearly enough, Lucas. Not nearly," she crooned, tasting each word, caressing each syllable.

"Now, Mike," he muttered thickly.

One look at his eyes and she knew she'd taken him as far as she could without destroying both of them. The need in her own body quickened.

"Now," she agreed and slowly, lovingly, lowered herself onto his length. She took him inside, inch by tantalizing inch, drawing out the pleasure for both of them until she felt as though she were about to burst.

He clenched his teeth and dug his fingers into the flesh at her hips, holding her down, pulling her hard against him, pushing himself higher, deeper inside.

Mike groaned and moved over him, grinding her hips against him, creating a delicious friction that sparked new flames within. She lifted both arms high and stretched, arching her back as she moved on him, rocking, swaying, setting a wild, fierce pace that thundered in the silence around them.

Cool ocean air rushed into the room, dazzling their hot bodies with the sweet kiss of the chill night. Moonlight played on their naked skin and shifted shadows around the room.

But all Mike could see was Lucas.

His eyes.

Watching her.

His jaw tight, rigid with control.

She felt his body inside her, aching, pushing, stroking, and she wanted him higher, deeper.

He dropped one hand to the spot where their bodies joined and Mike held her breath, not sure if she could stand one more sensation ricocheting around inside her.

Then he touched her, and she knew if he didn't *keep* touching her, she'd scream. He caressed that one, tender, fragile spot that held so much fire. He stroked her and she whimpered.

"Lucas . . ." Panting now, gasping for air that wouldn't come, she groaned his name again, helplessly caught in a whirlwind of her own making.

"Let go," he said, his voice harsh, strained. "Damn it, Mike, let go."

"I can't . . ." she laughed shortly, but it ended on another groan as she shook her hair back from her face, moving on him, riding him, rocking him.

"Don't want it to end," she admitted, licking her lips, feeling the challenge in speaking at all when every ounce of concentration she had was focused on what was happening to her body.

He touched her harder, stronger, stroking, coaxing.

"God, Lucas," she shrieked. She heard the high-pitched tone of her voice and winced, but couldn't help it. "Oh God, Lucas. Don'tstopdon'tstopdon'tstop . . ."

"Come, Mike," he urged her, voice soft, low, intimate and husky with the want she felt pulsing around them. "Come now and we'll do it all over again."

"Promise?" She laughed and wept and groaned at the same time as the first tremor shot through her system, stealing what was left of her breath.

"Promise," he ground out, pushing his body hard into hers. "Now go over, damn it, and take me with you."

She did.

And while she wailed his name and shivered atop him, Lucas followed blindly over the precipice and tumbled with her into a black void filled with stars.

"I've never met a more hardheaded woman," Lucas said, minutes, hell, maybe *hours* later, when he finally managed to find his voice again.

"Mmmm . . ." Mike practically purred as she lay bonelessly on top of him. "Stubborn," she murmured. "I prefer stubborn."

His hands slid up and down her back and then down to her behind, touching, caressing, squeezing. He couldn't seem to touch enough of her. He'd seen every inch of her body now and all he wanted to do was start over at the top and work his way down again.

He'd never felt like this with anyone else. Before tonight, he'd never imagined himself not only laughing during sex, but arguing, for God's sake—and having to badger a woman into an orgasm by promising her another.

A promise he intended to make good on as soon as the paralysis faded.

She wiggled against him and his body leaped into life again.

Okay, so much for paralysis.

"Damn, Rocket Man," she whispered and lifted her head to look down at him. "You've got some great hands on you."

He laughed.

Again.

"You're not so bad yourself," he said and rubbed her behind, just to watch her close her eyes and purr again.

She dipped her head to kiss his chest and something inside him quickened.

His heart?

He pushed that thought away fast.

This wasn't about hearts.

This was about flesh.

Lust.

Grade A lust, but lust, pure and simple.

It had to be.

Anything else was just unacceptable. He couldn't— *wouldn't*—do love again. Down that road lay nothing but misery.

"So," she said when she raised her gaze to meet his one more time, "I remember someone promising me another ride on the love train."

He grinned. "Is that right?"

"Damn skippy," she said, smiling down at him. "Trust me, without that promise, I'd still be riding you like a bronco in a rodeo, dragging that moment out forever."

"You think so?" God, she had him panting again.

"Oh yeah, I've got great control."

"Now see," Lucas said, flipping her quickly onto her back and looming over her. "You say something like that to a scientist and he's forced to prove or disprove that theory."

Her mouth curved and, God, it was a great mouth.

"So what? Like a contest?" she asked. "See who can hold out the longest?"

"Please." He snorted, enjoying himself tremendously.

Mike Marconi was definitely one of a kind. "You wouldn't stand a chance against me."

Her smile widened, and just for a minute or two, Lucas let himself drown in the blue of her eyes. Then she wrapped her fingers around his erection and gave him a gentle squeeze and he went temporarily blind.

"We'll see about that, Rocket Man," she said and slid her fingers up and down his length in delicate strokes.

As she touched him, he cupped her center, and watched her eyes roll back as his fingers manipulated her sensitized skin. He couldn't take his eyes off her. He saw each dazzle reflected in her eyes. Felt her climb, felt her tension mount, felt her control.

And he knew she was stubborn enough to hold on forever to keep him from "winning" their little game.

Shifting over her, he tasted her nipples again and again, suckling, drawing deep on the tender flesh until Mike moaned and twisted beneath him, arching her body into his mouth, silently demanding more.

He gave her more. Over and over again, he tasted every inch of her body, and when he'd finished, he flipped her over onto her stomach and kissed his way down her spine. She moved like a satisfied cat, stretching and sliding beneath his touch, moving into his hands, groaning and moaning.

Lucas smiled against her skin and used his hands to caress her body while his mouth sent her higher than she'd been before. Not enough, he told himself and wondered if he would *ever* have enough of her.

She looked at him over her shoulder and licked her lips. "Lucas . . ."

He slipped one finger, then two, into her depths and watched her eyes roll back. "Yeah?"

"I surrender," she whispered and rocked her hips into his hand as her climax hit her hard and fast.

"Me, too," he admitted, his voice hardly more than a breath.

Everything in him tightened. He moved over her, spread her thighs and entered her fast and hard. She groaned, went up on her knees and opened for him, welcoming him. He braced his hands on her hips and held her steady while he shoved himself home, giving her everything he had, everything he was. He moved with her, following the rhythm she set, and knew that a blinding, heart-stopping release was only moments away.

Her tight, damp heat surrounded him as he felt her body convulse around his and he gave himself up to the inevitable. Holding her, he jumped into the yawning abyss in front of them and took her with him as he fell.

A few minutes later, they were both lying on their backs in the moonlight, struggling for breath.

"I can't feel my legs," Mike muttered thickly on a half-strangled laugh. "That can't be a good thing."

Lucas snorted. "My legs are good, but the arms are gone."

"Great. Together we make one whole person."

"One whole very *happy* person."

"Goes without saying," she said softly.

Turning her head on the pillow, Mike looked at him, and even in the pale light, Lucas saw her eyes shining in the shadows. Amazing eyes, he thought, really amazing.

And her hair, long, blond curls tousled around her face, lying across her breast, tempting him.

Then she smiled.

"What?" he asked.

"Just thinking."

"About?"

She laughed shortly. "I thought this fund-raiser thing was gonna be boring."

"Usually are," he admitted.

"And this time?"

"Not really."

"Good to know."

He rolled onto his side and set one hand lightly on the curve of her hip. She sucked in a gulp of air, closed her eyes and released it on a sigh. "What're you up to now?"

"About seven inches."

She laughed, and the full, throaty sound of it rolled through the moonlit room, ricocheting off the walls and landing in his chest to bubble there with a magic he hadn't felt in a long time.

"Rocket Man," she said when she caught her breath again, "I think I'm starting to like you."

"Yeah?" Lucas grinned at her and moved closer, wrapping one arm around her waist to pull her tightly to him. "I might be getting a little fond of you, too."

He kissed her, his mouth moving over hers gently at first and then more insistently. Desire spiked inside him, like a sudden fever, and he held her harder, closer, gathering her into him and holding on for all he was worth.

Time ticked to a standstill.

He broke the kiss, stared down at her in wonder, and felt . . . words crowding his throat. Words clamoring to be set free.

Before that could happen, though, a tinny chorus of "Jingle Bells" sang out into the room.

"What the—"

She flashed him a quick smile and rolled off the bed. Staggering slightly, she walked to the chair where she'd dropped her purse. Opening the small black bag, she said, "My cell phone."

"It plays 'Jingle Bells'?"

She shrugged. "I like Christmas. Sue me."

"Don't answer it," he said suddenly as she pulled the phone free of her purse. She stood in a splash of moonlight that made her seem to nearly glow. And he knew. He wasn't ready for their alone time to be over. Wasn't ready for the rest of the world to come crashing back in. "Just turn it off."

"Don't answer a ringing phone?" she asked, clearly stunned. "That's genetically impossible for a woman." She flipped it open and glanced at the screen. "Besides, it's Sam. She wouldn't call if it wasn't important."

Punching a button, she smiled and said, "Sam? I warn you going in, I'm not really coherent at the moment and—"

She frowned.

Lucas watched her.

She was so easy to read.

Her emotions clouded her features and widened her eyes. He pushed off the bed and took an instinctive step toward her.

"Got it," she said sharply, holding one hand up to

him as if to keep him at a distance. "Right. I'll be there as fast as I can."

She closed the phone, smoothing her fingertips across the cool metal surface. She pulled in a long, shuddering breath before she lifted her gaze to him.

"What happened?"

Eyes wide, pain shimmering in those pale blue depths, she shook her hair back from her face and stared at him in stupefied shock.

"Mike," he asked quietly. "What is it?"

"It's my father." She lifted one hand to the base of her throat. "He had a heart attack."

10

"Sit down, Jo, you're not helping anything with all the pacing."

Jo flashed her brother-in-law a hot glance, then immediately dialed down her temper. It wasn't Jeff's fault that her insides were tied up in knots that kept getting tighter by the minute. This *helpless* feeling was one she couldn't handle. She couldn't stand the thought of not being able to take charge of a situation.

She supposed that if a shrink ever got hold of her—which would never happen—the doctor would tell her that she had *issues*.

Well, *duh*.

"I can't just sit here. We've been *sitting* for an hour."

Jeff Hendricks stood up with a smile for his wife, then crossed the mint-green lobby to stand in front of Jo. Dropping both hands on her shoulders, he said, "There's nothing we can do but wait."

She snorted and forced herself to stand still beneath Jeff's comforting hands. But she felt something inside her tremble dangerously and she couldn't allow herself to give in to the fear crouched within. Swallowing hard against a tide of vulnerability that could drown her if she wasn't careful, she said, "I'm not good at waiting."

"None of us are," Sam said, standing up to join her husband. "That's why we've got each other."

Jo nodded, but she wasn't convinced. Hanging together didn't make this any easier. In fact, it was a little harder. It was bad enough worrying alone. But watching people you love worrying was just another little pebble added to the landslide that was already crushing her heart.

As if sensing her sister's proximity to the edge, Sam took her husband's hands in her own and squeezed. "Honey, it's going to be a while here. Would you go over to Carla's? Check on Emma? Make sure she's okay?"

"Emma's fine," he said, then pulled her close for a brief, hard hug. "But I'll go, if you two need a little time to yourselves."

"Thanks," Sam said and went up on her toes to kiss his cheek. Once he was gone, through the double doors leading to the parking lot, Sam turned to face her sister. "Papa's going to be fine."

Sam looked sturdy, assured, confident.

All the things that Jo wasn't—at the moment.

"You don't know that."

"Nope. But I believe it."

"Why?"

"Because he *has* to be."

Jo nodded, then turned away, not wanting her sister to see the fear in her eyes. Just because you wanted something to go a certain way was no guarantee that it would. If anything, Jo'd always felt that fate had a twisted sense of humor. The harder you wanted something, the more likely it was that you wouldn't get it.

Hadn't she found that out for herself years ago? Hadn't she learned the hard way that *wanting* things to turn out right didn't mean a damn thing?

She reached up and rubbed the throbbing headache lurking behind her eyes. She understood how Sam felt. After Jo left college and came home, she'd hung on to that same wild, irrational hope. When Mama was sick, she'd prayed and chanted and lit candles and gone to mass and promised God *anything*, if He'd just come through for her this one time. She'd promised that she'd never blame Him for what had happened to her. She'd vowed to become a better person—all if He'd only let Mama be okay.

But it hadn't changed anything.

Mama died anyway.

And took what was left of Jo's faith with her.

Sighing, she glanced at an older man, hunched in one of the dark green plastic chairs, his gaze fixed on the muted television mounted high in one corner of the room. Hospital waiting rooms were hideous places. Crowded with tension, draped in mourning, and shaded with shattered fragments of hope.

Not to mention the smell.

"We should have called Mike sooner," she said.

"It's the middle of the night."

Jo shot her a look. "You called *me*."

Sam wrapped her arms around her own middle and hung on. "That's different and you know it. Mike's out of town."

True. Jo nodded abruptly and changed the subject. Didn't matter when they had called Mike. The point was, she was on her way here now. She could only hope that by the time Mike arrived, they'd have some good news for her.

"He'll be okay," Sam said again, and Jo wasn't sure who her sister was trying to convince. Then she jerked when a disembodied voice murmured over the loudspeaker before dissolving into silence again.

"Of course he will," Jo said, playing the game because to do otherwise was just unthinkable. She'd keep her fears and her doubts to herself. As she always had. "Where's Grace?"

Sam inhaled sharply. "She went to try and find out some information."

Jo snorted. "They won't tell her anything. She's not family."

"Actually," Sam said, following her sister as Jo headed for the heavy door separating the waiting room from the inner sanctum of the emergency department. "They will. I told the doctor that Grace is our stepmother."

Jo skidded to a stop and shot her a look. "What?"

Sam glared right back and her voice was just a notch below hysterical. "Seemed easiest at the time. I didn't feel like explaining that my father and his girlfriend were on a date when his heart went wonky."

Taking a deep breath, Jo nodded and reminded herself that she was the oldest here. It was her responsibility to make sure the family stuck together. To make sure they all made it through this scary night.

No matter what she believed.

"Right. It's fine." She dropped one arm around Sam's shoulders and said, "So, let's go join our new mom and see if we can find out what's going on back there."

Lucas drove like a crazy man and she would have thanked him for it if she could have gotten her voice to work. She appreciated the fact that he hadn't asked questions. He'd just helped her throw clothes into the suitcase and then get to the car and get moving.

Now, the first pale streaks of dawn were just sneaking across the sky, chasing the last few stars into hiding. The world felt hushed, as if the planet itself had taken a breath and held it. On her right, the ocean shone like black glass and the roar and sigh of it felt like a heartbeat.

The car's headlights gleamed in twin white slashes in front of them on the nearly deserted coast road. Lucas steered them around a sharp curve and the sweet little convertible hugged the road like a Formula One race car.

Mike's heart ached.

Her stomach spun.

And her breath seemed clogged in her chest.

Change.

It kept coming back to slap at her and she didn't like it one damn bit.

Never had.

When she was twelve and got her first period, *everything* changed. She went from being thought of as a first baseman to a "girl." Okay, the upside of that was pretty good, on the whole, but she'd still lost a piece of who she was. Then when she was sixteen, her mother, Sylvia, got sick. Of course, at first, no one knew *how* sick.

But slowly, things changed. Soon, Mama wasn't waiting in the kitchen with a snack and a smile when Mike got home from school anymore. Most days, she was taking a nap or sitting in a chair with her rosary in one hand and the TV remote in the other.

Naturally, Mama'd refused to see a doctor at first, claiming that there was no reason for that—it was just the "change" hitting her hard.

Change.

An ugly word, even back then.

But it wasn't *the* change, it was cancer, which brought along its own version of change. And by the time it was discovered, it was too late to do anything but fill up the days and weeks with as many memories as they could.

The whole family had shifted, as if they were all trying to fill in the hole Mama's illness had made in the family circle.

Jo came home from college, Sam too, eventually. Papa spent more and more time taking long drives alone and Mike . . . Mike ran.

She sighed, propped one hand on the car's window frame, and held her aching head up as her brain continued to spin through the years, back and forth with a wild, frenzied pace.

All the running she'd done and she never got far, thanks to the native-drum system operating in and around Chandler. She'd grown up in that little town and everyone there knew who she was and where she belonged.

Even when she hadn't known the answer to that question herself.

So they'd called the cops.

Called Papa.

Called Jo.

And every time Mike ran, they brought her home again.

Until that last time—

She shuddered and sucked in air.

"You okay?"

"Yeah. Fine." Sure. She was great. Racing home in the dawn, sitting beside a man who'd just taken her body to all kinds of new places, running to find out if Papa was alive or dead.

Yeah.

Fine.

She's out getting laid while Papa's at home maybe—

"Damn it, I should have been there," she blurted, lancing the pool of guilt inside and letting the venom spew.

"What?"

She turned her head to look at him. In the glow of the dashboard lights, his profile was harsh and lined with shadows. His hands were fisted on the steering wheel and he never shifted his gaze to her. Thankfully. Since on her right was the ocean and a damn steep cliff.

"I said I should have been there when Papa needed me."

"Bullshit."

"Excuse me?"

He took the next curve at a speed way higher than the one recommended by the road builders. Mike grabbed hold of the window frame with one hand and checked her shoulder strap with the other.

"I said bullshit," he repeated, jaw tight, eyes narrowed. "Don't start beating yourself up over this. Sometimes shit just happens and there's not a damn thing you can do about it."

Mike just stared at him for a long minute. She pushed her hair out of her eyes and blinked when the wind icing through her open window slapped it right back across them again. What kind of "shit" had happened to *him*?

For two months they'd known each other and it was only now she realized that though she'd told him practically everything about *her* family, she knew next to nothing about *his*.

"Speaking from experience?" she asked.

"You could say that."

"Want to talk about it?" She shifted a look at the darkness stretched out ahead of them.

"No, I don't. Especially now."

"What's that mean?"

"What part of 'I don't want to talk about it' wasn't clear?"

"What're you so tense about? *I'm* the one with an emergency, remember?" She turned in her seat to face him and watched as his jaw tightened even further. Much more and his face might snap. "For God's sake, I thought you might want to talk. Keep my mind off what's happening with—"

He shook his head and snorted. "I don't want to talk.

Not looking to share and bond here. Just because we had sex, doesn't make us a *couple*."

"Screw you." Mike reared back as if he'd hit her. All those hours with him. Intimate, open hours where she'd given him more of herself than she'd ever given to anyone. And apparently, they'd meant *nothing*.

Good to know.

God.

She felt more alone than she ever had and she was sitting practically on top of him. Damn little cars. No room to move away. Nowhere to go to escape.

Nowhere to run.

He slammed one hand against the steering wheel. "Look, I'm . . . sorry, okay? Didn't mean to—"

"Oh," she said tightly, "don't back off now. I think you said *just* what you mean."

"You're upset and—"

"Ya think?"

"I'm just trying to say—"

"Oh, trust me, you've said enough, Rocket Man."

He looked at her, and in the dashboard lights, his eyes were shadowed, dark and dangerous. "You want to unload on me because you're worried—"

"You think *this* is unloading?"

He shot a look at the road, then his gaze was on her again. "You don't know me."

"And don't want to."

"But I know you."

"Wow, psychic, too." Anger churned, blurred her vision, cut off her air.

"I know you well enough to know you're mad at me so you don't have to be mad at your father."

"For a smart man," she said quietly, "you're an idiot. You should really shut up now."

"You're the one who wanted to talk."

"Not anymore."

"Tough shit."

She laughed harshly, and it scraped her throat, making her eyes tear. That's what was bringing tears. Not him. Not hurt. Pain. "Gee, such an intelligent comeback. You must be a scientist."

"Damn it!"

His shout startled her.

She flicked a glance at the road and screamed, *"Lucas!"*

"Shit!" He stepped lightly on the brake, pumping it as he turned the wheel into the curve in the road. The tires squealed against the pavement and sounded like a terrified scream.

Mike grabbed hold of the window frame and squeezed, fingers white, breath strangling in her chest, eyes wide as the white guard rail loomed ever closer.

The sleek little car responded like a dream, narrowly missing the rail that wouldn't have been nearly strong enough to keep them from plummeting down the side of a cliff.

When he had the car under control again, he pulled in a deep breath, dropped their speed and drove on. "That was too close."

"Too much talking, not enough concentrating."

"Damn it, Mike. You don't understand."

"Don't want to, either." Her insides went cold and stiff. Her heart ached and what was probably a good dose of self-pity was already setting up shop in one corner of her soul. Fine. She'd deal with it later.

"Just shut up and drive, okay?"

Lucas dropped her off at the hospital.

He watched her drag her suitcase behind her as she walked away without a backward glance. His chest tight, he thought about following her. Grabbing her. Making her listen.

But what the hell could he say?

"No." Better this way. Better that they both back off and try to get a little perspective.

Steering the car back out onto the street, he headed through the quiet town of Chandler, which was just beginning to wake up, and tried not to think. Hell, it'd be best if he could just wipe the last twenty-four hours from his memory.

But somehow, he couldn't make himself want that.

What he'd found with Mike in those few hours had been better than anything he'd experienced in the last four years. Hell. *Five* years.

He drove down Main Street and noticed the lights on at the Leaf and Bean. He almost stopped for coffee, but he'd have had to be civil and, at the moment, that was asking for a little too much.

Damn it.

He shouldn't have shut Mike out like that.

But it was instinctive.

He'd been keeping his life *his* life for so long now, he didn't know if he *could* let anyone else in. Because the last time he had, tragedy had taken a chunk out of him that he'd never really gotten back. And because he was so busy pulling back from her, he'd damn near sent them both over a cliff.

"Good job," he muttered and scraped his hand over his face.

Once off Main Street, he made a left and passed the darkened movie theater on the way to the lake road. Lamplight glimmered in a few of the houses he passed and he welcomed each one. Nothing worse than feeling completely alone in the dark.

But then, hadn't he *chosen* to be alone?

"Too damn early for self-examination," he said firmly and squeezed the steering wheel tight enough to break it in two.

He worried about Mike.

About her father.

About what he'd done to her with a few harsh words.

But he quashed the beginnings of guilt. He'd already done enough of that to last a lifetime and he was done with it.

Above him, dawn lightened the sky into pale shades of rose and gold. On either side of the road, trees loomed close like silent sentinels watching him pass. He pulled the car into his drive, drove straight to the side of the house, and turned off the engine. Leaving his bags in the trunk, he headed around to the front door, steps dragging, mind racing.

All around him, nature was waking up.

He heard the ducks on the lake.

The birds in the trees.

The lap of the water against the shore.

And a too familiar voice.

Cold splintered inside Lucas and the jagged shards sliced at him. He felt as though he were breaking into pieces. He almost expected to rattle as he took first one step then another, forcing himself to move forward even when everything in him was telling him to leave. Get back in the car and drive away.

He rounded the corner of the house and stopped dead.

"Justin."

The man and woman sitting on the front steps turned to look at him. The woman, a tall redhead, with loose curls flowing down her back, stood up slowly and moved to stand in front of his brother in a protective gesture that was unmistakable.

"Hello, Lucas," Justin said and reached for the woman's hand, pulling her back to his side. "You really should've answered those e-mails."

Lucas swallowed back the rising tide of fury that was nearly choking him. His gaze locked on the twin he hadn't seen in four years and his hands curled into fists at his sides.

In the first, gentle light of dawn, Justin looked hideous. His face was drawn, his eyes deeply shadowed, and his clothes were hanging on him as if they'd been made for a much bigger man. Quickly, Lucas looked at the woman, and even in the soft light, he saw and noted the glint of battle in her narrowed green eyes.

He swallowed hard and shifted another look at his brother. When he thought he could force the words past his tight throat, he said, "Justin, you look like shit."

A brief ghost of what had once been his twin's charm-filled smile crossed his face. "Yeah, well," he said with a shrug, "that's what dying will do for you."

11

"Are you going to stand there staring at us all morning as though we're animals in the zoo?" the redhead asked, one hand at her hip. "Or, now that you're finally home at the very creak of daybreak, will you invite your brother in to sit down?"

Lucas blinked, and shook his head as if that might help him understand what was going on. It didn't. The tall, pretty woman was staring at him as if she already hated his guts. "Who're you?"

"This is Bridget," Justin said, giving her a half-smile. "Bridget Donohue."

"Just Bree," she said, returning that smile before shifting to give Lucas a look most people reserved for a rabid dog just before they shot him. "Now, will you be opening that door or must I put a brick through a window?"

He didn't doubt she'd do it. She looked like an Irish Amazon. Long red hair in thick, heavy curls fell nearly to her waist. She had a stubborn chin and creamy white skin scattershot with golden freckles. Her mouth was pinched and thinned into a razor-sharp line and her eyes were still shooting arrows at him.

Chest tight, Lucas stalked past the couple, taking the steps two at a time and muttering under his breath. Last night had started out great and ended with a thudding crash. Looked like his morning wasn't getting any better. He unlocked the front door, pushed it wide, then stepped back. He didn't want to look behind him at Justin.

Didn't want to face the brother he hadn't seen in four years.

Didn't want to have to acknowledge the change in the man who'd once been considered the most eligible bachelor in San Francisco.

Because Justin was dying.

Even if he hadn't said so, the truth was plain enough.

And there was only one reason Justin would come to him now.

He'd come to be forgiven.

But Lucas couldn't—wouldn't—give him that.

"There now, love, just a few steps and you're inside, out of the damp." The song of Ireland laced Bridget's voice, words sliding one after the other with a kind of rhythm and music that no other country could claim.

But more than her accent came through in her tone. It was affection, concern.

Love.

A cold fist tightened in the pit of his stomach. Even now, dying, Justin had found something Lucas had given up on four years ago.

Bitterness roared into life and his brain raced with memories he usually shut down the moment they appeared. This time, though, he let the images come,

flooding him with remembrance, strengthening his re-
solve against his brother. He'd allowed himself to be
talked into trying to bridge the gap between them once
before—four years ago—and it had cost him more than
he'd ever thought possible.

He closed his heart to whatever was coming next
and walked into his house. Each footstep sounded out
against the dark red tiles like a solitary heartbeat.
But when Justin and the woman followed him inside,
that solitude was shattered.

"Nice place," Justin said breathlessly.

"Thanks."

"Come on, love, onto the sofa." Bridget steered
Justin toward the main room and the pair of forest-
green sofas facing each other. Sofas Mike had picked
out, sitting on a patterned dark green rug he'd had to
fight her to keep. Even when she wasn't here, Mike's
presence was felt. At least by him.

"Rest a minute and I'll make you some tea." She
lifted her sharp, accusing gaze to Lucas. "You do have
tea?"

"Yeah." He shrugged one shoulder. "I, uh, think so."

Justin chuckled. "Luke's a coffee man, honey. Tea's
for girls and grandmas, right?"

Luke. Justin had always been the only one to call
him that. And as a kid, Lucas had liked it. Made him
feel less a nerd and more like one of the guys. But that
was a long time ago. They weren't those two kids,
joined at the hip, facing the world down together anymore. And hadn't been for a long time.

And he resented the hell out of the fact that Justin
was acting as if he still *knew* him.

"There's tea," he said and tossed his car keys onto the closest table. They skidded across the polished surface and fell to the floor, clattering against the tiles. He left them there and shoved his hands into his pockets. "In the pantry."

"Fine, then," Bridget said, with a studied look at him that clearly warned him to watch his step. "I'll just go and make some."

Lucas stared her down as she passed him. Damn it, how had his life come to this? That two strong-willed women stomped all over his world and made him think about looking for cover? And this one, he didn't even know.

"Watch out for her," Justin said on a laugh as she stalked away. "Got a head like a rock and a temper that'll singe the hair off your head."

"Who is she?" Lucas asked, stepping into the living room. Not because he wanted to talk to his brother, damn it, but because he'd be damned if he'd stand hiding in the hallway while Justin made himself at home in *his* house.

"I told you—"

"Yeah. Bridget. But who is she and why is she in my house?"

Justin sat up straighter on the overstuffed cushion, but still looked as if it took all his will simply to hold his head up. "I met her a few months ago. In Ireland."

"You were in Ireland?"

He nodded. "Went to see where our folks came from. Mom and Dad never really wanted to go back, but remember how we used to talk about going?"

He did. They'd once planned grand adventures together. Then those plans had been lost in time as goals changed—hell. As *they'd* changed.

"I was staying at Ashford Castle. Great place, by the way," he said, with a hint of the smile Lucas had once known. "Grand fountains, its own golf course, and right next to this tiny village where they filmed that old movie, *The Quiet Man*. It's called Cong."

Lucas snorted. "As in King?"

Justin laughed quietly. "Trust me, they don't like that pun. Anyway, Bridget worked in a pub there and we got to be . . . friends."

Not surprising. Justin'd always had a way with women. *All* women, he remembered tightly, feeling a flash of old pain and envy reach up and snag him around the throat. He tried to let it go. He glanced around the living room, enjoying the play of early sunlight streaming through the leaded windows to fall in diamond-shaped patterns across the furniture.

He reminded himself that a lot of things had changed in the four years since he'd seen his brother. He wasn't the same man he'd been then. He didn't have to let Justin—dying or not—come back into his world just to shake it up.

Scraping one hand across his face, he looked down at his brother and tried not to notice how worn and tired the other man looked.

More, he tried not to *care*.

"She's really something. Bree, I mean. Never took any of my shit. Gave it right back to me every time." He shook his head slowly, obviously lost in memories he enjoyed. "All my best lines fell flat. She laughed at me, Luke. And finally, when she found me after a long night of drinking toasts to my dwindling health, she told me I was a disgrace to myself and my good Irish name."

Hmm. Maybe he and Bridget would get along, after all.

"And after she got finished reaming me," Justin was saying, "she kissed me and said she thought there might be a man inside me somewhere and she was just curious enough about it to stick around and find out." He shrugged. "She's been with me ever since."

Admiration flickered to life inside Lucas. She'd stuck with Justin even through this illness. Which made her a very special woman who loved him—or, he thought, a woman who was trying to get her hands on the Gallagher money quick, before her meal ticket could die on her.

Lucas determined to find out which.

"And before you start thinking she's after the family money," Justin said as if reading his mind, "forget it. She didn't know about it when we met. And she won't take anything from me now that she *does* know. Hell, I had to fight her to get her to come on the family jet rather than fly here on Aer Lingus."

Lucas pulled his hands from his pockets and walked closer to the sofa. "You used the family jet? Why didn't I hear about that?"

Didn't surprise him any. Justin had been living the high life off their father's invention for years. He hadn't bothered getting an actual *job*. He much preferred the life of a do-nothing playboy.

Go with your strengths.

Justin shrugged. "Whatever you think of me, I'm still a Gallagher. I can use the damn plane without checking in with you first."

"I didn't mean—" Hell, he didn't know what he meant. It was a lot to take in all at once.

Justin dying, a pissed-off Irish barmaid in his kitchen, Mike furious with him, her father in the hospital.

Jesus.

Could somebody just stop the damn world so he could catch his breath?

"Anyway," Justin said, "Bridget's the reason I'm here."

"Meaning?"

"Meaning," he said on a sigh, "she wouldn't give me any peace until I agreed to come and see you. To try to—"

"What?" Lucas interrupted, moving to take a seat on the arm of the sofa opposite his brother. "Apologize? Again? No, thanks. Not interested."

His brother's eyes, so much like his own, glittered with emotion, but Lucas refused to be drawn back in. He wouldn't be Justin's straight man again. He wasn't going to give his brother the chance to fuck with his life. Not this time. Not when he'd finally found a little peace himself.

"Tell your girlfriend this is a waste of time."

"I did."

"She doesn't listen real well."

"Tell me about it," Justin muttered. "Damn woman's got a head as hard as those stone fences rambling all over her country."

Hell. Lucas knew what dealing with a woman like

that was like. And instantly, his brain shifted to Mike. Damned if he didn't wish she were there.

"So we understand each other."

"Hell, yes. It's Bridget who doesn't get it." He shook his head slowly and a lock of hair fell across his forehead. He started to reach up to push it away, but then apparently decided he was too tired and let his hand drop to his side. "She comes from a big family. Four brothers, a mother, and a million or so cousins." He smiled. "I swear, she's related to half of County Mayo. Anyway, she thinks family's everything."

Definitely a lot like Mike, then, Lucas thought, remembering the stark panic on her face as they drove through the night to the hospital. Worry and love for her father had pulsed around her like a neon light blinking on and off. And when she'd tried to draw him out, get him to talk about his family as she did hers, he'd slammed the door in her face. Not just because he didn't want to tell her about Justin and the long, miserable road of problems behind them—but because as close as she was to her sisters, he knew he'd never be able to make her understand how he and his brother could be so far apart.

And damn it, he didn't want her pity.

Didn't want her feeling sorry for him because he didn't have what she had.

Justin leaned forward, bracing his elbows on knees that looked bony right through the fabric of the too new jeans he wore. He stared hard at Lucas. "Do you think I wanted to be here?"

"Then why the hell are you?"

Justin smiled. "I told you. I'm dying."

No doubt about that.

There was no way for anyone to fake looking as bad as Justin did. His skin was sallow, his hair lank, and weight seemed to have dropped off the man who'd once been athlete of the year in college. Dying.

Justin was dying.

And all Lucas felt was . . . resentment.

What the hell kind of dick did that make him?

"What is it you want me to say, Justin?" Lucas asked, congratulating himself on keeping his voice steady, even.

"I don't know," he admitted. Sighing, he added, "I know you don't want to see me. But I guess I wanted to see you."

"Typical." Lucas slid off the arm of the sofa and landed on the cushion. Anger snapped and crackled inside him. "What Justin wants, Justin gets, and screw the rest of the world, is that it?"

A matching temper flickered in his twin's eyes for a moment before it was replaced with the wry spark of humor that Lucas would always associate with him. "Damn straight. Leopards don't change their spots, right? And bastards don't earn halos by dying."

"That what you're shooting for?" A bark of incredulous laughter shot from Lucas's throat. "A halo?"

"Hell no." Justin laughed again, and this time, the laughter dissolved into a fit of coughing that had his face turning beet red as he gasped for air.

Lucas curled his hands into the cushion and fought his own instincts to go to him. His brother had been getting along without him for four years; he could make it through a coughing jag without him, too.

Finally, after what seemed like an eternity, Justin caught his breath, held up one hand as if refusing help that hadn't come, and said, "I don't think there's a halo waiting for me, Luke. Just a pitchfork and a front-row seat in front of the fire."

Reaching up, Lucas stabbed his hands through his hair, dragging his fingernails across his scalp as if he could distract himself with pain. It didn't work. And he had to know. "What's wrong with you?"

"What *isn't*?" Justin quipped, then a moment later, shrugged and said, "Cancer."

"I guessed that," Lucas said. He'd done enough research in and around hospitals to know the signs of a body eating away at itself. "What kind?"

"Does it matter?"

"Humor me."

Justin shrugged again and his jacket slid around on his body as if it had been made for a much bigger man. "Pancreatic."

"Jesus."

"Hey, don't be blaspheming when I'm this close to being able to tell you if it pisses the Big Guy off or not."

"Is everything a damn joke to you?"

"Hell yes," Justin said and pushed himself to the edge of the sofa, leaning forward and bracing both hands on the gleaming apothecary-bench table in front of him. "Don't you think it's funny? All the shit I've gotten into and out of in my life and my own fricking *pancreas* kills me?" He shook his head. "What the hell *is* a pancreas anyway?" He held up one hand again. "Never mind. I know you can tell me and I really don't give a rat's ass. All I know for sure is, mine stinks."

Scraping one hand across his face again, Lucas fought for air. He hadn't wanted to see Justin. Hadn't wanted to ever speak to him again.

But he also hadn't wanted him dead.

Apparently, he just wasn't going to get what he wanted.

"How long?" Lucas leaned forward, too, bracing his hands on his side of the coffee table. He couldn't help glancing down and noting the difference in their hands. His own were calloused and brown from the hours he'd spent outside this summer, doing some work on his house—and yes, trying to keep Mike out of it.

Justin's hands were fine boned and fragile. The skin was stretched so tightly that Lucas was sure he could count every tendon and muscle. Then Justin's hands trembled and Lucas had to look away, choking back the annoying—and unexpected—lump in his throat.

"How long have I got?" he asked. "Or how long have I known?"

"Either. Both."

Justin sighed and cocked an ear toward the kitchen, where the sounds of cupboards opening and closing and water running assured him that Bridget was still busy. "I found out about eight months ago."

"Eight months?" His twin brother received a death sentence nearly a year ago and he hadn't known. Hadn't felt it. Weren't twins supposed to be linked? Psychically or spiritually? Shouldn't he have *felt* Justin's pain whether he wanted to or not?

But if he had, would he have paid attention? Wasn't the truth that whenever he thought of Justin, he automatically shut his brain down and turned everything off? He hadn't *wanted* to know about Justin. Had pretended, for four long years, that his brother didn't even exist.

Lucas had written his twin off a long time ago. Was the fact that the man actually *was* preparing to disappear really that important?

Yes.

"You should have told me."

"Right." Justin flopped back against the couch, as if the strain of sitting upright had just been too much. He gave a bone-rattling sigh as he settled in, then added, "Because we're so close. I should've called you right away and you would've come running."

Lucas's jaw tightened. "What happened between us wasn't my doing."

"Don't you think I know that?" He sounded tired. So damn tired.

The rising sun filled the main room with warm golden light and Justin turned his face into it greedily. He smiled and closed his eyes, letting the warmth pouring through the window soak into his skin.

"Did you ever really watch a sunrise?" he asked idly, shifting the subject so quickly that Lucas just stared at him for a long second or two.

"What?"

He opened his eyes and turned to look at Lucas. "I have. A lot in the last few months. Sunrises and sunsets, and did you know, none of them are ever the same? Kind of like snowflakes, I guess, though we've only got the word of scientists for that one. No offense."

A tea kettle whistled into the sudden stillness between them and they both knew that Bridget would be back in a moment or two. Lucas shot a look toward the kitchen, then turned his gaze back on his brother.

"I don't know what I'm supposed to feel. To say."

"Maybe you don't have to say anything."

"What do you want from me?"

He sighed. "I don't want anything, Luke. Just a place to stay for a while, then Bree and I will go. We'll head into the city and stay at the family apartment."

The apartment that had stood empty for years. Ever since their parents had died. And they'd died because . . . Nope. He wasn't going there. Not now anyway.

"What do your doctors say?"

"Who listens?"

"Damn it, Justin, *you* should."

"Why? So they can stick me in a hospital room and jab me with needles?" he countered. "No, thanks."

His words rattled around in Lucas's brain like marbles at the bottom of an empty can. "Are you telling me you're not being treated?"

"Yep."

"Are you insane?"

Justin grinned halfheartedly. "Probably."

"It's still a bit chill in here," Bridget said as she walked back into the room carrying a tray loaded with three steaming cups of tea and a plate of cookies. She set the tray down onto the table and then shot Lucas a look. "Will you start a fire in the hearth or will I?"

Justin grinned.

Lucas, still not sure what the hell was going to happen next, got up to build a fire.

• • •

"How long does it take to run some tests?" Mike shot a glare at the closed double doors and then looked back at her sisters.

"Too damn long," Jo muttered and jumped up out of the uncomfortable green plastic chair. "And what's Grace doing back there?"

"Sitting with Papa," Sam answered and stood up to join her sisters. "She didn't want to leave him and—" She shrugged.

"Right." Mike took a deep breath and blew it out. She'd been at the hospital for a half hour already and she still didn't know a damn thing.

Head pounding from that last furious conversation with Lucas, all she really wanted to do was go home and lie down in the dark. But if she went home, the house would be empty.

Papa wouldn't be in the living room, falling asleep in his battered recliner.

Instead, he was here, hooked up to machines that blinked and hummed and ticked off the seconds of his life in some sort of macabre countdown.

"Can't we *do* something?" she muttered.

"We can wait," Sam said and held out one hand, looking from one of her sisters to the other. "Together."

"Together," Jo repeated with a nod and laid her hand on top of Sam's. "But if we don't get some answers soon, I say we find a doctor and let Mike kick his ass until he talks."

"Finally," Mike said, "a plan." She dropped her hand on top of Jo's.

With fear hovering in every corner, the smell of anti-septic stinging the air, the three of them stood, linked. As they always had.

The Marconi sisters.

Never alone.

"Good. You're all here." Grace pushed through the double doors behind them all of a sudden, and the heavy doors slapped angrily at the air before thudding to a stop.

"Of course we're here," Sam said.

"What's wrong?" Jo demanded.

"Papa?" Mike almost squeaked the one word out.

"No, no," Grace said quickly, reassuring them all with a faint smile. "Your father's stable—for the moment. The doctors are still reading the tests and they've hooked him up to an electrosomething or other."

"Okay, that's good. I guess," Jo said, shooting a glance at the door separating her from her father.

"There's something else I have to tell you," Grace said and her calm blue eyes shifted from one of them to the other, each in turn.

Mike stared at her warily. The tiny pixie of a woman looked worried. And that sure as hell didn't bode well. She felt as if she should be crossing herself. Or maybe trying to ward off the evil eye, like Nana always had when she had a bad feeling about something.

"Just say it, Grace," Jo urged.

"Fine, then." The older woman took a deep, steadying breath and folded her hands together at her waist. "I think it's time we called Jack and his mother."

Mike glanced at her sisters, then shifted her gaze back to Grace. Blinking like a deer frozen by head-lights, she heard herself ask, "Who's Jack?"

Grace swallowed and winced a little, as if she were trying to choke down razor blades.

This couldn't be good.

"Jack," the older woman said calmly, "is your father's son."

12

"He's Papa's *what*?" Jo's voice spiked and echoed off the mint-green walls of the waiting room.

Mike rocked back on her heels, stunned right down to her bones.

Papa had a *son*?

Stupidly, all she could think about was how many times she'd heard her father teasingly say, "I should have had boys." Always, they'd laughed at it. Always, because Papa had never, *ever*, been less than proud of his daughters. Their whole lives, Papa had been there, teaching them what he would have taught sons—and taking special pleasure in the fact that his *daughters* were better at their jobs than most men would have been.

There'd never been one moment in Mike's whole life when she'd thought that Papa felt regret about not having a son.

And why should he? a small voice inside whispered, he *has* a son.

A son none of them knew about.

"You're telling us that Papa's lied to us our whole lives?"

"No," Grace said, "it wasn't like that."

"Yeah? Well, why is it that *you* know, and his children *don't?*"

"He only told me a year ago," the older woman countered as worry etched itself into her features. "And he—"

"A *year* ago?" Jo interrupted. "*You've* known for a *year* when we didn't?"

Mike's head pounded. She lifted one hand to rub at a spot between her eyebrows. No way was it going to help.

"Slow down, Grace," Sam said quickly, then added, "And shut up, Jo."

Jo's mouth snapped closed, but Mike could have sworn she saw steam coming out of her sister's ears.

Oh God.

"Henry didn't want you to find out like this, but all in all," Grace said, still keeping her fingers tightly locked together, "I think it's only fair that Jack be here. That he have the chance to see his father just in case—"

Okay, *that* was harder to take than the notion of Papa having a son that no one knew about. The idea that Papa was going to *die?* No.

Unacceptable.

Mike shook her head. She couldn't believe this. Had to be a mistake. Maybe Grace had misunderstood. Maybe Papa had told her something and she just made a mistake. Maybe . . . She spoke up fast, before Sam could say anything else. "This Jack. He's Papa's son? Really?"

"No, it's impossible," Jo snapped, "he wouldn't have done something like that and never told us about it.

Grace just has a wicked sense of humor." She narrowed her gaze on the older woman. "Not to mention *timing*."

Grace flushed right to the roots of her snow-white hair. But she didn't back down under Jo's withering stare. Instead, she lifted her chin and said, "I know this is hard."

Hard didn't even come close to covering this situation. Mike's ears were ringing and her heartbeat was suddenly so fast, she thought for sure her heart was going to jump out of her chest, race across the green-flecked linoleum, and head out into the sun-splashed parking lot.

Just as she wanted to.

Oh God.

She hadn't changed so very much after all, had she?

The first thing she thought of in a pinch was running away.

The difference being that now, she wanted to run— and wouldn't.

"Girls," Grace said, and any other time, Mike might have mentioned that they were all way too old for anyone but Papa to think of them as "girls." But today, that seemed insignificant.

"I know you're all upset right now, but calling Jack and his mother is the right thing to do."

"The *right* thing to do?" Jo gaped at her, sucking in air and blowing it out again in a rush of tangled breaths that sounded as though she were hyperventilating. "Our father's lying in there with a heart attack and no one will tell us how he's doing and now you come out to calmly break the news that we should call his *son*? A son none of us ever heard of before now?"

"Why?" Mike stepped in front of Jo, like a human shield, and stared down at Grace. "Why do we not know about what's-his-name? Jack. Where is he? How old is he?"

Grace's mouth tightened and Mike braced for the next blow. She had a feeling it was going to be a beaut.

She wasn't disappointed.

Grace sighed. "Jack is almost ten."

"Ten." Jo's whispered voice sounded broken. She pushed Mike out of her way. "Almost ten. So that means—"

It meant that while Mama was sick . . . *dying* . . . Papa was off . . .

"Uh-uh. I don't believe it," Mike said flatly, lifting her chin and facing them all, one at a time. "No way do I believe that while Mama was dying, Papa was off screwing some other woman."

"Why not?" Jo snarled. "He's doing it now."

Grace stiffened as if she'd been shot. "Your father's not a monk, Jo," she said after a minute or two.

The uncomfortable silence that followed stung them all. Jo had the decency to look ashamed of herself. But not by much. "Sorry, Grace. Not your fault. I know that. It's just—"

"Hard," Sam said, lifting one hand to clap over her mouth as if she were sick.

Jo held up both hands, backed away a little, and shook her head as if she could shake loose everything she'd heard.

Mike knew how she felt. Her own stomach was boiling, rumbling and rolling as it had the one time she'd gone on a spinning Ferris-wheel ride at a carnival.

She'd been eight years old, stuffed with cotton candy and hot dogs, and that damn ride had insured that she'd spent the next hour revisiting every snack she'd shoved down her throat.

And Papa had been there, holding her head and soothing her tears.

"Oh God." She whispered the plea and felt chills crawl up and down her spine, along her arms. This couldn't be happening.

Not Papa.

Not the one man in the world she'd always believed to be perfect. He was her hero. He'd been the one stable point in her universe, her whole damn life.

All those times she'd run away, when Mama was so sick. All those nights Papa had sat with her, holding her hand, telling her not to worry. That the family would survive. That Mama would *want* them all to survive.

He was bigger than life.

Stronger than Superman.

Now? Now, she finds out that Papa was just a man?

How was she supposed to live with that? How would *any* of them get past this to reclaim their lives?

"We have to call now," Grace said, an eerie calm to her voice, a soft shine of understanding in her dark eyes. "I know you don't want to hear it. I know you're still in shock. So I'll do it if you want, but it's the right thing to do."

"How can it be right? How can any of this be *right*?"

"Jo, will you lower your voice?" Sam looked worried as she flicked a glance past Jo and Grace toward the double doors and the crowded hallways beyond.

"Oh yeah," Jo said tightly. "Wouldn't want anyone

to hear us talking about this. *That* would be the real tragedy."

"You're not helping," Mike told her.

"There *is* no help for this, Mike. Weren't you listening? And when the hell did *you* get so accepting? Why aren't *you* as pissed as *I* am?" Jo blew out a breath and shook her head, her dark brown ponytail whipping from side to side at the back of her head. She lifted both hands again, palms out toward them, and backed up with long, uneven strides. "You do what you have to do," she said. "I need some air. I'm—"

She turned fast and stomped toward the door leading out into the parking lot. She hit the door with both fists and kept right on moving.

In the sudden silence, the three women looked at each other like strangers.

Which is just how Mike felt. As if she'd been dropped into a world where she didn't know anyone. Didn't know the rules. Didn't know what she was supposed to say and feel. And damn it, she didn't like it.

Jo was wrong. She wasn't *accepting* anything. She was just too lost to know what to do.

Last night, she'd been in Lucas's arms and found more excitement, more tenderness, more . . . *everything* than she'd ever expected to find. Just remembering those few hours had Mike wishing she could turn back time, relive it all again and somehow . . . postpone what she was now dealing with.

But then, the night with Lucas hadn't ended all that well this morning, and if she turned back time, she'd just have to relive *that* part of the festivities over again, as well. No, thanks.

She pulled in a breath and winced at the taste of antiseptic in the recycled air. Man, this weekend had gone to hell in a hurry.

"What now?" Sam ground the words out, biting each one off as if they tasted bitter.

"I'll call Carol."

"That's her name?" Mike asked. "The bitch?"

"Mike . . ."

She shook her head as she felt her old standby, fury, rising up within her to drown all of her doubts and fears in a sea of righteous indignation. And she was grateful for it. A raging temper was so much easier to deal with than confusion.

"Sorry, Grace," she said tightly, "but you're telling me that this *woman* and our father were bouncing on sheets while Mama was dying. That doesn't put her up for sainthood in my book."

"People make mistakes."

"They don't generally *hide* them for ten years," Mike countered and felt a twinge when she saw she'd scored a point. Damn it, she didn't want to make points off Grace. The older woman hadn't done anything to deserve it. It was Papa's fault this was all coming down now, and they couldn't even yell at him because he was hooked up to so many damn machines . . .

Oh God.

"Carol and Jack live in San Francisco," Grace said quietly. "They can be here in an hour or so."

San Francisco.

All the weekend trips that Papa had made into the city over the last several years came rushing back to haunt Mike all at once. She'd wondered why he always went to San Francisco instead of spreading his wings a little.

Hah.

Turns out he'd spread his wings *plenty.* Her stomach lurched, her heart ached anew, and her soul shriveled up and wept.

"Call them," Sam said and stepped in front of Mike, preventing her from jumping back into the argument. "Papa would want them to know."

Grace nodded and left, after one last, uneasy glance at the two of them.

Silence stretched out for what seemed forever before Mike said, "What Papa wants? Do we really *care* what Papa wants at the moment?"

Sam whirled around to face her, eyes snapping, teeth bared. "We damn well better care, Mike, because for all we know—" She lifted one hand and jabbed her index finger toward the double doors. "Papa's in there dying. Do you really want to prevent a little boy from seeing his father for the last time? Will that make this easier on us? Will that make everything okay?"

"No, but—"

"Hell," Sam said, on a tear now and picking up speed, "maybe when they get here, you can take the kid outside and kick him for a while. And Jo can beat up his mother. That'll be good. After all, the hospital's right here."

Mike shifted uncomfortably. "Jesus, Sam, get a grip."

"I've got a grip," she snapped and suddenly whirled around to face the lone man in the waiting room, now avidly watching *them,* the muted TV forgotten. "As for you," she shouted, "mind your own damn business. Watch your stupid TV and don't you repeat a word of anything you heard today or I swear to *God*"—she paused to inhale sharply—"I will find a way to make you sorry."

"Yes, ma'am," the guy said, eyes wide and terrified.

Smart man, Mike thought, as he slumped down into his chair, making himself as small a target as possible. But strangers listening to the family secrets wasn't real high up on her list of things to worry about at the moment.

"What the hell are we supposed to do with this, Sam?" Mike grabbed her sister's arm, turning her back around to face her. "Are we supposed to greet this kid with open arms?" she demanded. "Tell his mother that all's forgiven and aren't we a happy family? Hey, Thanksgiving's coming up! Well, forget it. I never wanted a brother, you know, and I still don't."

"You think I do?" Sam asked, peeling Mike's fingers off her arm, one at a time. "But you know what? Unlike you and Saint Josefina out there, stomping around, filled with the Holy Glow of Certainty, I *know* what it's like to make a mistake." She lowered her voice and the words hissed at Mike, making them that much harder to listen to.

"I know what it is to do something so wrong, so heartbreakingly awful—" She paused again, to get the tremble out of her voice. "So awful that you can't live with yourself."

Mike knew where she was going with this and cut her off at the pass. Just a couple of months ago, Sam's husband, Jeff "Weasel Dog" Hendricks, had come back into her life. She'd been forced to relive old tragedies to eventually find a miraculous ending. And Mike understood how she felt. God, her heart hurt for Sam, but, "This isn't about you. This is nothing like what happened to you."

"Of course it is," her sister said softly. "I was sad and miserable and empty and lonely for Jeff. Just as Papa was for Mama. And I did something stupid. Unforgivable, really. *I gave up my own child.*"

The raw pain in her sister's voice stabbed at Mike and her eyes filled with tears of empathy. Around Mike, no one cried alone. Papa used to say she had the most sympathetic tear ducts in the world.

Papa.

Her heart ached.

"Trust me, Mike," Sam said, stepping forward to wrap her arms around her sister for a fierce, brief hug. "I know what it is to do something you regret. Something you'd rather no one else ever knew about. And I know what it is to be so bone-deep lonely and scared that nothing makes sense." With her arms still tightly locked around Mike, Sam continued. "I heard him, Mike. At night, I used to hear Papa crying, when he thought we were all asleep. The thought of losing Mama pushed him to the edge. Is it so hard to understand that he grabbed hold of *something* to keep from falling over?"

The images Sam drew were hard to stand against. The thought of her strong father giving in to tears was something that she'd never really thought about. Stupid, she guessed, but he'd always been the rock. And frankly, she'd been too wrapped up in her own pain then to feel anyone else's.

Mike held on for a long minute, reining in her tears and giving Sam time to do the same. When she was sure she could look at her sister without crying again, she freed herself and stepped back.

"Okay," she said, "you understand. You get why Papa might have done what he did. And maybe . . . maybe I sort of do, too. But answer me this, Sam . . ."

She waited.

Mike took a deep breath and let it go again. "What about Mama?"

Sam's mouth worked and her eyes filled up again.

But Mike kept going, determined to have her say. "Mama was dying and Papa was out with some bimbo, making the *son* he always wanted. What's that say?"

"I don't have all the answers, Mike," Sam said wearily, and let her shoulders slump, as if she were a balloon with a slow leak. "I just know that there's more here than a few stark facts. And I figure we owe it to Papa to hear his side of things. Just like we owe it to this boy to let him see his father."

Mike's teeth ground together and she swallowed back a sudden, tight knot of fear. She didn't want to *owe* a child she'd never met. One who had as strong a claim on her father's heart as she did herself.

"And if Papa dies? What then? We *never* find out why he did what he did?"

"Didn't I just say I don't have all the answers?"

"Right." Mike nodded and shoved her hands into the pockets of her black slacks. "Well, since all we've got are questions . . . here's another one for you. How the hell do we know this kid is really Papa's?"

Lucas felt trapped in his own home.

He couldn't stay in the living room. Justin might be there. Bree had taken over the kitchen. And going to his office and pretending to work was pointless.

Only one thing left to do.

"I'm going out," he said, and realized that it was the first time in four years that he'd had to say that to anyone. He'd lived alone for so long, doing what he pleased, when he pleased, that this habit of "checking in" felt . . . alien. But if he lived a sometimes lonely life, it was one he'd chosen deliberately.

"I'll be gone a while," he said abruptly, more to cut off his own thoughts than because he thought the Irish Warrior gave a good damn.

"Bring some ice cream back with you, then," she said, stepping into the main room from the kitchen, wiping her hands on a blue and white checked dishtowel.

"Please?" He stopped, hand on the doorknob, and looked at the woman who was still glaring at him.

"Your brother enjoys it and he doesn't eat much anymore," she said, instead of the one word he'd requested.

And Lucas felt like an ass.

Justin was dying and he was an ass.

Great.

"Fine." He opened the door and stalked out, needing to be away from the house that he'd spent so much time planning. So much time looking forward to.

Now, it was as if he didn't belong there. Justin was inside.

Dying.

The drive into Chandler didn't take more than twenty minutes. Huge gray and black clouds raced across a deep blue sky and the wind pushed at the trees lining the lake road, making them bend toward him in elaborate bows. He hardly noticed.

Even on a Sunday morning, Main Street was busy. Tourists clogged the sidewalks and cars crawled as if in a parade.

But he was in no hurry.

Parking the car outside the Spirit Shop, he stepped into the morning sunlight and let the weak autumn warmth seep into his bones along with the chill, ocean wind. The roar of the waves was louder here and almost sounded like music. Maybe that's what he needed, he thought. A walk on the sand. Clear his head. Get some perspective.

But first, coffee.

He stepped up onto the sidewalk, and weaved his way in and out of the mob of people strolling or simply stopping to window-shop. Hitting the door to the Leaf and Bean, he stepped inside and a wall of conversation rushed to greet him.

The place was packed. Lucas stalked across the gleaming wood floor to the counter, paying no attention at all to the people clustered at the scattering of round tables. But their voices and snatches of conversation followed him as he made his way through the store.

"So the recount's over . . ."

"Yep, Jackson won again."

"No chads?" A snort of laughter.

Lucas smiled in spite of his mood.

"Rachel Vickers is fit to be tied, I hear . . ."

"Feel sorry for Mayor Vickers. Living with a queen who's been dethroned. Won't be pretty . . ."

Life went on, Lucas thought, idly sorting through the chitchat for a few pieces of town news.

"High school's first football game is next week . . ."

"Autumn Festival looks bigger this year . . ."

Lucas smiled to himself, waited his turn in line, then gratefully moved up to the counter to place his order.

"Lucas," Stevie Candellano said, a worried smile on her face. "Here on a coffee run from the hospital?"

Small towns, he thought, and wondered how Mike's father was doing. Hell, how was *she* doing?

Amazing how fast news got around this place, though. They were better than the CIA at intelligence gathering.

"No," he said, finally answering Stevie's question as he leaned both elbows on the shining glass countertop. "I just need one cup. For me."

"Oh."

One word and yet it held a world of disapproval. Seemed he couldn't do *anything* right with women these days. As she started on his usual order of a latte, she looked up at him and asked, "Any word about Papa Marconi yet?"

He sighed and admitted, "I don't know. I dropped Mike off there a couple of hours ago and—"

"Yes," she said, nodding, "I knew you were off at some big splashy party yesterday."

One eyebrow lifted. "Word travels fast."

"In Chandler?" She laughed aloud. "Please. There's no such thing as a secret in this town. Believe me, it's been tried."

Which meant, he thought, that by this evening, news of Justin and Bree's arrival would be the hot topic in Chandler.

Perfect.

"How was Mike doing when you saw her last?"

The espresso machine hissed and spat and the hot milk frothed with millions of bubbles. He stared at it as if the foam-covered surface held the answers to every question ever asked.

How was Mike doing when he last saw her? Pissed off at him and worried as hell about her father. And he'd driven away. Left her there to find out— Whatever it was she was finding out.

Jesus, no wonder the women in his life hated him.

He really was a dick.

"She was scared," he said quietly, remembering the shadows in Mike's amazing eyes. Then he glanced around to make sure no one was listening. No one was looking directly at him, but he wasn't fooled. Everyone here was interested in the Marconis because they belonged to Chandler. They were part of the whole.

And when a single thread was disturbed in this little tapestry, all of the other threads felt the loss.

"Not surprising," Stevie answered thoughtfully. "Bet she could use a shoulder right about now . . ."

Yeah, Lucas told himself, she probably could. And the very least he could do for Mike was to bring her some coffee. Hospital coffee was enough to poison the very people it was supposed to fortify.

He sighed and reached for his wallet. "I guess you know what the Marconis usually order?"

"Is my husband the most gorgeous man on the planet?"

"Huh?"

"That was a yes. And," she added with a grin, "I've already started making them. Plus one extra. Grace is there, too."

"Grace?" He thought about it. "Oh, the woman they were doing all that work for this summer."

"That's the one." Stevie leaned toward him and lowered her voice. "*And*, Grace is also Papa's girlfriend, so I know she's there."

"If you say so."

"Oh, ask anybody, I'm always right." She thought about that for a minute. "Well, don't ask Carla, because she thinks *she's* always right, so—"

"I get it," Lucas said, laughing slightly in spite of everything. "And you'd already started making the drinks even before I ordered them, hadn't you?"

"Yep."

"Pretty sure of yourself."

"Sort of. But mostly, I was pretty sure of you," she countered with a smile.

Good that somebody was, he guessed.

13

Bree emptied the dishwasher, enjoying the mindless, soothing task. She carefully put everything away until the room looked as tidy, as *unused*, as it had the moment she'd arrived. A shame, she thought, this big, beautiful house, home only to a solitary man with a heart of stone.

She frowned. Although he had his reasons. Reason enough to want to turn his back on his twin—the other half of himself. But it tore at her to know that Justin might be facing death without the comfort of the one person in the world whom he most needed.

Hard to believe she hadn't even known him eight months ago. Hard to believe there'd been a time in her life when she wasn't in love with Justin Gallagher.

Crumpling a blue and white checked dishtowel in her hands, she squeezed the fabric and leaned back against the gleaming black granite counter. She stared out the window opposite and focused blindly on the trees in the distance, watching the play of the turning leaves as the wind danced through them. And as the silence of the house dropped around her, Bree remembered . . .

So handsome he was, with a smile made for devilment. Bridget took one look at him, sitting in the

corner booth of her family's pub and knew that here
was the one she'd waited for most of her life. For four
nights, she watched him, alone and friendless, oblivious to the noise and laughter surrounding him.

Most tourists came to Ireland looking to become a
part of life there, if even for a while. But this one man
left the glory of Ashford Castle every evening to come
here, to a neighborhood bar, to sit alone. He intrigued
her. Drew her to him as no one ever had before.

Of course, that wasn't to say he was perfect. Just
perfect for her.

Smiling, she asked, "Are you going to sit and drink
your life away, then?" as she served him another pint
of Guinness.

He looked up at her. "Seems as good a way to go as
any."

"And if I were to offer an alternative?"

One corner of her mouth tilted. "Such as?"

She glanced behind her at the bar and signaled to
her older brother that she'd be taking a break. Then setting down her tray on his table, she said, "Take a walk
with me."

"What? Now?"

"You've something better to do?"

"Actually," he said, "that's the best offer I've had in
a month."

There was something sad and lonely about him that
called out to her. Then he really focused on her for the
first time and a slow smile spread across his handsome
face.

"Too real for an angel," he said, "too tall for a
leprechaun. So you must be a fairy princess."

Bree laughed, shook her head, and didn't miss the way his gaze locked on the long fall of her hair. "Oh yes. That I am." She swept her arms out, encompassing the pub, and added, "This is my fairy raft and you've just been captured. So here you'll stay for the next hundred years—" She grinned. "Or until I tire of you."

"Sounds like a good deal to me," he said, standing up to look down into her eyes.

She tipped her head to one side and met his gaze with a wink. "Ah, but we've yet to see if the deal is as much in my favor as in yours."

"Oh, I can tell you now, Your Majesty," he said sadly, "it could never be that."

Sorrow welled up in his eyes until she almost couldn't bear it. Then he seemed to find himself again and banished the pain for a glimmer of a smile. "But I'd like to take a walk with a fairy princess anyway."

And just like that, she'd been caught. Caught in a fairy raft of her own making.

All these months later, she could see no way out but one. She wouldn't be escaping Justin. *He* would soon be leaving *her*.

And her heart wanted to break with the knowledge.

She straightened up from the counter, folded the damp dishtowel and draped it over the oven door handle so that it fell squarely, neatly. Then she smoothed her fingertips along the edge until even *she* was forced to admit that she was stalling.

She wasn't ready to climb those stairs and check in on Justin. Wasn't ready to admit that every day he was a little paler, a little weaker, a little closer to leaving her behind.

Still, she left the kitchen, because avoiding trouble never made it go away. The heels of her sensible brown loafers clicked softly against the cold, hard tile floor.

"He made a good choice with that," she muttered. "Wood floors have warmth. These tiles are as cold as he is."

Laying one hand on the banister, she skipped up the stairs softly, trying for as little sound as possible. If Justin was sleeping, she didn't want to wake him. He slept so fitfully these days. As if even in his dreams he could find no peace.

And oh God, she wished she could give him what he sought.

She walked stealthily along the hall to the guest room and quietly opened the door to peek in. The bed was empty, the quilt atop the mattress barely mussed. His weight was so slight now, he was already ceasing to make impressions on this world. As if his soul had already started its journey and all it needed was for his body to catch up.

Stepping into the room, she whipped her head from side to side, scanning the large, comfortable room for signs of him, terrified she might find him unconscious on the floor. But there was nothing. Panic stirred within, but she fought it down. Instead, she poked her head into the sleek adjoining bath, but he wasn't there, either.

"I'm over here."

His voice. Softer than it once had been, but still so smooth, so familiar.

She followed that voice as she had for so many months now and walked out onto the balcony overlooking the lake at the back of the house.

Justin sat on a white chair, his feet propped up on a

low wicker table in front of him. "Pretty out here, isn't it?"

"So it is," she said, and took a long, deep breath of air sweetened by both ocean and lake. It reminded her of home. The green meadow that encircled the lake and the cool, still water that rippled with every breath of the autumn wind. "But you shouldn't have come out here, Justin. At least not without a jacket or something."

"I'm fine." He reached up and took her hand, pulling gently at her until she sat on the floor beside him. His grip was so slight, his fingers so frail, she felt as though she were holding a wounded bird every time she touched him.

How could it have happened so fast? How did a strong, hearty, laughing man become this wraithlike creature in less than a year? And how would she ever live without him?

"I told you we shouldn't have come," he said, lifting his hand now to stroke her hair in long, tender caresses.

"He's a hard man, your brother," she muttered, leaning into him, just to have the comfort of his touch for as long as she could. "Are you sure you're twins?" She shot him a wry look. "He might be a changeling."

He laughed, then coughed, then gagged until his eyes watered and hers did, too, in sympathy. Then shaking his head, Justin said, "You're not seeing Luke at his best. And that's my fault. He has reasons. I told you."

"Aye, you did. And I grant you, they're powerful reasons." Bridget stretched out her hand and smoothed his hair back from his forehead. "But Justin, you're his *family*."

He shook his head slowly. "We stopped being that to each other a long time ago."

"Your Lucas is a hard man, but you're hard*headed*. so maybe that makes you equals, after all," Bridget snapped, irritation surging inside her. "Talk to him, Justin. Explain."

"He won't listen."

"Not if you don't even *try*."

For one instant, a flash of something hot and wild sparked in his dark eyes and then it was gone again. "I have tried. Lucas doesn't want to hear it and I can't blame him."

"Well, I can." She went up on her knees and focused her gaze on his. "You're a fool if you're willing to sit here and do nothing. You've come thousands of miles, Justin, to make this right. Will you stop now that you're home?"

"Hey," he complained, a spark of humor in his eyes, "don't be mean to the dead guy."

Dead.

She swallowed hard, forcing a knot of anger, pain, and fear down her throat to tangle in the pit of her stomach. "I hate it when you do that."

"I was just—"

"Kidding, I know, yes." She nodded and sank back to sit on her heels. "But the thing of it is, it isn't *funny.* None of this is funny. Not to me."

"I know," he said softly, letting his head fall back to rest against the chair. "But damn, Bree. It is to me. The joke of the century." Then he sighed and turned his head to look at her.

Love shone in his eyes and Bree wanted to cling to it. To etch this moment on her brain so that in the years to come, she'd have it to pull out and remember over and over again. And it wouldn't be enough. She knew it would never be enough. She'd found love. She had his heart.

And she was losing him.

"Fine, then. If you won't talk about Lucas, we'll talk about the other."

"God, you're like a dog with a bone."

"A beautiful dog, no doubt," she said, frowning slightly.

"Oh yeah. At least a collie."

"An Irish setter, I think," she said, swinging her hair around to lie across her shoulders. "And you're changing the subject."

Now he frowned. "I'm ignoring the subject."

The wind freshened, brushing past them both with a sigh.

"It won't go away," she said. "I won't let it."

He looked at her and smiled. "Wish I'd met you when I was alive. I think we'd have had some good times, Bree."

"Stop talking like a dead man," she snapped, hiding the fear that lurked inside with the brisk tone she always took with him when he started feeling down. "You're not dead yet, you know."

"I'm not going to let you marry a walking corpse."

Her heart pinged slightly as that little dart hit home. "If you're saying no because you're worried about your blessed money, you can stop. I don't want a thing from you but your name," Bree said quietly. "Give me that along with your heart, Justin, and it will be everything."

"Damn it, Bree, I know you don't give a damn about the money and we've talked about this enough."

"Not nearly enough, since I've yet to convince you."

"Are all Irish as stubborn as you?"

"There's the big black pot screaming at the kettle."

He smiled but still said, "No."

"Justin, you're *alive*. And you'll stay that way if I've anything to say about it."

"Bree . . . not even you can win this one."

She leaned in and kissed him, hard on the mouth, letting their lips linger together on a sigh of memory and regret. Then she pulled back and winked at him, leaving the familiar argument for the moment. She wouldn't give up. Not on him. Not on them.

Not on what they had of the future.

But there would be other times. Other chances to convince him.

"Don't you put money on that bet, Justin Gallagher."

He studied her for a long, thoughtful minute, then his eyes flashed with something warm and lovely. "Okay. If you're that set on it, I just won't die."

It was an old game now. One they played every week or two. When he felt bad and she felt closer to losing him. They'd say their parts, act out the roles, and each pretend to have consoled the other.

"Promise?" she asked, cupping his cheek in the palm of her hand.

"Promise," he lied, and turned to plant a kiss in the heart of her hand.

Lucas drove to the small community hospital on auto-pilot. With the carrying tray of coffees resting on the seat beside him, he asked himself what the hell he was doing. He should be steering clear of Mike.

They'd taken a step last night that couldn't be undone, but that was no reason for him to come riding in on a white horse. For him to give her the wrong idea. He was no errant knight out looking for damsels to rescue.

He had enough problems of his own. More, in fact, at the moment than he knew what to do with.

"So why're you here?" he muttered, as he threw the gearshift into park and cut the engine.

It wasn't just to avoid going back to the house that was no longer his. It wasn't just because he thought she could use some coffee. It wasn't even because he was feeling a little guilty about just *dropping* her off after first *pissing* her off.

"The plain damn truth is, I just want to know she's okay." Man. Somebody shoot him now.

He got out of the car, reached back in for the tray stacked unevenly with five drinks. Four on the corners for the ladies and one in the center for him. Now if he could just find them.

But just as he thought it, he spotted Mike storming out of the hospital and crossing to where an obviously irritated brunette was kicking a trash can.

By the time he was close enough to hear them, Lucas knew he was walking into a combat zone.

"Damn it, Jo, if I thought it would do any good at all, I'd *help* you kick the damn trash can into San Jose. But it won't change anything."

"Who says I'm trying to change something? Maybe I'm just so pissed I can't see straight." She glared at

Mike. "And who the hell are you, anyway? And what did you do with my sister Mike? Because if she were here, she'd have beat me to the kicking."

"You're a pain in the ass, you know it?" Mike sniffed and wiped her eyes with the backs of her hands.

"Like I've never heard *that* before," Jo muttered, and suddenly noticing they weren't alone, she spun around, nailed Lucas with a glare, and demanded, "What the hell do *you* want?"

"To live." And he backed up a step, just in case.

"Lucas?" Mike looked at him as if she couldn't really believe he was there. Then pleasure drifted into irritation and her pale blue eyes fired off a few sparks. "This isn't a good time."

"Yeah, I'm getting that." He ignored the death stare that both women were firing at him and held up the tray, like a fanatic offering up his firstborn child to the Sun God. "I brought coffee."

Instantly, some of the tension drained away and Jo's defensive posture relaxed a bit from combat ready. She blew out a breath. "Thanks. That was nice of you."

Mike looked at her sister, then back at Lucas. "Wow. A miracle. You hardly know her and you defused Nuclear Jo in your first try."

"Pay no attention to her," Jo snapped, stepping forward to take the tray from him. "I'm not the pain in the ass in the family. That's her job. Damn good at it, too. Usually."

"Suck coffee, Jo."

"Plan to."

"Wait." Lucas stopped her when she turned away. "Middle one's mine." He snatched it.

"I suppose the whipped-cream-and-caramel-topped froufrou drink is for Grace?"

Mike pulled one of the other cups out of the tray and nodded. "She loves those frothy, sweet drinks."

"Jesus," Jo muttered. "I'd be too embarrassed to order one." She sighed heavily and looked at Mike. "But I'll take it to her. Make *nice.*"

Mike smiled tightly. "That's a good mad dog. Good girl."

"Bite me," Jo said on a choked laugh, then tossed Lucas another look. "Seriously. Thanks for this. Appreciate it."

"No problem." He watched her stalk toward the double doors, then looked down at Mike standing beside him. "Do you want to go back in?"

"God no." She shook her head and started for the low concrete wall along the edge of the parking lot. "Come on. Sit with me for a while."

Lucas frowned slightly, but followed her. He hadn't really meant to stay, but how could he leave her out here all alone? Her sister looked psychotic—or at least borderline—and Mike's eyes were still shadowed.

Surprised the hell out of him just how much that bothered him.

Neatly tended grass bordered the retaining wall and the wind scuttled in from the ocean to wrap itself around them in a cold embrace.

Mike perched on the wall, then patted a spot beside her.

He sat down and took a gulp of coffee before asking, "Bad day?"

Mike blinked at him, then laughed.

He hadn't expected that.

But the laughter sounded way too close to the edge of hysteria for comfort. Instinctively, he reached out and laid one hand on her knee. "Mike?"

"Sorry." She pulled in breath after breath, in an attempt to steady herself. "It was just the 'bad day' thing. Oh man, Lucas, when days go to hell, they go fast."

"Tell me about it," he muttered, thinking of his own set of problems waiting for him in his brand-new house.

Mike, though, took him at his word.

She launched into an explanation of everything that had been going on at the hospital since he left her there. He watched her eyes fill, spill over, and fill again. He watched her mouth flatten, curve, then firm into an unforgiving slash. He heard the catch in her voice and the tear in her heart as she finished. And everything in him wanted to comfort her.

But what the hell could he possibly say?

Mike sighed. "Jo's kicking inanimate objects, Sam's beating her breast like some chained martyr waiting for the dragon, and Grace is running around clucking her tongue."

"And what're you doing?"

"You mean besides talking your ear off?" She took a long sip of her coffee, then wrapped the cup between her cupped palms. "I don't even know. I mean, I feel like Jo, you know? I want to punch something until my hand hurts. But what am I supposed to hit? The trash can? Yeah, that helped. This boy?" She shook her head and her blond hair lifted and danced about her face in the wind. "Oh God, Papa has a son and he's coming here."

"I don't know what to say to you," Lucas said softly.

She lifted one shoulder in a shrug and sniffed. "Me, neither. And I *always* know what to say. Now, I don't even know what to *feel*."

Lifting one hand, she pushed her hair back from her face and admitted, "I don't even want to go home. Not that I could leave while Papa's . . . but later, I mean, tonight. I can't go back home. It's too empty. Papa's not there." She took another drink. "I should have rented Stevie's place," she muttered, more to herself than to Lucas. "Thought about it. Stupid to not just do it. Then I'd have my own place and it wouldn't feel empty because I'd be used to being alone and—"

The very thing he was craving, Lucas thought— *solitude*—was the one thing Mike was trying to avoid. The irony wasn't lost on him. The suggestion that popped out of his mouth, though, surprised them both.

"Come home with me," he said suddenly.

"What?"

He couldn't believe he was saying this, but it felt right. "You don't want to be alone. So don't."

She shook her head, even though she looked as though she were considering it. "Might not be such a great idea after last night—"

"We don't have to do that again."

She took a sip of coffee and paused a moment before asking, "But what if we *want* to do it again?"

His body lit up like a power plant—despite everything. "Then we'll decide."

"Lucas, you *like* being alone in that house."

"Yeah, I do, but I'm not now anyway, so—"

"Whoa. Back up. Rewind and hit play again. What do you mean you're not alone now anyway?"

He shifted his gaze from hers, squinted into the distance, and said, "My . . . brother. Justin and his girlfriend are there." He scowled and added, "They were waiting at the house for me when I got there this morning."

"Wow." She snorted. "So. We both got surprise brothers today."

He glanced back at her and actually smiled about the subject of Justin for the first time. How weird was that?

"Karmically speaking," she mused, "what were the odds?"

"As a scientist," he said, still smiling, because how could he help it when looking into her eyes? "I can tell you they're damn high."

Her lips curved. "Very scientific of you."

"Hey, I'm a genius."

"And humble."

"Goes without saying."

"Thanks."

"For what?"

"For making me smile today when I didn't think I'd be able to. When I was wondering if I ever would again."

"Same goes."

Mike shivered and took another long drink of coffee, enjoying the spill of warmth rushing through her. It wouldn't last. Wouldn't do anything to get rid of the bone-deep cold that had settled around her heart. But at the moment, she was grateful for any warmth at all.

And oh God, she was grateful for Lucas.

They hadn't exactly parted on the best of terms a

few hours ago, but right now, he was looking like her only safe harbor in a really choppy sea.

"If you were serious about that offer," she said, watching his eyes carefully, "I accept."

"Good."

She'd worry about what this might mean, what this might change between them, later. Right now, it was enough to know that she wouldn't have to be alone tonight. Or tomorrow.

"Mike?"

Her head whipped around and she spotted her sister stepping around the corner of the hospital. She stood up slowly, as if braced for another blow. Lucas rose to take up a spot beside her. She didn't even see him move. He was just suddenly, simply, *there*.

"What is it, Sam?" Mike asked. "Is it Papa?"

"No. Sorry. Shouldn't have scared you." She pursed her lips, then chewed on them for a second or two before adding, "They're here. Jack. And his mother."

"Oh God. Okay. I'm coming."

Sam went back the way she'd come and Mike grabbed hold of her coffee cup and clung to it as if it were a life preserver and she was going down for the third time. Then she shifted a glance at Lucas. "It's him. The new little brother."

"I'll go with you."

She smiled. "Was kind of hoping you'd say that."

They rounded the building, and Mike felt him just a step or two behind her. Funny. This morning when he dropped her off at the hospital, she never would have guessed that he'd be back here now, offering support.

And boy howdy did she need it.

Her gaze locked on a tall woman in gray wool slacks and a soft yellow shirt. Her short, dark blond hair was stylishly cut to chin length and she was carrying a Prada bag to match her truly great shoes.

She wasn't pretty, in the traditional sense. Her features had too much character for that. Strong nose, wide mouth, high cheekbones. She was attractive, though, almost exotic looking. But Mike quickly lost interest in the woman her father had cheated with so many years ago. Instead, she focused her gaze on the boy looking up at Sam as she introduced herself.

His hair was the same shade of brown as Jo's. He was already tall, and judging by the size of his feet, he was destined to be a lot taller than Papa.

But the most arresting thing about him were his eyes.

Papa's eyes.

Marconi eyes.

Mike swallowed hard. She'd been so hoping that this was a mistake. That maybe the woman had lied to Papa and he, being male and pretty much putty in a woman's hands, had bought the whole story, hook, line, and sinker.

But there was no mistake about this.

That boy was her brother.

And she was just going to have to learn to live with it.

14

Mike kept a solid grip on Lucas's hand as she took the last few steps separating her from her sister, the boy, and his mother. As she got closer, her breath strangled in her chest and her heartbeat skittered wildly. She swallowed hard and clenched her coffee cup so tightly, she was vaguely surprised her fingers didn't splinter through the cardboard.

Sam turned as she joined them and Mike noted the acceptance that flashed in her eyes. But then, Sam had already been prepared to forgive Papa. To accept this boy. Because of her own past, she was naturally inclined to acknowledge this new and totally startling relationship.

Mike didn't know if she could do the same.

Hell. Didn't know if she *wanted* to.

Then the boy turned to look up at her.

His too long hair fell across his forehead, and as he swiped it aside, he blinked Marconi eyes and gave her a tremulous, wary smile.

"You're my sister Mike," he said softly.

It was that easy.

And that hard.

And that complicated.

Whatever she and Papa would have to say to each other later, this boy wouldn't be a part of it.

"Yeah," she said, swallowing hard and forcing the words out of a throat too tight to breathe. Blindly, she tightened her grip on Lucas's hand and kept her gaze on Jack *Marconi*. "I'm your sister."

Hank Marconi opened his eyes and knew immediately that something was different. For starters, he was in a hospital room with tubes and plugs jutting out of his body and a roomful of machines burping, clattering, and beeping. For seconds, Grace was at his side, looking as if she were planning a funeral.

"Hey," he said, and cleared his throat when his voice sounded rusty.

Grace's head snapped up, her gaze shot to him, and a beatific smile creased her face. "Henry. Oh, thank God."

"Jesus, Grace." He tried to move but found he didn't have the energy, so he slumped back against the pillows. "What the hell am I doing here?"

"You had a heart attack."

"I did?" Strange. He didn't remember anything like that. Sure, he'd felt a little tired and maybe achy. But shouldn't a man *remember* if his heart goes out on him? "Are you sure?"

She laughed and the sound of it was great, the one normal thing in the midst of this confused mess.

"Henry, you're enough to make me old before my time."

"Not a chance," he murmured and reached for the hand she held out to him. "When do I get outta here?"

Grace moved closer, scooting around the machinery surrounding his bed as it continued to click and beep like a weird science experiment. He scowled and fought down a quick jolt of fear.

He'd never liked hospitals. Especially not after what had happened to his Sylvia.

"Go into a hospital alive and come out dead," his father used to say. And back when Hank's father was a kid, it had probably been true more often than not.

These days, though, things were different. His head knew that. It was just his gut trying to tell him different.

"The good news is," Grace said, and Hank told himself to pay attention, "the doctor said it was a minor episode of angina."

"Minor?" He glanced down at his arms, with the IV tubes and the oxygen meter stuck to his finger, and at the array of machinery. "This is how *minor* is treated?"

"Henry, be quiet."

His eyebrows shot straight up. When Grace got that "no nonsense" tone in her voice, a wise man settled back and waited for the storm to pass. "All right."

"You scared us all to death." She pulled in a shaky breath and smiled again, stroking the back of his hand with her fingertips. "We know *now* that it was something minor. But we didn't know. Not for hours. The doctors didn't want to take any chances and rightly so. But . . ." She paused to look at him again, as if assuring herself that he really was alive and kicking, so to speak. "But the waiting was dreadful. We were all so worried."

"My girls?" he asked, instantly picturing his three daughters, frantic, making the hospital staff's lives a living nightmare. Hank knew his girls. "They know I'm all right now, don't they?"

"Yeesss . . ."

He narrowed his gaze on her as a small worm of concern slithered through his insides. "Something's wrong, Grace. Don't treat me like a sick old man," he ordered. "Tell me."

"I am. In my own way."

She let go of his hand and smoothed her hair in a nervous gesture he'd first picked up on two years ago. Whatever was up, it had Grace worried. And he figured it wasn't just his health causing it.

"The doctors said you'll be fine. You have to stay here for a day or two—"

"Stay *here*?"

"—for observation," she continued blithely as if she'd never heard the interruption. "And you'll have to change your diet and maybe start on some blood thinners."

"That's crazy," he blustered, waving one hand despite the IV line attached to his arm, "I'm fine."

"Fine for a man hooked up to a heart monitor," she snapped and he saw the flash of tears in her eyes and immediately felt contrite.

He might not remember this heart attack, but clearly Grace did. And she'd been suffering while he'd been blissfully asleep. Best not to argue with a woman when she had too much on her side in the fight.

"I'm sorry if I scared you, Grace. Scared the girls." He watched her carefully. "But there's something else you're still not telling me. Are the girls all right? Are they here?"

She swallowed hard and nodded. "They're all fine and, yes, they're outside in the waiting room. And so is someone else."

Now he felt a twinge in his heart. Along with a jolt of something surprisingly like panic. "Who?"

She lifted her chin and straightened her spine. "Jack and Carol are here, too."

All the air left him in a rush. "Ah God . . ."

"I called them, Henry," she said, tilting her chin even higher in defiance, just in case he had it in his head to argue with her or yell at her for making such a decision on her own. "They had a right to know. Just as much as your girls did."

"You shouldn't have told the girls," he whispered, and for the first time, Hank Marconi felt like an old man.

"You're right," she said, leaning over the metal bedrail to get close enough to plant a kiss on his forehead. When she pulled back, she looked directly in his eyes and said, "*You* should have. A long time ago."

He'd thought about it. Prayed over it. Had a million one-sided conversations with his long-dead Sylvia about it. But somehow, he'd never been able to have the confrontation he knew he should have. Because he simply couldn't bring himself to risk his daughters' love.

And more.

He couldn't bear the thought of seeing disappointment—disapproval—in their eyes.

"I couldn't," he muttered. "That's just not something a man can tell his daughters."

"That's the point, Henry," Grace said, smoothing one hand over his neatly trimmed beard, "they *are* your daughters. *You* and Sylvia taught them how to love. How to forgive. You should have trusted them."

"I do," he argued, idly plucking at the flannel sheet covering him. "I just—"

"They're hurt and angry and confused. But they'll find their way past it."

He lifted his gaze to hers and admitted his own self-ishness. "I can't lose them, Grace. I don't think I could live without my girls."

"Foolish man, you couldn't lose them if you *tried*. They love you. As I do."

Henry looked up into her shining dark eyes and, de-spite the fear of what his daughters were thinking of him, felt like a man who'd been blessed.

Twice in his life, he'd known love. Real, honest, soul-deep love. First there'd been Sylvia, the love of his youth, the mother of his precious girls. When he was losing her, he'd felt his own soul following her. She died in inches and took pieces of him with her as she went. If not for his girls, he never would have been able to hold on to what was left of his life.

And now, he loved Grace. This tiny, infuriating, ex-asperating woman had shown him that the heart never really grew old. She'd awakened his soul, enlivened his days, and filled his nights with a warmth he'd missed with a bone-deep need.

Two women had touched his heart.

But there'd been another. He hadn't loved her. But he'd needed her and cared for her, in a dark and empty time. She hadn't really touched his heart, his soul.

But she'd touched his life in a profound way.

She'd given him a son.

Shown him life in the middle of death.

And though he felt the shame of his actions, he couldn't completely regret them—because to do that he would have to wish Jack away. Something he could never do.

"They won't forgive me," he said quietly and admitted, if only to himself, that he wouldn't be able to blame them for it.

Grace's heart was in her eyes as she said, "Maybe not at first. The hurt goes deep. But they will, Henry. Eventually, they will."

He clung to those words like a convert clutching a rosary during an earthquake.

God, Mike hated hospitals.

She'd spent more than enough time in them for one lifetime, thanks very much. All those days and weeks with Mama. Not to mention the weeks she'd spent stretched out on her own hospital bed.

And she wished she hadn't sent Lucas home an hour ago. But once they knew Papa was going to be all right, it hadn't seemed fair to keep him there with her out of pure selfishness. Now of course, she was rethinking the whole selfish thing.

Because at the moment, she really missed the warm strength she'd found in the grip of his hand on hers.

"Is Papa okay now?"

Mike shifted in the uncomfortable green plastic chair and looked down into her brother's eyes—so

much like her own. She wanted to not like him, damn
it. By rights, he shouldn't exist. By rights, her father
would still be the paragon of perfection she'd always
assumed him to be.

But she couldn't hate Jack.

Couldn't even resent him.

He was just a kid. He hadn't asked to be born. He
hadn't set out to break up a family.

Now, he was only a frightened little boy, looking to
his big sisters for comfort. And damn it, he had a right
to expect it.

"Yeah," she said, forcing a smile. "Papa's going to
be fine. You can go in and see him as soon as Sam
comes out if you want."

Jack nodded, let his gaze slide to the closed double
doors, and then back again. "Mike, how come Jo
doesn't like me?"

She blew out a breath. "It's not that," she lied, wishing her oldest sister were in front of her so she could
kick a little ass. Jo hadn't been mean to the kid, but being Jo, her emotions were written on her face, and
even a little boy could see that something wasn't right
there. Still, Mike said, "Jo's just . . . worried. About
Papa."

"Oh." His face scrunched up as he thought about it,
but it said something about how he'd been raised
that he accepted Mike's word for the situation a moment later. "My mom says we shouldn't stay, but I
don't wanna go yet. I wanna see Papa's house here.
And meet Bear. And—"

"Jack, sweetie," his mother said, coming up behind
him to lay a protective arm around his shoulders.

"Why don't you go and get a soda from the machine in the hall?"

She handed him a dollar and Jack shrugged before moving off, dragging each foot to make sure the women knew he was going reluctantly.

The minute the boy left, Mike felt . . . *exposed*. She didn't want to be this close to the woman who'd slept with her father. She didn't want to be in the same room with her, if it came down to that.

The air in the waiting room still stank of antiseptic and despair. The mint-green walls had closed in on them all hours ago and Mike wanted nothing more than to race outside and fill her lungs with the air of freedom. But she was stuck. Rooted to the spot as Carol Benedetto faced her.

"Thank you," the woman said stiffly.

Mike stiffened, too. Jack's existence wasn't *his* fault, but nobody said she had to make nice to the woman standing in front of her right now. "For what?"

"For being nice to my son."

"We rarely beat the shit out of little boys anymore," Mike sneered.

Carol's wide, expressive mouth worked a minute or two, then she inhaled sharply and tucked her Prada bag under her arm. "Look, I know what you and your sisters must think of me—"

"Oh, I doubt that," Jo said, stepping up to join the little chitchat.

"Jo . . ." Mike knew how her sister felt. But taking the elegant-looking woman by the throat and choking her for a few hours just wasn't the answer. No matter how good it sounded.

Jo held up one hand for quiet and turned her steady gaze on Papa's past fling. "If you did know what we think of you, you wouldn't be standing so close."

"Look, think what you will," Carol said hotly, fighting Jo's fire with a little heat of her own. "But you know your father better than I do and even I know that he's an exceptional man—"

"We agree on that," Sam said, arriving just in the nick of time to flank Jo's other side.

Mike didn't doubt she could take her big sister down, but it wouldn't be easy—especially since she sort of agreed with how Jo was feeling at the moment. So she was grateful to have Sam there, just in case.

Carol shot a glance toward the hall to make sure her son was out of earshot. Then she faced the daughters of the man she'd known on the sly for more than ten years.

"I don't much care what you guys think of me, you know. But Jack's been seeing pictures of the three of you since he was old enough to look at them." She shifted her gaze from one to the other of them. "Your father was always so proud of you. He wanted Jack to know his . . . *sisters*."

Jo flinched.

Mike moved closer.

"If you want, we can talk," Carol offered. "I'll tell you whatever you want to know. But not now. Not in front of Jack." She worried at her bottom lip, scraping off a little of the dark peach lipstick she wore. "I don't want him to know what you three think of me, if you don't mind."

A long moment of silence passed. But it wasn't completely silent. Mike actually *heard* the hum of tension rattling around them all. She felt it crackling in the air, like static electricity. She almost expected their hair to lift straight up.

"That sounds fair," Sam said quietly, glancing at her sisters.

Mike nodded. "Works for me." Thinking that at some point, yes, she would like to know how her father had slipped off his pedestal. And what he'd found in this woman that he couldn't find at home. You know?

With his *wife*?

"Yeah. Whatever," Jo said tightly, then looked over her shoulder, also checking to make sure Jack was nowhere near. Satisfied, she leaned in toward Carol, and keeping her voice at a low hiss of disapproval, she said, "Jack's a kid. We keep him safe because . . ." She took a deep, ragged breath. "Because he's *family*. He's a Marconi and Marconis stand together."

Carol jerked a nod.

"But make no mistake," Jo continued. "*You* are nothing to me. *You* are just the woman who stole a dying woman's husband."

Carol winced, but took it.

Mike felt a grudging admiration for her.

"And as far as I'm concerned," Jo finished, "that makes you less than just about everything on earth."

"Fine. Then we understand each other," Carol said quietly.

"Damn straight," Jo muttered, just as the boy came back, clutching a dripping soda.

"I spilled it," he said. Unnecessarily, since orange soda was liberally sprinkled across his white T-shirt and dribbling down his arm.

"No problem," Jo told him. She dropped one arm around his shoulders, turned him around, and headed back to the hallway. "I'll show you where the bathroom is."

Lucas saw the headlights streak across the darkness and knew Mike had arrived. And he'd never been more happy about seeing her.

For two months, every time he saw her truck pull up in the driveway, it had irritated him, set him on edge, wondering what the hell she was going to do next. Now, he was so eager to see her he felt like a kid on Christmas Eve.

Abandoning the book he'd been pretending to read, he stalked across the living room, opened the door, and stepped out onto the porch.

Overhead, clouds pushed and shoved at each other as thunder rumbled ominously. The wind kicked up out of nowhere, rattling through the trees, making the dry leaves whisper together in a hush of sound that was horror-movie worthy.

He went down the stairs, walked onto the damp grass, and stepped into the wind, enjoying the air moving over him. It made him feel *alive*. And after an afternoon of watching Justin die, he needed that simple, physical reassurance.

Mike climbed out of her truck and instantly the wind lifted her long, loose blond hair and flew it around her head like a banner announcing her presence. She slammed the truck door and then leaned against it as if she were too tired to take another step.

Not surprising. After no sleep the night before, she'd been running on pure adrenaline today. Bound to crash.

She turned her head slowly to look at him, then smiled and tipped her face into the wind. "God, it feels good out here."

"It does." He stuffed his hands into his pockets.

"Always liked the wind. Sam never did, though. Always worried about her hair." She laughed quietly as her own hair flew like blond snakes. "Jo likes a good storm, too. Not surprising, I guess, considering how much alike our temperaments are." She paused. "I wonder if Jack likes 'em."

"You should ask him."

"Yeah. Maybe."

"So where is the little brother?"

She sighed and reached up to shove both hands through her hair, tangling it, lifting it until the wind was all around her. "Grace took Jack and his mother home to her place. She dropped me off at home so I could get my truck. Had to feed Bear, too—Papa's dog. Then Jack and the dog became such good friends, Grace took him home, too." She shook her head. "Poor old dog's too old to have to put up with Grace's goats."

"Goats?"

"Long story."

"Right."

"Where's *your* brother?" she asked.

"Upstairs." *Dying.* But he didn't say it aloud. There would be time enough to tell her about Justin.

She nodded and closed her eyes.

"God, I'm tired," she whispered, her voice fading

into the sigh of the wind, becoming a part of it. "I feel like overcooked pasta."

"Huh?"

"You know, all limp and tasteless?" She waved a hand. "It's an Italian thing."

Lucas sensed her exhaustion. Would've felt it, even if he hadn't seen it etched into her features. Pulling his hands free of his pockets, he finally moved, walking toward her with long, slow steps. When he was close enough, he did what came naturally and opened his arms.

She fell into him, sighing again as his arms came around her, holding her tight. "You know, Rocket Man," she said softly, "I could really get to like you."

"Same goes," he said and heard the stiffness in his voice. He wondered if she did. If she was as surprised by his admission as *he* was.

She snuggled her head against his chest as if trying to find a comfortable position on a pillow that was just too hard.

"Who knew, huh?" she asked, voice tired, slurred. "I mean, you sort of sneaked up on me."

He knew exactly what she meant. But he didn't say so.

He chuckled shortly. "You're just saying that because I'm holding you up instead of letting you collapse into the dirt."

"Well," she said, tipping her head back and smiling. *"Yeah."*

Her eyes. A man could get so lost in those eyes that he'd never find his way out again. At the moment, he didn't even think he'd mind.

"Where's your stuff?" he asked.

"Back of the truck. Do we have to move now?"

"The bed's more comfortable than the grass."

"You just said the magic word," she murmured. *"Bed."*

He laughed again. "Well, you're easy."

She looked up at him, all seriousness suddenly. "You know? I never was, before."

"Mike . . ." He lifted one hand to touch her cheek, her jaw, to feel her skin sliding beneath his.

She reached up and caught his hand in hers and gave it a squeeze as she smiled. "Sorry. Didn't mean to go all thoughtful and deep on you. It's too late and I'm too tired to get introspective, okay?"

"Yeah," he said, smiling down at her. "Who needs deep, anyway?"

She gave him a quick grin as a reward. "You know, there's a lot to be said for shallow."

"Puddles need love as much as the ocean," he said, stepping past her to reach into the bed of the truck. He grabbed a huge navy blue duffel bag and hoisted it out. Carrying it in one tight fist, he draped his free arm around her shoulders and pulled her up close to him.

Less than twenty minutes later, Mike was showered, changed, and stretched out on his bed. She wore a tiny dark green tank top and boxer-style bottoms that rode low on her hips, allowing him glimpses of the diamond-topped gold bar piercing her navel.

He climbed into the bed beside her, turned off the light on the table, then reached for her, drawing her into the circle of his arms. She curled into him, snaking one arm across his bare chest and tucking her head into the curve of his shoulder.

"I'm so tired," she said softly, her breath dusting across his chest.

"Then sleep, Michaela," he murmured, stroking one hand up and down her back, in long, rhythmic strokes. "Just forget about everything and sleep."

"Mmm . . . sounded nice," she said, her voice fading into the quiet of the room. "I like the way you said my name . . ."

"Michaela," he said again, drawing the name out until it sounded like music.

She drifted into sleep, and long after her even, steady breathing told him she was dreaming, Lucas lay awake. Staring up into the darkness, he thought about what she'd said to him earlier. How he'd "sneaked up on her." Well, she'd done the same to him.

He didn't know quite how it had happened, but with Mike here in his arms, for the first time, this house really felt like *home*.

15

While Mike slept a few miles away, Jo sat in the darkened church and listened to thunder rolling through the sky outside. Rain fell in angry sheets and battered at the walls of St. Joseph's with furious fists. The wind howled and swept through the gaps in the window casements to flicker the flames of the candles on the altar and at the feet of the statues of the saints.

Jo thought the raging storm was a fitting accompaniment to the emotions churning inside her. She sat in a pew in the middle of the old church and stared at the crucifix attached to the gray stone wall behind the altar. Her hands clenched tight in her lap, her eyes filled with tears she refused to allow to fall, she glared at the pain-filled image of Jesus' face.

"You just keep piling it on, don't you?" she muttered, her voice fading into the rush of wind and the crash of the rain. "People look up to you, ask for help, and you slam-dunk 'em. Is it any wonder I don't spend more time here?"

She pushed off the pew, stood up, and walked to the wide center aisle.

When she was a kid, the Marconis were here in St. Joseph's every Sunday. Mama never missed mass and wasn't about to let her family miss it, either. Sylvia Marconi had probably spent a good half of her life on her knees in prayer. Said enough rosaries to wear her fingertips to the bone.

And blindly believed in a God who'd let her die anyway, despite the frantic prayers of her family.

Jo walked up the center aisle, listening to the quiet click of her boot heels against the stone floor. For years, she'd done everything right. She'd gone to mass, said her prayers, believed everything her parents had encouraged her to, and what was her big reward? Losing her innocence *and* her mother in the same year.

The closer she got to the altar, the angrier she became. Outside, thunder rolled, and through the stained-glass windows, lightning flashed, sending bursts of wildly colored light dancing through the shadows. Jo hardly noticed.

At the gleaming, mahogany altar rail, where she and her sisters had made their First Communion and their Confirmation, she stopped. Memories rushed through her mind. Mass with her family. Weddings. Baptisms.

And the night she'd made a confession—her darkest secret and shame rippling from her to the ears of a priest who could never repeat what he'd heard.

Jo closed her eyes tightly, banishing that memory as she tipped her head back, opened her eyes, and stared directly into the delicately carved eyes, of the Son of God. Rage bubbled up inside her, frothed through her veins, until it reached the pit of her stomach where it churned and roiled until she felt sick with it.

Inhaling sharply, deeply, she spoke and there was enough of the old-school Catholic inside her still to make her wince at the loudness of her own voice in this quiet place.

But it didn't stop her.

"That's it," she said. "We're finished, You and me." Her voice broke on the strangle of tears clogging her throat. "I believed. All along, in spite of everything, I still believed. I tried to pretend I didn't. Didn't come to see You. Didn't pray. Haven't said a rosary in *years*. But I believed."

She dropped her hands onto the altar rail, felt the cool, slick surface of the polished wood beneath her hands and held on as if it meant her life.

"Now, though, it's too much. My father. The one man I trusted more than *anyone*." She sucked in a trembling breath. "He's not who I believed he was. So that tells me *nothing* I believe in is real. Which means, You're not real."

She laughed shortly and lifted one hand to clap over her mouth to keep that laughter from spiraling into hysterics. When she had control of herself, she let her hand drop to her side.

"Stupid, huh? I'm standing here, telling You that You're not real—but if I'm talking to You, You *are* real. So let's put it another way, okay? Even if You are . . . we're done. I'm through being disappointed. I'm through hoping for the best and getting kicked in the teeth." She let go of the rail, stood up and jammed both hands into her pockets. "You go Your way, I'll go mine."

For the first time in her life, she didn't genuflect in front of the altar. Didn't show that respect that had been pounded into her brain from the time she was a child.

Tonight, she just turned and stomped out of the church, boots clomping in rhythm to the fury of the storm. And when she hit the double doors at the end of the aisle, she slapped them hard with both hands and kept right on walking.

"You should have let me say something."

Monsignor Gable stared at the doors through which Josefina Marconi had disappeared for a long moment before turning his gaze back on Father Tim Holden, the young parish priest beside him.

"She was disrespectful and should have been stopped."

Monsignor Gable, an old man, who knew exactly why Jo Marconi was so furious, only smiled. "Faith like that should be welcomed," he said, "not hushed."

"*Faith?* Didn't you hear her?" The younger man still quivered in outrage.

"I heard her," the old man said. "But I wonder if you really did."

"What do you mean?"

St. Joseph's pastor patted his young colleague's shoulder patiently. "The fact that she felt comfortable enough with Our Lord to come in and give Him a dressing-down speaks to a deep faith. How many people believe in God enough to shout at Him when they're hurt and angry?"

Father Tim looked stunned.

Monsignor Gable only smiled. "Even by telling God that she was through with Him, Jo made the connection to the faith that has seen her through some dark times."

He frowned, remembering the confession she'd made so long ago. The one that had broken his heart. "She'll be back."

"How can you be so sure?"

"Because it's who she is," he said softly, then steered his young friend out the sacristy door, headed for the rectory and home. "Now, about the Forty-Niner game next Saturday. I'll give you three-to-one odds . . ."

"You should've told me," Mike said, facing Lucas down under the overhang of the front porch the next morning. "Could have *warned* me at least."

Lucas sighed and shifted his gaze to the still stormy sky. All night it had poured as though the skies were trying to empty themselves. This morning, the rain was still falling, though with a little less gusto than the night before. Which pretty much described the situation between him and Mike, too.

She'd awakened early, gone downstairs to make coffee, and found both Bridget and Justin in the kitchen.

He'd been hearing about the awkwardness of the whole situation ever since.

He didn't look at her as he said, "Not something you can just drop into conversation. 'Oh, did I mention that the twin brother I haven't spoken to in years is *dying*?' "

Mike, wearing a faded blue MARCONI CONSTRUCTION T-shirt and the worn, nearly threadbare jeans that clung to her legs, stared at him. She felt her gaze even though he still couldn't quite meet it. "Did you know?" she asked. "Before he got here. Did you know?"

"No."

"God, Lucas."

He blew out a breath and stuck one hand out from under the porch to let the rain puddle in his palm. Then he pulled his hand back, shook it dry, and shoved it through his hair. "He tried to tell me. I wouldn't listen. Didn't want to hear him."

"Are you listening *now*?"

He glanced at her, irritation flashing. "He's here, isn't he?"

"Yeah," she said and walked closer, perching one hip on the porch rail and tipping her head back to look at him. "But he's inside and you're outside. So basically, you're still not answering his e-mails—even the 'in person' ones."

He knew damn well what he was doing and didn't need Mike pointing it out to him. Last night, falling asleep with her in his arms, he'd felt more relaxed—at peace—than he had in years. But this morning, the truth was, Mike didn't know what had happened between him and his twin and he didn't know if he wanted to tell her or not. Dredging it all up again wouldn't help anything. Would only make him relive things he'd spent too much time trying to keep buried.

But wasn't it all alive again now, anyway? With Justin here, Lucas couldn't avoid the past. It continually slapped at him whether he wanted it to or not.

"Are you gonna talk?" Mike asked in an over-the-top movie-villain voice. "Or am I going to have to get nasty?"

He glanced at her. "Funny."

"Yeah, you shouldn't laugh so hard," she said. "You'll hurt yourself."

His hands fisted in his pockets. "I don't—"

She cut him off with a wave of her hand. "If you're about to give me the 'we're just having sex we're not a couple' speech again, skip it. We might not have planned any of this—but we've moved past the 'ships that bump in the night' thing anyway and you know it."

He nodded. They were more than just bed partners. He just didn't know *what* they were. Wasn't sure he was ready to find out, either.

"Look, don't think of this as pillow talk. Think about it like we're just two friends spilling our guts. God knows, I've spilled enough of mine all over you."

"Friends?" he asked. "Is that what we are?"

"Works for now, doesn't it? Besides, there're worse things to be."

"Good point." Trust Mike to cut through the bullshit and get right down to it.

"So do you want to tell me now, before I go to the hospital to see Papa, or when I get back?"

"I get a choice?" he asked wryly.

"There's always a choice, grasshopper."

"You getting deep on me?" he asked with a brief snort of laughter. "What happened to a love for shallow?"

"I'm changeable. Sue me."

He ignored that. "If there's a choice, I vote for later."

"Not surprised," Mike said and scooted off the porch rail. She stepped up to him and laid the flat of her hand on his chest. His heartbeat quickened under her touch and he realized that his instant reaction to Mike was the *one* thing he could depend on lately.

"You realize," she said, meeting his gaze squarely, "I won't let this go."

"When have you *ever* let something go?"

She smiled, reached up and hooked one hand behind his neck. Pulling his head down to hers, she gave him a long, hard, smacking kiss and then released him again. "Rocket Man, you're getting to know me, aren't you?"

"I'd say so."

"Can't have that," she said with a shake of her head that sent her blond braid into a pendulumlike wave, "so I guess I'm going to have to find a way to surprise you."

"You usually do."

"What's life without surprises?"

"Peaceful?"

"Boring." Then she patted his chest, grabbed her shoulder bag off the closest chair, and sprinted down the steps and through the rain to her truck.

Most women he'd known would have had an umbrella, protecting their hair if not their clothes. Mike, though, was a law unto herself. He watched her easy grace, the way her legs moved in long, lazy strides. And he admitted, at least to himself, that he'd much rather have surprises in his life—even if it meant having a dying brother show up on his doorstep or trying to keep one step ahead of Mike.

Papa's already ruddy face flushed nearly beet red. His full gray beard stood out in sharp contrast against his skin and his eyes were wary as he watched Mike approach his bed.

"How you feeling, Papa?" She grabbed the top rail of the bed and let the feel of the cold metal ground her. It hadn't been easy, walking into this room. But it would have been even more difficult to stay away.

She'd been worried about this. Talking to him for the first time since finding out about the secrets he'd protected for so long. Facing him, knowing that her father wasn't the man she'd always thought him to be.

But now, looking down at him, Mike felt the sweet rush of love pour through her. She knew it wouldn't be easy, sorting through her wildly confused feelings. But the bottom line was, this was Papa. The man she'd loved her whole life. And God, it was good to know that feeling was still inside, despite the pain and the disappointment. She couldn't have borne losing Papa.

"I'm fine," he said softly and his hands opened and closed on the flannel sheet covering him up to his chest. "Just . . . *worried*."

She squeezed the top rail a little tighter. It seemed they were going to have the talk now. Here.

Was she ready?

Nope.

Mike's stomach churned.

"Your sister Samantha was here this morning. We talked."

"And now we have to?" she asked.

"I think so."

"Papa," she said, suddenly sure she really didn't want to go there. "Why don't we just pretend we did and leave it at that?"

"The time for pretending is over."

She blew out a breath and met his gaze. Pale blue

eyes stared back at her. Misery shone in those familiar depths, along with hope.

She knew those feelings. She'd been so terrified yesterday, that they were going to lose him. She thought about Lucas at home, dealing with a brother he was *going* to lose, no matter what. And she felt . . . confused? Oh yeah. Grateful? That, too. And still, just a little hurt.

To protect herself, delay the inevitable, she said quickly, "The last time we were together in a hospital, *I* was the one in the bed."

"I remember," he said, his gaze locked on hers.

"I was scared then, too." Her voice dropped to a hush as memories reared up, demanding to be noticed.

She didn't remember the accident. That was probably a blessing. She *did* remember hitchhiking and a guy stopping to pick her up.

The minute she was in the car with him, she smelled the alcohol. The whole car reeked of it. He was happy. Celebrating some big business deal. And he'd told her she shouldn't hitchhike. Too dangerous. But she was safe with him. She tried to make him stop—even runaways knew better than to drive with a drunk. He didn't stop, though. Just kept driving and talking and laughing and then he shook a cigarette out of a pack and stuck it in his mouth.

The car weaved back and forth across the highway while he fumbled with a lighter. Mike yelled at him to be careful, but he laughed again. Then the car drifted farther, into oncoming traffic.

Headlights speared in through the windshield. The

man screamed and that sound echoed in her brain over
and over again as Mike slid into darkness.

When she woke up, the cops told her the drunk had died, along with the guy they'd hit. She was the lucky one. She lived. Of course, her internal injuries were so severe they'd had to remove most of her ovaries. And at seventeen, she'd had to look up into a kind doctor's face as he told her there was a ninety-six percent chance she would *never* have children.

She'd paid a heavy price for running. Now Papa was paying a price of his own.

"I remember lying in the bed, feeling so damn sorry that I'd run again. That I'd disappointed you and scared Mama, again."

"We understood, Michaela. We hurt because *you* hurt."

She nodded, her grip on the bedrail tightening as the past faded and the present slammed hard into her heart.

"Did Mama know?" she blurted, surprised by the words because she really hadn't known that question was inside her, waiting to come out.

"No." He understood what she was talking about now and reassured her as fast as he could. Reaching for one of Mike's hands, he said, "I would not have hurt her by telling her the truth only to make myself feel better. Confession is not always good for the soul."

Mike shook her head and sighed. She knew he believed that. But the truth was, a woman always knew. Husbands might think they could keep indiscretions separate from their real lives. But wives always knew.

"Papa, even if she didn't know—it hurt her."

"Do you think I don't know?" he asked quietly, his voice barely more than a breath. "Do you think I haven't lived with my own guilt, my own shame, all these years?"

"Why, Papa?" Her eyes filled with tears and she lifted her free hand to brush them away. "Why would you do it?"

He sighed and it seemed to come from the bottom of his soul. "It was a hard time, Michaela. Your mama was sick. I was scared."

"You? Scared?"

A brief, sad smile curved his mouth and was gone again in an instant. "More scared than I've ever been before in my life. I couldn't help her. Couldn't do anything for her. She was slipping away from me to a place I couldn't reach."

Oh God, she remembered it all so well. Mama sick, closing herself off in her room—her own pain and misery making her look for a cave to hide in.

Papa sleeping on the sofa, so he wouldn't disturb her in the night. Him standing outside their bedroom door, wanting to at least see her, but unsure if he should bother her or not. If she'd welcome him or not.

She remembered she and her sisters creeping through the house, not wanting to make any noise. All of them afraid to admit that Mama was dying. Afraid to look at the crumbling world around them.

And God, she remembered how she ran.

All the times she ran and hid, wanting to escape. Wanting to run from the pain and the fear of losing Mama. Until that last time, when she'd ended up in a hospital and seen the fatigue and sorrow in Mama's eyes.

In her own way, Mike had made it all so much harder. She hadn't helped. She'd been that one last straw on the back of an already crippled camel.

"So you ran away, too," she said quietly.

Surprise flashed in his eyes and she knew he was grateful that she could understand. "Yes. I ran. I'm ashamed. But I ran. I went to a bar in San Jose. Someplace to hear people talk about things other than death and sickness. To hear music and remember life was still going on. And I talked to a nice young woman—a waitress there—who was in college at night. She was alone. And I . . . *felt* alone."

"Carol." One word. One name. And it hung in the room like a neon banner flashing ADULTERER.

"Yes. Carol." He scraped one hand across his face, smoothing his beard unnecessarily. "She had problems of her own. And we . . . talked. It helped. Talking to someone who didn't *need* something from me. Someone who didn't *expect* me to have all the answers."

Mike's insides twisted. She wanted to yell at him. To ask him if he really thought that explanation made everything okay. But she could see in his eyes that he didn't.

"And it happened," he said softly, letting it go at that, and Mike really didn't need a picture drawn, thanks very much.

"When Carol found out she was pregnant, she told me," he said. "She wanted the baby. And how could I ask her to get rid of a child?" He shook his head. "I couldn't. So she went to San Francisco. Got a job. Had the baby. I went home to watch my Sylvia die and I helped Carol—and Jack—when I could."

"Jack knew about us."

Papa frowned. "You're his sisters. He should know you."

"He's our *brother*," Mike said flatly. "We should have known *him*."

Yes," he admitted, his voice tired. "You should have . . . now you can."

That was too much to think about at the moment, so she simply shrugged as if it didn't matter to her one way or the other and said, "Maybe."

Papa cleared his throat and asked, "Where is Josefina? I haven't seen her."

Mike shifted her gaze to the far wall, where an oversized clock was ticking off the seconds. "Jo was here yesterday, waiting with us. She's—"

"Mad at her papa."

"Yeah, you could say that."

He nodded thoughtfully. "And you, Michaela? How do you feel?"

She blew out a breath. "I'm still a little mad, too," she admitted, wondering if that feeling would ever completely go away. "But maybe I understand better because of what happened to *me* when Mama was dying. And I love you, Papa. That doesn't change."

His eyes filled with tears and he bit down hard on his bottom lip to keep from giving in to them. When a strong man breaks, it's not an easy thing to watch.

Carefully, she released the latch on the guard rail and leaned over him to lay her head on his chest. Mike felt Papa's arms come around her and she closed her eyes on a silent prayer of thanks that he was still a part of her life.

The rest, they'd have to work on.

Bridget stomped down the back stairs, avoided the rocky path leading down to the lake's edge, and instead walked through the grass toward the meadow. The storm had passed, the sky was clear, and the wind sharp with the scent of fresh rain.

But the storm inside *her* was still raging.

So mad she could spit, she kept moving until the house was far behind her. Only then did she drop to the ground and stare back at the place. A lovely home, to be sure, but inside that lovely place lay a man more stubborn, more hardheaded, more exasperating than anyone she'd ever met.

"Who's the fool, though?" she muttered, letting the wetness of the grass soak into her jeans. "The irritating man or the woman who loves him in spite of himself?"

"You know," Mike said as she dropped to the ground beside her, "I've asked myself that very question a couple of times lately."

Bridget scowled and flipped her head back, swinging her hair in a wild, fiery arc. "I didn't know you were there."

"Surprise." Mike grinned, drew up her knees and wrapped her arms around them. "Didn't mean to sneak up on you—but in my own defense, if you hadn't been talking to yourself, you probably would have heard me."

She looked so at home, Bridget thought with a slight pang of envy and a wave of homesickness so thick she could almost taste it. Mike Marconi had an easy way about her, compassionate blue eyes and a temper to match her own. Under other circumstances, they might have been friends. But as Bridget loved a man being shunned by the man Mike loved, she doubted that would be happening now.

"I've come out to get a bit of distance between me and those two in there," she said, careful to keep a tight rein on her temper.

Mike flicked a glance at the house behind her. "They're arguing?"

"It would be better if they were," Bridget scoffed. "Instead, Justin pretends to be strong and brave and Lucas pretends his brother isn't there at all."

"Family's not easy," Mike muttered.

"No, they're not," Bree said, thoughtful as she pictured her four older brothers and a mother who thought herself the queen matchmaker of County Mayo. "My own would drive the saints screaming right out of heaven. But to be without them would be worse, I think."

"True, though the thought is tempting from time to time," Mike said wistfully. Then her demeanor shifted and her eyes narrowed. "So I'm guessing that Justin's making you nuts?"

"In a word." Grabbing up a handful of wet grass, Bree shredded it between her fingers, making green confetti that she threw skyward as soon as she was finished. "The man's a fool."

"And you love him."

"I do," Bridget snapped. "So I don't know which of us is the bigger dolt."

"Never an easy question."

"And you? Does that coldhearted man of yours make you happy?"

Mike stiffened. "He's not cold, he's just—"

"Heartless?"

"You know," Mike said, her voice low and tight, "I came over to see if I could help and you're just really starting to piss me off big time."

Bree looked at her for a long minute, then blew out a disgruntled breath. "I'm sorry. It's not *you* I'm furious with. Your only sin is being handy."

"Been there, done that. *Many* times."

Smiling a bit, Bree watched as Mike, too, pulled up a handful of wet grass and shredded it absently. "Why would you be offering to help?"

"Good question," she said, taking her time about answering. "I guess Lucas is as important to me as Justin is to you. I thought maybe we could look at it like women versus men. Never hurts to have a little backup, does it?"

Some of the tension in Bridget's chest eased a notch or two and she took a long, deep breath to enjoy it. "It's kind of you," she said, "and I'm glad to have the offer. But this problem with Justin is not so easily solved."

"Why not tell me the problem and find out?"

"Fine, then." Bridget ground her teeth together, feeling the anger creep back into her heart. She'd needed someone to talk to. Someone to understand. Mike's offer of friendship had come at just the right time. "Justin's not only dying, he's dying *stupid*."

"Well, he *is* a man," Mike reminded her.

A reluctant smile curved Bridget's lips briefly. "Too true."

"What's he done?"

"It's what he *hasn't* done that matters," Bridget said,

with a furious shake of her head. "What he *refuses* to do. I've told him. All I want from him is his name. I don't give a flyin' damn about his money or anything else. Just his name. I want to be his wife. But he won't do it. Said he won't make me a widow at twenty-six."

She glared at the back of the house as if she could stare right through the walls and peel a layer of skin off the man she loved with just the heat of her stare. And then more words rushed from her as if they'd been dammed up too long, and now that her walls had been breached, there was no way to keep them locked away anymore.

"As if *not* being married will make me less of a widow when he leaves me. Does he think that I won't mourn?" she demanded, wagging a finger at Mike. "Does he think that as long as I'm single, I'll be fine? Doesn't he know that by marrying me, he'll be helping me?"

Her shoulders slumped, her chin hit her chest, and she felt every bit of air slide from her lungs, as if she were slowly deflating, disappearing.

"You're pregnant, aren't you?" Mike whispered.

Bridget's head whipped up and she stared open-mouthed. She considered denying it, but then asked herself why she should bother. It wasn't as if she were ashamed. She loved Justin. Knowing that she would have his child—something of him after he was gone—was the only thing holding her together.

· "Aye, I am. Justin doesn't know," she said before Mike could ask. "I thought to tell him, wanted him to know that something of him would live on. That something of *us* would live on. But I can't. Can't bring myself to tell him, knowing that he'll never see his child. Never hold it. Never love it." She inhaled sharply as if she couldn't quite get enough air. "I don't want to add to his misery. Isn't it enough that he's dying? Would he want to know that he was leaving a child who'll never *know* him?"

"Oh God, Bree . . ." Mike's heart broke.

She dropped both hands to her still flat abdomen and lifted her gaze to Mike's again. "In Ireland, things're changin'. Slowly. But still, an unwed mother has a hard road. If I had his name, the baby's life would be that much easier."

Mike went on instinct. Moving in close, she wrapped her arms around Bree and held on tight. The other woman cried, softly, desperately, and Mike wondered if life was ever going to right itself again. She wondered if there was a saturation point on pain. Bree's tears soaked Mike's shirt and all she could think of was Justin, dying, not knowing what he was leaving behind. And Lucas. What would he think, to know that his brother's child was alive and well? When Justin was gone, would Lucas ignore the man's child as he had the man himself?

She closed her eyes and said again, "God, Bree. I'm so sorry."

"I'm not," she whispered, shaking her head even as tears clogged her voice. "Not about the baby. Only about losing Justin this way. And not being his wife."

"Baby?" a deep voice asked from close by. "What baby?"

16

Lucas stared down at the two women and held his breath while this latest bit of news dropped to the pit of his stomach like a stone.

A *baby*?

Trust Justin.

Even dying, he'd not only managed to find love, he'd made a baby.

Bitterness filled his mouth, his heart, and he wanted to shout. To curse whatever fates were handing out joker cards, because he'd sure as hell been given a full deck of 'em.

"Didn't hear you come up, Rocket Man," Mike accused, as though he'd sneaked up on them deliberately.

"You were a little busy talking. About a baby."

"Sounds as though you got an earful," Bree snapped. "Do you often listen in on other people's conversations?"

"Hey, I'm walking across my own damn lawn here."

"Lucas, chill out."

"Chill out?" He echoed Mike's words and felt the top of his head lifting off. "You expect me to relax? I find out Justin's up to his old tricks again and I'm supposed to chill out?"

Mike glared at him. "What's up with you?"

"You don't know him," he said, words rushing from him as anger pushed them out his throat. "This is just so damn typical. He does whatever the hell he feels like doing and screw the consequences."

"Consequences?" Bree glared at him. "My baby is not a *consequence*."

He shook his head and laughed. "Hell, you're being left holding the bag and still you're defending him."

"I am, and I will," she said, "to you and to anyone else who thinks they can say what they will about Justin."

"Damn it, I'm on *your* side in this."

"Who asked you to be on *my* side? And if you were, by the way, you'd be a damn sight kinder to your brother."

"Kind? Justin doesn't need kind. Justin needs his ass kicked," Lucas told her hotly. "The man goes through life with a damn shield around him. Nothing gets through. Nothing hurts him. He just leaves misery and chaos in his wake like a . . . damn garbage scow, leaking crap into the ocean."

"Crap now, is it?" Bree's voice was thin and dangerous.

"Lucas, swear to God, you're digging a hole you might not get out of."

"Damn it, Mike, the man causes turmoil and never has to pick up the check. Nothing gets past his armor. He walks through minefields and comes out shining."

"Not now he's not," Mike pointed out quietly.

The simple truth of those words plowed a hole through the middle of his gut and Lucas had to take a step back as reality crashed down on him. For years, he'd held a grudge against his twin. For years, he'd cursed the fact that no matter what, Justin sailed through life, untouched by the chaos that surrounded him.

But now . . .

"Your brother's *dying*, man," Bree said, ignoring Mike and focusing solely on the man she'd been taking little bites out of for days. "But he might as well already be a ghost as far as you're concerned. He's dying with every breath he takes and you won't *look* at him."

Lucas shook his head, vainly trying to find a footing from which to continue his fight. "Looking at him won't change anything. Talking to him won't change anything."

"It would give him peace," Bree argued.

"And why do I *want* him to have peace?"

"Jesus, Lucas . . ."

Stunned disbelief colored Mike's tone and he wanted to defend his position. The one that he'd been defending for five years. But suddenly, his defenses seemed petty. Small. His chest ached and his lungs heaved for air that didn't seem to help.

Bree stared at him for a long moment. "I know he hurt you. He's told me. But don't you think he's being punished enough? Don't you think he's suffering enough? How much more does he have to endure until you're satisfied?"

He reeled and had to stagger to keep his balance. Was he punishing Justin? All these years, he'd been convinced that he was protecting himself— but maybe that wasn't really the truth. Maybe it had been more about meting out penance than about self-preservation.

"And if you don't give *him* peace, do you think you're likely to find any when he's gone?"

"You're right," he said softly.

"Ah, I'm right, am I?" Bree shook her hair back from her face, unmoved by whatever Lucas was going through at the moment. "Me being right changes nothing. You saying it changes nothing. If Justin were drowning, would you throw him a life rope, or watch him sink?"

"Okay, Bree, that's it." Mike's words were short, sharp, and to the point. "You've had your say. You've made your point. You don't have to hit him over the head with it."

Instantly, the Irish woman turned her hot, fierce eyes on Mike. "And what do you know of it?"

"I know Lucas. You don't. So why don't you just dial it down a notch or two before this gets ugly."

A small stab of warmth pierced his heart as Mike defended him—even though he knew there was no defense for what he'd been doing.

"That's fine. The two of you building a wall against a man who can't fight back." Bree pushed herself to her feet, brushing damp grass off the legs of her jeans. "Mind you, though, I *can* fight for him. And I will, if either of you brings him more pain than he's already living with."

"Man," Mike muttered, jumping up herself to look the woman in the eye. "I thought *Italians* were drama queens. Listen up, Bree. No matter what you think, Lucas is not the ogre you're making him out to be."

"That's yet to be seen, isn't it?"

"If you can't see it," Mike countered, "then you're

as blind as *he* is." She jerked a thumb at Lucas. "You're seeing only Justin's side just as Lucas is seeing only his own. How does that make you right and him wrong?"

Bree's mouth clamped together, her lips thinned into a grim slash. But she didn't argue again, so maybe that was something.

"Can we get back to the point of this?" Lucas demanded, and wondered how he kept losing control of every damn conversation.

When they were quiet again, he looked at Bree.

"You're pregnant?"

"Yes," she said, tears still staining her cheeks and fire leaping to life in her eyes. "And as it's none of your business, you'll not be mentioning this to Justin."

"No." He shook his head, then glanced into Mike's pale blue eyes. "You were right before. Is *everyone* pregnant?"

Mike's eyes flashed. "I'm not."

Damn it.

She couldn't have children. And he'd forgotten. Moron. Idiot.

"I'm sorry," he said and squeezed her hand briefly. "I'm just—"

"Surprised?" she offered, with a hint of a smile.

"There's that word again," he said, holding on to Mike's smile like a starving man grabbed at a steak. Somehow, she'd become the one stable point in his wildly rocking world.

Shifting a look at Bridget, he asked, "What're you going to do?"

"Right now," she said, "I'm going inside to make a

nice pot of tea and see if I can get Justin to eat something."

She started past them and Lucas grabbed her arm, stopping her in her tracks. She let her gaze fall to his hand and he got the message, letting her go instantly.

"Bree," he said carefully, walking as wide a path around this woman's temper as he did Mike's. "Why don't you let me do that?"

"What?"

"Yeah," Mike echoed. *"What?"*

He sucked in a big gulp of air and swallowed it while he tried to think of a way to explain himself. He hadn't exactly welcomed Justin into his home. Hadn't found the time to talk to him. To listen to him.

If he were going to be honest, at least with himself, he could admit that he hadn't wanted to give Justin the chance to ease his conscience. Hadn't wanted to make it easy on him.

Easy.

God. The man was dying a little more every day. Nothing about this was easy.

Truthfully, he wasn't real eager to do it now, either. But the plain fact was, he was losing his brother . . . his only family. If things didn't get said now, they'd never be said.

He couldn't let that happen.

Letting go of Mike's hand, he shoved his own hands into his pockets and rocked uncomfortably on his heels as the women watched him. "It's just—you look like you've been crying . . ."

Bree instantly lifted her hands to her cheeks, swiping away the last of her tears.

"I thought maybe you and Mike could take off—"

"Trying to get rid of us?"

"—go to town," he said, emphasizing the last word for Mike's benefit. "Get some coffee. Get a break from . . ." He nodded in the direction of the house.

Bree tilted her head to one side and studied him for a long minute or two. "I'm to believe that you're suddenly willin' to look after Justin?"

His jaw clenched. He felt Bree's and Mike's gazes on him and wanted to flinch. These women had a way of seeing too much. Of looking into his heart, his soul. And right now, he wasn't sure it was much of a view.

"I'll look after him. I give you my word."

"Rocket Man keeps his promises," Mike said softly and went up on her toes to plant a kiss on his cheek.

Lucas felt as if he'd been handed a medal. He smiled at her, then shifted another look at Bree. "I won't tell him about the baby."

She nodded.

"But you should."

"No," she said instantly. "I won't be doing that to him. It would only make his going harder on him than it has to be."

Was she right?

Who the hell knew?

"Up to you," he acknowledged and pulled Mike in close, just because suddenly he needed her there, tucked up against him. He felt more alone than he had at any time since the gulf between him and Justin had first been forged.

And damn it, he was tired of being alone.

He dropped a kiss on top of her head, then said, "You guys go ahead. We'll be fine. *Justin* will be fine."

"If he's not," Bree threatened, leaning in to make sure he read the danger in her eyes. "You'll have *me* to deal with, Lucas Gallagher. And bet your life, that's not something you want to have happen." Then she turned and started for the front of the house.

Mike looked after the woman for a moment before grinning up at Lucas. "She's really mean. I *like* that in a woman."

"Apparently," he said on a sigh of acceptance, "so do I."

Still smiling, Mike said thoughtfully, "You know, I think she's almost as scary as *me*."

He laughed. God, it felt good too, however briefly it lasted. "Nobody else is *that* scary."

She grinned up at him. "Aw. You're just saying that 'cause you know I like it."

Damned if he didn't like it, too. Which said plenty about how his life was going lately.

Jo knew this was the best place for her. She had plenty to keep her busy and no chance at all of running into her father. Not that she wasn't glad as hell that he was going to be fine. She was.

She just didn't want to talk to him.

Not now.

Maybe not for a while.

She attacked the rotten shingles on the roof of the Leaf and Bean and yanked them up before sliding them down off the edge of the roof to land in the alley behind the shop.

Good work. Steady work. Mind-numbing work. Didn't have to think. Didn't have to wonder about the fast-moving whirlpool that was her life. Didn't have to think about anything except not falling off the roof.

"Hey!"

She wobbled unsteadily and caught her balance again before shooting a look into the alley. "Damn it," she yelled, when she spotted Cash Hunter looking up at her. "Do you want me dead? Is that it?"

"That's not how I want you . . ." He smiled and even from a distance that smile was pretty potent stuff.

Sighing, she shifted until she was sitting on the roof, legs drawn up, arms resting across the tops of her knees. Her hammer hung lightly from her right hand and she swung it carelessly, just for something to concentrate on. "What *do* you want, Hunter?"

He stood there, looking like the poster boy for Dangerous Guys. His black hair was wind ruffled, his worn jeans hugged his long, muscular legs, and his black T-shirt strained across his broad chest. All in all . . . amazing. Which only pissed her off. She was in no mood for anything remotely like a turn-on.

"Heard about your father."

She cringed inwardly.

"How's he doing?"

"Better," she said tightly and hoped he couldn't hear the tinny note in her voice. "Fine, I mean. He's going to be fine."

"Good news."

"Yeah." It really was. She knew that. Her heart knew it. It was only her twisting guts and her racing mind that wanted to shriek and howl.

"What about the other thing?"

"Huh?" She blinked at him.

He glanced around to make sure the narrow alley was empty. "You know, your *class*?"

"Shut up about that!" Jo tightened her grip on the hammer and thought about throwing it. But then she'd only have to climb down the ladder to get it again, so she settled for putting a choke hold on the scarred, wooden handle. "I told you to never talk about that."

He folded his arms across his chest and looked up at her, apparently going nowhere until she'd answered his question. She took a quick look up and down the alley before saying quietly, "It's fine."

"Fine."

"Better."

"Better."

"What're you? An echo?"

He grinned. Damn, the man had one hell of a smile. "Did the book help?"

The book. *Astronomy for Dummies*. She should have thanked him for it days ago. Should have had the guts to call him and say she appreciated it. But she hadn't been able to make herself do it. She hadn't wanted anyone to know. And now, after the thing with Papa, it all seemed so much smaller than she'd been making it.

"Yeah. It did." She paused a beat or two. "Thanks."

"Wow. Sounded like that actually hurt."

"What?"

"Thanking me."

She scowled at him. "Did you drop by just to irritate me?"

He laughed. "Damn, Josefina, I don't have to be anywhere *near* you to irritate you."

"True."

"Look," he said, pushing his hair back out of his eyes with one big hand. "I stopped to see you because I wanted to tell you I'm leaving town for a while."

A ping of something she didn't want to identify bounced around inside her. "And you're telling me this *why*?"

He shook his head, still grinning. "For one thing, because I hired your family to redo the guest cottage?"

"Oh. Yeah." She'd forgotten about that. God, her brain was like a colander. Too many holes where thoughts were draining out like hot water rinsing off hot pasta. "Okay. Whatever."

"That's it?"

"What?" she asked. "You want a party? A real send-off with balloons and everything?" She waved a hand at him. "Go. Fly free."

He muttered something she didn't quite catch and when he looked up at her, eyes narrowed and jaw tight—she figured that was probably just as well.

"I don't know why in the hell I try to be nice to you."

"Me, neither," she snapped.

"You've got a nasty disposition."

She lifted the hammer. "And a mean throwing arm."

"I'm not worried."

"Why not?"

"Because you'd miss, then you'd have to come down here—by *me*—to get it back."

"I could wait till you're gone to get it."

"I won't go."

Her temper snapped. She'd had enough. Too many people pulling too many of her strings and she just was so damn tired of being Chandler's favorite marionette.

A sharp, cold wind sliced in off the ocean, picked up a few stray pieces of paper in the alley and hurled them along like soccer balls. Black clouds, heavy with rain, raced inland, and as they blanketed the sun, she shivered.

"I've got to get this plastic on Stevie's roof before that storm starts."

"Right. I'll let you get to it." He turned and took a couple of steps, then stopped and looked up at her over his shoulder. "I'll be back in a month or so."

"Wait," she said dryly and patted her shirt as if looking for a pocket that wasn't there. "Let me get a pen so I can circle the date on my calendar."

One corner of his mouth lifted. "Yeah. Nasty disposition. Why does that fascinate me?"

She gave him a tight smile. "Masochism?"

"Miss me, Josefina."

"Bite me, Cash."

Lucas stepped out onto the back deck and, unobserved, watched his brother for a long minute. Justin sat on one of the wooden Adirondack chairs, his blanket-covered legs resting on a stool drawn up in front of him. The man's face looked more gaunt than it had just a couple of days ago and his pale hand rested idly on the blanket's edge. He was staring out at the lake, watching a couple of ducks doing doughnuts on the still surface of the water.

The reeds on the shoreline dipped and swayed in a dance with the wind and the soft hush of the turning autumn leaves sounded like a symphony of sighs.

"Just gonna stand there and look at me?"

Caught, Lucas walked out onto the deck, sat down in a chair close to his brother, and held out one of the two beers he'd brought with him.

One of Justin's eyebrows lifted. "Harp. You still like Irish beer?"

"Is there any other kind?" Lucas asked and set Justin's bottle on a small table beside him.

"Thanks," his brother said. "I'll have some in a bit."

"No hurry."

"See," Justin said, lifting that pale, weak hand and pointing his index finger. "That's where you're wrong. There *is* a hurry, Luke. I'm running out of time."

Something inside him fisted, squeezed like a vise, then relaxed again to allow him to draw breath. "I know."

"It's beautiful here," his brother said softly. "Quiet. You should sit out here more often."

"I do," he said, though he knew damn well he hadn't really taken enough time to come out here and admire the view. He was working on the book or researching or rushing around to do something else. He almost never stepped out onto the deck to just *sit*.

"Yeah," he said, shifting his gaze to the ducks on the lake. "I should."

Justin smiled and let his head fall to the chair back. "Don't look now, but I think we're having a Kodak moment."

Lucas snorted and took a swallow of beer. "Everything's still a joke to you."

"Jesus, Luke. If I didn't laugh, I'd have to cry, and who the hell wants to see *that*?"

The wind was cold and the clouds looked like they meant business. But now that they were finally talking, Lucas didn't want to move. Didn't want to suggest they go inside, where walls might spring up again.

Justin apparently felt the same way. "The night Mom and Dad died—"

"We don't have to—"

"Yeah, we *do*."

Lucas closed his eyes and held tight to the bottle of Irish beer. His father's favorite brand, Harp, had become Lucas's and Justin's favorite, as well. Their father had been a giant of a man to them. He'd had all the answers. Hell, he even knew all the questions.

They'd both looked up to him.

They'd both loved him.

And late one night five years ago, Justin had killed him.

17

"Why'd you really come here to me, Justin?"

His brother turned his head on the chair back to look at him. Brown eyes, already a little hazy, as if they were staring beyond this world and into the mysteries of the next, met Lucas's. "Because I couldn't die with you hating me."

"I never hated you."

"Sure you did. Hell. *I* hated me for a while."

Lucas shrugged, cupped the icy beer bottle between his palms, and admitted, "Okay, maybe I did. Once."

And never more than on that dark, cold night five years ago.

Justin had crashed another one of the fast cars he seemed determined to kill himself in, but this time, there'd been an open bottle of beer on the back seat. He hadn't been drunk. Just careless. But still, he was arrested and, naturally, he called his twin to come bail him out.

But that last time, Lucas said no.

He was busy, he'd said; working, he'd said. But the simple truth was, he was sick of being Justin's backup plan.

So their parents went instead.

Then, with Justin driving them home, they'd died on a rain-streaked road when he lost control and slammed into a tree.

Images filled Lucas's mind and it was as if he were back there. Standing in the rain beside the twisted hulk of his father's Mercedes.

Plastic tarps covered his parents' bodies. Steam lifted from under the crumpled hood, and the head-lights, knocked out of line on impact, streamed brightly into the darkness. One speared toward heaven and the other toward hell. The flash of revolving red and blue emergency lights pulsed in the air and Lucas fought back tears as heavy as the rain.

Paramedics were working on Justin. Lucas over-heard one of the cops muttering to his partner. "Too bad. Man killing his own parents like this. A hell of a thing to have to live with."

Pain whipped through him, fresh and raw. It clawed at his soul and ripped at his heart and he squeezed his eyes tightly shut in an effort to hold it all in.

"It wasn't my fault," Justin said, and it took a minute or two for his soft voice to get through the roar of blood rushing in Lucas's ears.

"Bullshit." He took a long drink of beer. "Of course it was." Gritting his teeth, he squinted into the rising wind. "If we're going to go through all this, at least be honest."

"I am." Justin sighed, his voice weak and trembling. "Mom was in the front seat."

Lucas took another long drink of his beer and the

taste was bitter. As his brother talked, he returned to that empty road and the flashing lights in the rain.

"We were headed up the mountain. Just a mile or two from the house."

Lucas remembered. So close, he'd thought at the time. So close to safety. And still so far.

"A deer jumped out in front of the car. Came out of nowhere. Just stood there." Justin sighed and closed his eyes, as if he, too, were reliving it all one more time. "I probably could have avoided it. But Mom panicked. Grabbed the wheel and twisted it to keep me from hitting that stupid deer."

Lucas's stomach fisted. That would have been so like their mother. For her to react instantly in an effort to protect an animal. She'd always been the one mom on the block who took in every stray cat or dog and even pet rats and mice that other mothers couldn't handle. Her heart was as soft as her will was strong.

But if that was true . . . Lucas jumped to his feet, paced to the edge of the deck, then turned around and stomped right back again. His mind churned, his heart ached, and his stomach was spinning like he was on a cheap ride at a carnival.

"You're saying the accident was *Mom's* fault?"

"No. It was all my fault no matter what actually happened on that road. If I hadn't called them . . . If I hadn't gotten arrested . . . They never would have been there. They'd have been safe. At home."

Back teeth clenched, Lucas muttered thickly, "And if I hadn't turned you down—"

"No." Justin cut him off sternly with a slow shake of

his head. "You don't get a share in this, Luke. It's on my head. Just like you always thought. It just happened. So fast. So damn fast, I couldn't get us out of the spin. Mom screamed, the deer jumped clear, and then—nothing." He sighed and closed his eyes. "I woke up in the hospital three days later and they were already buried."

Lucas swallowed hard. Even though he'd been furious with his brother—so sure that his recklessness had killed their parents—he'd always felt a little guilty about that. About Justin not being there for the joint funeral. But there hadn't been a lot of choice, either. "We didn't know. We thought you were going to die, too."

Justin snorted. "Should have. Would've been faster. And easier. On everybody. And maybe then . . ."

Lucas cut that train of thought off quick—he wasn't ready to detour on this little forced march down memory lane. "Why the hell didn't you tell me about this *then*? When you got out of the hospital? Why did you let me blame *you*?"

"Because I blamed me," Justin said, pain ripping through his voice and wracking his body. "If I hadn't been in trouble *again*, they wouldn't have been there to get me out of it. If I'd been more like you and less like *me*, none of it would have happened."

Lucas dropped onto the chair again, as if his legs had given out. Shaking his head, he stared at the man he'd avoided so carefully for so many years and wondered what might have happened if they'd faced their own shame and guilt long ago. "Damn it, Justin, I was mad at you, but I was blaming *me*."

"For God's sake, *why*?"

He glanced at him, then picked at the label on the beer bottle with his fingernails. "Because you called me to come get you and I said I was busy. I wasn't. I was with—"

"Alice."

"Yeah."

Alice Doyle. The woman Lucas had once believed himself in love with. The woman he'd planned to marry. The woman—

"Nothing happened between us," Justin said.

Lucas lifted his gaze from the neck of the beer bottle to his brother's eyes. "I know that. But it didn't matter. She still chose *you*."

Another price of their battle. After their parents' deaths, Lucas had shut himself off from Justin. Didn't speak to him, wouldn't take his calls. Alice, though, couldn't stand the breach between the twins. She'd wanted him to make peace with his brother.

She called Justin on her own, told Lucas she was going to visit her mother for a few days, and instead flew to San Diego to see Justin.

"She told me you sent her," Justin said now, smiling in spite of the tremble in his hands and the pain flickering in his faded eyes. "I was glad. Took her out to dinner. Showed her around town. Tried to score a few points with my brother's girlfriend. Hoped she'd help fix things between us. Instead—"

"A few days with Mr. Charm convinced her that she didn't really love me after all," Lucas finished for him.

Alice had come home from San Diego and everything was different. She told him that she'd seen Justin.

That she'd *felt* something for him. That she knew now that she didn't love Lucas enough to marry him.

Hell, if he tried . . . which he wasn't about to do, he could almost hear her saying, *"We're lucky this happened now, Lucas. Better to find out before we married. Before we had children."*

Oh yeah.

Better.

Justin winced. "Nothing happened. I wouldn't have done that to you."

"Hell, I know that. I even knew it *then*." He took another pull of his beer. "But when I lost Alice, I blamed you again. It was easier than admitting that I'd been wrong about her. I thought she loved me. She didn't."

Justin laughed briefly and leaned over, feebly reaching for the beer.

Lucas grabbed it and handed it to him carefully.

After a long drink, his brother said, "She wasn't good enough for you."

"I wanted her," Lucas said simply. "And she wanted *you*."

"She wanted me because she didn't have me. That's all."

"The hell of it is," Lucas added wryly, "once she was gone, I didn't miss her. Then being mad at you became more about wounded pride than anything else."

"Hey," Justin pointed out, "sometimes pride's all we've got left."

This honesty thing was getting easier. Lucas's soul felt as if it had been drained of the black, oily spill he'd been carrying around for so many years. His heart felt lighter, his soul a little less chilled.

He wasn't *healed*. He wasn't willing to go that far. But talking to Justin had not only opened old wounds, it had aired them out enough that the chance for healing was finally there.

But with Justin dying, all of this was coming too late. Regret rocked him to his bones as he thought of all the years lost. His own damn fault. He'd let Justin take the full blame for everything that had gone wrong between them because that had left *him* off the hook. It had relieved Lucas of carrying a shared burden.

But in avoiding guilt, he'd lost his brother.

And it was time he'd never get back.

Looking at his twin, the other half of himself, Lucas saw him not as he was now, frail and slipping away daily, but as he once was. Tall and strong and laughing. *That* was the memory he'd hold on to in the coming years. *That* was the Justin he knew. The man who faced every trial with a joke. The man who sucked as much fun out of life as he possibly could and then went running back for more.

God, he'd missed so much, cutting himself off from Justin.

How much they'd both missed.

"Hell," Lucas finally said, a reluctant half-smile on his lips as he buried the regret, knowing Justin wouldn't want it. "Women always liked you best. That charm of yours won 'em over every time."

"Yeah, I got the charm, you got the brains."

Lucas smiled sadly at the old joke.

The ducks on the lake swam in lazy circles, as if pushed by the wind still rippling the surface of the water. The trees whispered to each other and storm clouds chased each other across the sky.

"Bree loves you." He blurted it out, not sure why, but sure that he had to say something. Bree didn't want Justin to know about the baby, so he wouldn't tell him. But he had to try something. For Justin's child's sake.

"Yeah." He smiled. "She does."

"Marry her, you idiot."

"Idiot? Is that any way to talk to a dying man?"

Lucas snorted. "Gonna ride that one down to the ground, aren't you?"

"Use what works," Justin said with a tired shrug.

"You've got a woman who actually *wants* to marry you and you'll tell her no?"

Justin shot him a look. "Why would I let her marry me now? Like this?"

Lucas met that look. "When the hell else will she *get* to marry you?" He swallowed hard. "Now is all you've got."

He shook his head slowly and rested the bottom of the beer bottle on his chest. "Not fair to her."

"Not fair to love her and *not* marry her."

"I don't want to hurt her."

Lucas leaned forward and lowered his voice as he met Justin's gaze. "You're hurting her by *refusing*."

"Maybe." Sighing, Justin said softly, "I wish there was more time."

Reaching out, Lucas laid one hand on his brother's arm. "So do I."

. . .

Late that night, Mike stretched on Lucas's big bed and grinned into the darkness. "Rocket Man, you've got some great moves."

He smiled against her skin and slid down the length of her body, skimming his lips and teeth over her flesh. "I feel . . ."

"How?" she asked, propping herself up on her elbows to look down at him. Lifting one hand, she smoothed his hair back from his forehead and looked into his dark eyes, glimmering with too many emotions to identify.

He'd been . . . *different* since the moment she and Bree returned from town. Whatever had passed between him and Justin had done more than clear the air. It had opened something inside Lucas that had been closed for too long.

As soon as they were alone in his room, he'd told her everything, and she finally understood where the pain that had haunted him had come from. He'd spared himself nothing, at last accepting at least part of the blame for the years lost between brothers. And in the telling, Mike was sure Lucas had found something he hadn't known in a long time. The very thing he'd come to Chandler looking for.

Peace.

"How do you feel?" she whispered, fingers threading through his thick, silky hair.

He kissed her abdomen, right below the diamond-topped gold bar in her navel, then looked up at her and smiled. "*Alive*," he said. "I feel alive."

Tears burned her eyes, but she blinked them back. This wasn't a time for crying. This was the time for celebrating the fact that he'd found his brother before Justin was lost to him forever.

So she grinned again and gave him a wink. "Well, then, let's see just how alive you can get, shall we?"

"Right there with you," he murmured and dipped his head to trail the tip of his tongue in lazy circles on her skin.

She hissed in a breath and let it slide free again on a lovely sigh. Her body was still humming. Her blood still pumping. And at her core, she was needy again. Needing *him* again.

"You know something?"

"Hmm?" Mike wiggled beneath him, trying to get his enormous brain focused on the task at hand again.

"I just noticed something about your scars."

She froze up and caught herself stiffening. "That they're not exactly gorgeous? Whoa. News flash."

"No." He went up on one elbow and studied the silvery pattern of lines streaking across her flesh, following them with the tips of his fingers. "They look like—"

"Lucas—" God. Didn't he understand that she was just a little self-conscious about the faint webbing of lines marking her body? Ever since their first night together, he hadn't mentioned them. Why now? Why tonight?

"—Pleiades," he said, a tone of wonder in his voice.

"Huh?" She lifted her head again to stare at him.

He looked . . . *excited.* As if he'd just made a rare and startling discovery.

"Pleiades," he said again, then tried to explain. He slid to one side, stretched out one arm and grabbed his glasses off the nightstand. Shoving them on, he looked at her again, then bent to examine her scars more closely. "The Seven Sisters."

"Still have no idea what you're talking about."

"It's a star cluster," he said, and excitement charged his voice as he glanced up at her. "In Taurus. It's the best known of all the star clusters . . ."

"Well, sure."

He heard the sarcasm and shrugged it off. "I know you don't know it, but it really is an amazing likeness."

"Good to know."

"And," he whispered, dipping to plant another kiss on her abdomen. "It's beautiful. In the sky and here. On *you*."

Her heart turned over.

Oh boy.

He smiled at her and used the tip of one finger to push his glasses back up on the bridge of his nose, and just like that—

She fell in love.

It was all so easy.

So incredibly *right*.

And so damned inconvenient.

Mike wanted to take a moment. To feel the rush and charge of finally being in love. But to do that, she'd have to tell him. And Rocket Man had already had a pretty full day.

Instead, she reached up, plucked his glasses off and tossed them in the general direction of the nightstand.

"You know," she said softly as he lowered himself over her, "that was the most romantic thing anyone's ever said to me."

"Yeah?"

"Oh yeah."

He wiggled his eyebrows, then dipped his head to nibble on her neck while he stroked one hand down her body until he could cup her center. Then he dipped one finger inside her heat and whispered, "Wait'll I tell you about black holes."

"Keep talkin', Rocket Man . . ."

A week later, things had settled into a routine. Mike was still living at Lucas's place, Carol and little Jack had gone home to San Francisco, Papa was at Grace's, and Jo still had a pole the size of a redwood up her butt.

Under cover of the kitchen table, Mike kicked her oldest sister, and when Jo gave her a look designed to singe her eyebrows, Mike jerked her head toward their father. *Say something,* she mouthed.

Shut up, Jo mouthed back.

Mike muffled a sigh by biting into a fresh breadstick. They'd agreed to a meeting here in the family kitchen, because, hey. That's where they held Marconi meetings. Papa was cooking, Sam was on the phone, and Jo was trying to pretend she was somewhere else. Mike kicked her again. Just for the hell of it.

"Grace's house is finished," Papa said and stepped away from the stove after giving his sauce a theatrical stir with a wooden spoon. "So, now we start on Cash Hunter's job."

"No hurry," Jo said, looking up from the file folders littered across the table.

"No, not at all," Mike countered, grabbing another breadstick from the cobalt-blue jar in the center of the kitchen table. "Unless we want to, you know . . . *eat*."

Which, she thought with a grimace, suddenly didn't sound like such a good idea. Mouth working around a sudden flood of saliva, she tossed her breadstick onto her plate, took a deep breath and listened up.

"She's got a point," Sam said, clicking off her cell phone and lifting a glass of Coke before taking a long drink.

"Only on her head." Jo blew out a breath that ruffled a stray lock of dark brown hair hanging across her forehead. "You've got time to take care of the Santos's pipes," she snapped, with a glance at Mike. "And Stevie wants the shop reroofed. I already started that last week. Wright Wood's delivering the new shingles in a few days and—"

"And Cash Hunter is expecting us to start work on the guesthouse," their father said, glancing at his three daughters, gathered at the table.

Jo's mouth puckered as if she was sucking on a lemon. At last, though, she looked up at her father and said, "Cash is out of town for a month or so. He said there was no hurry."

"So you're making the decisions now?" Papa asked.

Jo squirmed a little and Mike scooted her chair to one side. Always better to distance yourself from the one in trouble.

"No, Papa. All I'm saying is that Cash stopped to see me last week—"

"He did?" Mike perked right up. Hey, Sam had a husband, Mike was having regular sex . . . it was about time Jo got something going. Either that or sign up for the convent and get to wear the cool outfit. "When?"

"I just said, *last week*."

"You should have told me," Papa said, wiping his hands on a dishtowel, then coming to stand right in front of the table, blue eyes pinned on Jo.

"You were busy having a heart attack," she said.

"Whoops." Sensing imminent danger, Sam pulled out her cell phone, scooted back from the table, and said, "I'll just call Jeff. From outside."

"Good idea," Mike echoed, grabbing her purse and fumbling for her own cell. Her stomach pitched a little, but she paid no attention. "I'll, uh, be out front. Calling . . . *somebody*."

"Traitors," Jo muttered, but kept her gaze locked on her father's. It was the first time she'd been alone with him since he got out of the hospital and she still wasn't ready to talk to him about this.

"Josefina," he said, his voice a low rumble that held a world of love and memories for her. "You don't come to see me. You don't want to look at me."

"Papa . . ." Oh God. Her throat was tight, her eyes were full, and her lungs were empty. She couldn't do this. Not now. Not yet.

"I loved your mama."

"God, Papa, I know that." Too hard. Too hard.

"I love you. And your sisters. I am sorry I hurt you girls. Sorry I failed you."

"Can we please not talk about this?" she asked, and

her own voice was just a desperate whisper. Slowly she stood up, and her chair scraped loudly against the worn linoleum.

The scent of Papa's sauce bubbled in the air and the windows had frosted over, blocking out the cold night just outside.

"Josefina," he said again, this time reaching for her hand, "I love you."

She pulled her hand back, then lifted it to her mouth as if she couldn't quite believe she'd done that. Papa looked as though she'd slapped him and she wanted to cry. Not just for herself. For him. For Mama. For the fact that nothing would ever be the same.

"I'm sorry, Papa," she said, voice breaking as she grabbed her purse and sidestepped to the back door. "I really am. I *do* love you. But I can't do this yet."

"It's all right," he soothed her, as he would a frightened puppy, making no quick moves, keeping his voice soft and even. "Don't leave, Jo. Stay. Have dinner with your sisters and me. We won't talk about this again."

"Papa . . ."

"It's all right." He walked back to the stove, picked up the wooden spoon, and concentrated on stirring his sauce. "You take whatever time you need. I will be here. My love will be here. When you're ready."

When she was ready?

When would she ever be ready to tell him about how it felt to have the one perfect man in the world tumble off his pedestal? How it felt to keep a shameful secret from that "perfect man" for ten years—only to find that he carried secrets more shameful than her own?

· · ·

Three days later, Mike sat on the examining table at her doctor's office and absently tried to keep the edges of her paper blanket together. No good, though. The damn thing wouldn't fold and its stiff edges poked out at odd angles, offering periodic peep shows.

When the door opened, she looked up and smiled halfheartedly. "You know, with the cost of insurance and stuff, don't you think they could come up with a better blanket than an oversized Kleenex?"

Dr. Shelley Baker closed the door behind her, walked up to the examining table, and sat down on the wheeled black stool. She studied the chart in her hands, looked up at Mike, then checked her notes one more time.

"Okay, this can't be good."

"What?" The doctor glanced up. "Oh. Sorry. Distracted."

"Great," Mike said, as a sinking sensation opened up inside her. "Just what a girl wants to hear from her doctor."

She swallowed hard against yet another wave of nausea so thick and greasy, she felt sweat break out on her forehead. For God's sake, she'd been sick for days. Even Lucas was beginning to notice that she wasn't eating much.

She hadn't bothered to tell him that she'd figured there was no point in eating if she was only going to lose it later.

"So what's the problem?" she asked. "Flu? Typhoid? *Plague?*"

Dr. Baker set the file down on her lap and folded her hands on top of it. "You know, we ran a lot of tests."

"Duh. Can't figure out why you'd ask me to pee in a cup just because I've got the flu."

"Standard pregnancy test."

Mike swallowed hard and said, "Not funny, Shelley. We both know that's not possible."

"We both *knew* that was *probably* impossible."

"What?" Nausea rolled through her again and this time there were party favors. Her vision got all speckled like bits of confetti were floating in the air and her head went suddenly light.

"Mike, you're pregnant."

18

"Have another blanket," Bree said as she came up behind Justin. Snapping it open, she let the soft dark green spread drift down over him like a cloud. When it had settled, she tucked it in around him, lifting his arms gently to lay on top.

"Thanks," he said, tipping his head back to give her a ghost of the smile she'd once known.

Bree's heart ached, but she was used to it now. For months, she'd felt every twinge of his pain, every soft sigh, every groan. She'd taken his pain inside her and there it had blossomed until it was *all* she felt. Now those pains were her constant companions.

"Cold today," he murmured, shifting his gaze to the corner hearth where a fire blazed and crackled cheerfully.

She wiped sweat from her forehead and agreed quietly. "Going to be a cold winter here." Coming around the edge of the sofa, she sat close beside him and pushed a lock of hair off his forehead with her fingertips. "Reminds me of home."

She watched him as though, if she could only keep

her gaze on him, she could save him from the passing seconds that measured what was left of Justin's life from heartbeat to heartbeat. And though her own heart urged her to hold him closer, tighter, to keep him safe, her head knew that there would be no happy ending.

That with every second she spent with him, she was losing him.

"I'm glad we came," he said, his voice so soft, it was nearly lost in the snap and hiss of the fire.

"As am I," Bree said, lifting his hand and holding it carefully between her own.

She'd worried about this trip. Known that Justin would have to face a past that had haunted him for years. Known that in facing his brother, he would be opening himself to even more pain.

And yet he'd come through it and found the ease he'd needed so desperately.

For the last week and a half, things had been different in this house by the lake. Justin and Lucas had found their way back to each other—just in time to be separated forever.

"I've been thinking," Justin said.

"Have you now?" Bree leaned in toward him, inhaling his scent, trying to lock it deep within her. "What about?"

"About getting married."

She went perfectly still. "Is that right?"

He turned to look at her, meeting her gaze with his. Only months ago, she'd first seen those dark eyes and fallen in love—now, in those fathomless depths, she read "goodbye."

And her heart broke neatly in two.

"If you're sure you still want to," he said.

"I am, yes."

"Then marry me, Bree." He leaned toward her, until his forehead met hers. "Marry me tomorrow."

"Tomorrow? Can we do it that fast, then?"

"Changing your mind?" he asked, one corner of his mouth lifting.

"No," she said, smiling now despite the swirl of anguish churning within. "Not a bit. But can we? Licenses and—"

"Lucas arranged for the paperwork to be done."

"He *did*?" Fondness for Justin's twin surprised her. How that man had changed, too. The coldness that had set him apart, kept him from reaching for his brother, was gone now—as though he were trying to make up for the years lost.

"Yeah." He let his head fall back against the couch, exhausted from the effort of holding himself upright. "But be kind to me on the honeymoon, okay?" He gave a brief smile again. "Don't want to die early and miss something interesting."

"Ah, Justin . . ." Happiness and despair coiled together inside her, twisting, tangling. She fought them both down and concentrated solely on this one moment. Even the promise of the wedding she'd wanted so badly couldn't eclipse the beauty of this single moment in time, with Justin close beside her, their child nestled within, and the promise of one beautiful tomorrow.

For right now, that was enough.

• • •

"Breathe."

"I'm . . . trying . . . can't . . ."

No air. No air. No air.

Breathebreathebreathe . . .

Mike felt the doctor's hand on the back of her neck, pushing until her head was firmly between her knees. Slowly, the swirling patterns of bright lights faded enough that she figured she wouldn't be passing out anytime soon.

But still, air was hard to come by.

"Better?" Shelley asked.

"Than what?" Mike's voice was muffled against her paper lap robe.

Shelley laughed and let her up slowly. "I thought you'd be happy about this."

"Happy?" Still woozy, still wishing air was a part of her current lifestyle. But happy? Didn't even come close to describing it.

Slowly straightening up, Mike took a quick look around the examining room, just to ground herself. Yep. Still pale blue walls, dotted with posters showing detailed and completely gross pictures of internal organs. Blood pressure monitor hanging on the wall beside the tiny desk fitted into a corner.

Normal.

Everything was the same.

Everything but *her.*

Shifting her gaze to Shelley, Mike looked hard at the doctor she'd been coming to for three years. Shelley's short, stylishly spiky hair framed her heart-shaped face and her dark green eyes were filled with understanding.

"Are you sure?" Mike asked and cleared her throat when her voice sounded unsteady.

Shelley laughed. "It was a urine test. Trust me, I know how to read the results. I'm sure."

"But . . . how . . . ?"

"I'm guessing, the usual way."

"Good. That's good. Doctor humor." Mike shoved her hair back out of her face and tucked it behind her ears. "Ohmigod." She sucked in air, blew it out again, and muttered, *"I'm pregnant."*

"Just barely," Shelley said. "But yeah."

"And it's okay?" She slapped one hand to her tissue-paper-covered abdomen. "I mean, it's doing what it's supposed to do?"

"Yes, Mike. The baby's fine. Tiny, but fine."

"I can't believe this. I thought it couldn't happen. They *told* me . . ."

"You always had a four-percent chance of conceiving."

"Funny," Mike whispered, more to herself than to Shelley. "Never thought of it like *that*. Only considered it from the ninety-six percent chance of *not* conceiving."

"Surprise."

Mike's jaw dropped. How many times had she said that word to Lucas?

Oh God.

Lucas.

How was she going to tell him? What could she possibly say? He probably wouldn't believe her. He'd think she'd tricked him or something. Blood drained from her head to pool in the pit of her stomach.

"Whoa. You're looking pale again. Problem?" Shelley always had been quick to pick up on things.

"No," she said firmly, with a shake of her head. "No problem." Well, none that she was going to sit here and tell her doctor about.

"Okay, then," Shelley said, a little unconvinced but willing to back off. "I want to see you in here next month for another checkup. Make sure everything's as it should be."

Fear spiked through her in a flash of heat. "It will be though, right? I'm not going to lose it or something?"

"See no reason why you should," Shelley said. "Your condition made *conceiving* difficult. Not carrying the child."

Relief chased the fear away and though Mike's stomach was still doing a great impression of a roller coaster, she felt better. Weird, though, how fast her mood was shifting. But it didn't matter. *Nothing* mattered. She was pregnant. And the baby was fine.

"Good. That's good."

Still cradling her belly, Mike realized that in the last few seconds a decision had been made. Not that there'd ever been a doubt.

She was having this baby.

Didn't matter what Lucas had to say about it.

It wasn't every day someone handed Mike a *miracle*.

"She said yes."

"Did you think she wouldn't?" Lucas sat down on the sofa opposite his brother.

He sighed. "Not really."

"I'm glad."

Justin grinned. "Sure, *every* man's glad someone *else* is getting married."

The room was too warm and still, Justin was shivering. Lucas kept the smile on his face, but worry slithered through him. Worry, chased by regret. Why had they waited so long? he wondered now, when it was too late. Why had it taken *death* to make them come together?

And what good was it to think about it now?

"Is everything arranged?"

"Yeah," Lucas said, glad to have details to fall back on. He'd arranged for a license and had talked a minister into coming to the house tomorrow afternoon. "Everything's set. By this time tomorrow, you'll be a married man."

"Weird," Justin said softly. "I used to think that getting married was a fate worse than death."

"Now?"

"Now, turns out *death* is way harsher." Justin laughed and the soft chuckle became a cough that wracked his too thin body like a spoiled kid shaking a toy.

When the coughing jag eased, he winced and gasped as pain rushed through him, stealing his breath, stabbing at him, slicing deep. Every day, the pain got a little worse. A little sharper, a little stronger.

The pills weren't doing the trick anymore. Like putting a Band-Aid on a gaping chest wound. He knew he could change things. Go to a hospital. Get morphine in a drip. Get hooked up to machines that would allow him to control his own medication. Keep himself doped so thoroughly that the pain wouldn't be able to reach him anymore.

Nothing would reach him.

But he didn't want that.

He wanted to be alive while he was alive.

Focusing his will inward, Justin battled the pain, pushing it down, down, until it became an almost livable presence.

Across from him, Lucas fisted his hands and gritted his teeth. But he stayed where he was and Justin was grateful. He didn't want to be hovered over. Didn't want the people he loved torturing themselves by not being able to help. All he wanted to do was *be here*. For as long as he could.

He wanted to love Bree. He wanted to touch and be touched. He wanted to be a part of the world he was leaving—so that when he was gone, at least his memories would be clear.

And please, God, he'd keep those memories with him wherever he ended up.

Summoning a halfhearted smile, he looked at his brother and lifted one shoulder in a shrug. "Don't look so panicked," he whispered. "I'm not dying right *now*."

"Thanks for that," Lucas said softly, his fists relaxing. "Wouldn't want to face Bree and tell her the wedding was canceled."

"I'll make it." The words came firmly and Justin repeated them to himself like a mantra, willing his body to hold on. He couldn't die.

Not until he'd done this one last thing for Bree.

. . .

An hour later, Mike walked into the Leaf and Bean and nodded at a few of the familiar faces. Funny, none of them had ever looked so . . . comforting before today.

But then maybe it was just *her*. Maybe she was looking at the world around her and feeling just a little bit more . . . sappy about everything.

And who could blame her?

"Mike?" Stevie slapped one hand on the glass countertop and the sharp sound jolted Mike out of her thoughts and back to reality.

"Geez . . . take it easy, will ya?" Mike wondered if adrenaline surges were good for the baby—then figured it was half Italian, so adrenaline was probably a good thing.

Stevie grinned. "You were zoned out. Welcome back to earth. Where were you? Was it nice?"

"You know," Mike said smiling, "it really *is*."

"Okay, now you're being weird. Something up?"

"Something's always up in Chandler," Mike said, covering neatly. No way could she let her little secret slip onto the gossip train before she'd had a chance to tell Lucas.

Oh God.

Telling Lucas.

"Okay . . ." Stevie shook her head and said, "Glad you showed up. Your sisters wanted coffee and I wasn't looking forward to climbing that ladder to take it to 'em. And when I saw you coming, I poured a latte for you, too. On the house," she added, "since you guys are making my ceiling safe from rain."

"Right. The job."

Her sisters were up on Stevie's roof right now, trying to get it ready for reshingling. And they weren't real patient when waiting for their coffee.

"You sure you're okay?"

Mike snapped to attention. "Yeah. Fine."

She took the tray Stevie handed her. Lattes for her and her sisters. Good. She could talk to them. Marconi solidarity. That's what she needed right now.

She wasn't ready to face Lucas yet.

Oh God.

Lucas.

Mike's brain took off like the space shuttle. How could she tell him this? She'd sworn to him that she couldn't have children. Oh, he was never going to believe her. She could feel those dark, scientific eyes pinning her right now. He'd probably think this was a big setup. Like she was trying to trap his rich, cute self into marriage.

She gripped the tray a little tighter as she headed for the back door and the alley beyond. Her mind raced with thoughts of Lucas and how he was going to take all of this and she could feel her blood pressure spiking.

Joe Franklin was coming out of the restroom as she stomped by and he did a quick back step—probably reacting to the fury she knew was stamped across her features.

Trap him?

The more she thought, the madder she got. Why

would she trap Lucas into marriage? How could he possibly think she'd be desperate enough to sink so low as to trick him into making a baby? Did he really think he was *that* hot and tasty?

"Who does he think he is, anyway?" The nerd prince should have been grateful she'd gone out with him at all. Thinks he's such hot shit just because he knows what the hell Pleiades is.

Pleiades.

Just like that, fury drained away and warmth reached up and curled around the base of her throat. She swallowed a hot flood of tears along with another wave of nausea.

That was so sweet of him, to think her belly looked like stars. Weird. But very sweet. Who would have guessed when she'd stumbled across him almost three months ago that she'd love him? That she'd have his baby inside her?

Who would have guessed that things could get so weird so fast?

Shaking her head, she stepped into the alley, saw Jo's truck and the ladder propped along the back wall of the shop.

Something gross was in the nearby trash bin and Mike's stomach did a quick flip and wild slide. Oh, this was gonna be a thrill ride. Nine months of this and she'd be insane or something.

Nine months.

Ohmigod.

Pregnant.

Cradling the coffee tray in one hand, she used the other to grab hold of the ladder as she started to climb.

Jo's and Sam's voices, arguing, naturally, drifted down to greet her and Mike smiled.

The lattes smelled great and the higher she climbed away from that trash bin, the better she felt.

Hmm. Latte. Should she drink it? Was it okay for a baby?

"Hey, it's *my* baby, right?" she muttered. "And it's probably expecting its usual jolt of caffeine."

Her *baby*.

Oh God.

She poked her head over the edge of the roof and the first sister she spotted was Jo. "Hey, give me a hand, here," Mike called.

Jo whipped her head around, narrowed her eyes and snapped, "Where the hell have you been?"

"For God's sake, Jo," Sam yelled from higher up on the roof, "I told you like twelve times Mike went to the doctor. She's been sick."

"Still am," Mike said as she handed off the tray to Jo and climbed the rest of the way onto the roof.

From the peak of the building, you could see up and down Main Street. Cars clogged the narrow road, and the sidewalks were thick with tourists. The Autumn Festival was in full gear and the town's cash registers were ringing like an orchestra.

Out on the meadow at the edge of town, local craftsmen and artisans set up booths to showcase the jewelry, paintings, and carvings they'd made during the rest of the year. Tour buses filled with people looking for autumn beauty ended up going home with gift bags piled high with earrings, birdhouses, handblown glass vases, and God knew what else.

It was a yearly tradition around here, and Mike smiled at the thought of teaching her own kid about Chandler. Taking her—okay, or *him*—to the summer carnival, watching the street carolers during Christmas week, and oh God.

There were so many things she wanted to teach her. Him.

Whoever.

"You don't look sick," Jo said flatly as she gave her a quick once-over. "You look . . . spooky."

"Thanks."

"Thanks for the coffee." Sam inched along the shingled roof on her butt and got close enough to snatch one of the lattes out of the tray. "What'd the doctor say?"

"Yeah, Shelley said you're okay to work, right?" Jo asked, waving one hand at the only partially finished roof. "Because they say there's another storm due in day after tomorrow and I want to get as much of this done as we can before then—"

Mike took a breath and blurted, "I'm pregnant."

Stunned silence pretty much described the situation.

Mike's nervous gaze snapped from Sam to Jo and back again. She gulped at her latte and winced as the hot liquid singed her throat.

"You're—" Sam started.

"Pregnant." Jo finished.

"Yep."

"You're sure?"

She looked at Jo. "*Way* sure."

"How?"

She looked at Sam and lifted an eyebrow. "Did you *see* a star over the house?"

"Right."

"Lucas?" Jo asked.

"Of *course* Lucas," Mike said. "What am I, the Happy Ho?"

"How do you feel?" Sam stared at her.

"Amazing." She shrugged. "Scared. Happy. A little pukey."

Jo gaped at her, amazement clear on her face. "I thought they said you couldn't—"

"Shelley said that it *was* possible. It was just a four percent chance of happening—"

"Man, you beat some serious odds."

"Yeah." Mike took another drink. "I can't believe this."

"What'd Lucas say?" Sam asked.

"Haven't told him yet," Mike admitted and looked down at the white plastic lid of her latte.

"Why the hell not?" Jo took a gulp herself. "You're going to, right?"

"Yeah. I am. I'm just . . ."

"Nervous?"

"Good word. Another word is— Never mind. 'Nervous' works."

"What're you waiting for?"

She looked at Jo. "He's not gonna believe me. I told him I *couldn't* get pregnant."

"Why wouldn't he believe you?" Sam demanded.

Mike blinked at her. "Hello? Paying attention? *Pregnant* here."

"Yeah, but you don't lie."

Mike smiled at Jo. "Thanks. I know that. You know that. But how does *he* know that?"

"We can go with you. Like character witnesses," Sam offered.

Mike laughed shortly. "Thanks, but I don't really want my sisters there while I break it to Lucas that he's about to enter the Daddy Zone."

A wind straight off the ocean blew at the three of them, lifting their hair, twining around them, as if trying to bind them even closer together.

"Whoa, what's Papa gonna say?" Sam wondered suddenly.

"Oh man . . ." Mike hadn't even thought about breaking this to her father. Unmarried and pregnant is not most fathers' dream for their little girls. Although, she might have timing on her side. How much could he say when they'd all just discovered the existence of Jack?

"Don't worry about Papa," Jo said, not surprisingly, "what do *you* want to do?"

Mike held her latte in one hand and braced her other, palm flat, against her belly. "I want to have a baby. You guys," she said on a soft breath of wonder, "I never thought this would happen to me. I mean, I was okay with being the really cool aunt, but deep down, it hurt. Knowing I could never have what most women take for granted."

"Oh, Mike . . ."

"Don't cry," Jo told Sam gruffly, "your vision'll blur and you'll fall off the roof and then what'll I do for help?"

"You're so sentimental," Mike said wryly.

"I'm plenty sentimental." Jo smiled and held out her right hand. "I'm Italian. We're all about sentimental. And the shouting."

"Goes without saying," Sam said with a sniff and a smile as she laid her right hand on top of Jo's.

"I'm gonna be a mom," Mike said and dropped her own right hand on top of her sisters'.

Jo grinned. "God help us all."

19

Lucas felt like he'd been dragged behind a Porsche for a couple of miles, then run over just for fun.

He was tired, pissed off, and on edge. Watching his brother die was eating away at him and he couldn't find a cure. He should have told Justin about the baby. Should have given the man at least *that*. But since he'd promised Bree, he couldn't.

Damn it, Justin deserved to know.

Taking the stairs two at a time, he headed for his office. With Bree and Justin sitting out on the back deck, Lucas figured he could take an hour or two. Lose himself in some dry clinical research. Research on nanotechnology. The thing he *knew* would one day save patients just like Justin.

Only it wouldn't be in time to save his brother.

Watery winter sunlight slid through the tall, narrow window at the end of the hall, lying across the dark red tiles, making them shine. Lucas hardly noticed. As he stalked along the hallway, frustration kept pace with him.

It chewed on him, reminding him that he hadn't been smart enough, or fast enough, to make the technology of the future available *today*. If he was so damn smart, why hadn't he worked harder? Faster? Why couldn't he *do* something? Why did he feel so damn helpless?

"Lucas?"

He stopped fast, his running shoes squeaking on the tiles. Looking through the open door to his bedroom, he spotted Mike, watching him. God. Everything in him relaxed. When had she become the barometer of his emotions? How had she gotten so completely under his skin that one look into her pale blue eyes could ease tension or fire desire?

Office forgotten, he stepped into the room and frowned as she backed up a step. Although she was silhouetted by the afternoon sunlight streaming in through his bedroom window—she'd been right about that "solar flare" thing, too—he could still see that her features were taut, her eyes wary.

Instantly, he went on alert. "What's wrong?"

"Nothing," she said, and her tone convinced him she was lying.

"When did you get home?" *Home.* Jesus. When had he started thinking that his house was home to Mike? About the time the rest of his world fell apart?

"Just got here a few minutes ago," she said and took another step back, around the end of the bed.

"What's going on?"

"I—*we*—have to talk."

"Ominous."

"No, it's good." She grinned quickly, briefly, then waved both hands as if she didn't know quite what to do with them. "At least," she continued, "*I* think it's good. Great, really. Although you might not think so, and by the way, I'd totally understand if you don't, but the not knowing is why I'm a little shook here. Well, that and the pukey thing is back—"

"You're still sick?" he asked, concern ripping through him at light speed. Nausea might be nothing. But it could also be the forerunner of a lot of *somethings*, too. And with Justin . . . "What'd the doctor say?"

"Well, that's why I'm here."

She'd come directly from work, as always. Her jeans were faded and torn at the knee. Her boots were dry and cracked and the letters of MARCONI CONSTRUC-TION were peeling away from her dark blue T-shirt. Her blond hair was in its familiar braid, but her face was pale and her sky blue eyes looked . . . *worried.*

"What's going on?"

"I went by Papa's house before I came," she said, and waved one hand at the bed. "Wanted to get my medical records to show you."

Only then did he notice the stack of manila envelopes, loose papers, and a small, three-ring binder. Confusion had him shifting his gaze to her. "Why do I need to see your records?" Something cold fisted around his heart. "Is there something seriously wrong with you?"

"No, not at all. Not wrong. Really, *really* right."

"I'm confused." He shoved his hands into his jeans pockets and waited.

"Yeah, I'm getting that." She grinned again, then wiped the smile away with one hand. "Okay, the best way to do this is to just do it. Like pulling off a Band-Aid, right? Fast."

He took a step closer to her but she held up a hand to keep him at bay.

"Lucas, I'm *pregnant*."

Blood roared in his ears. His mouth went dry and he tried hard to swallow. Something a lot like panic coiled in the pit of his stomach, but Lucas ignored it. For the moment.

"Pregnant?"

"Yeah." She grinned again, then folded her arms in front of her. "Shelley says I'm just barely pregnant, but little whozit's in there all right."

"Shelley."

"Baker. My doctor."

"Right."

"Are you okay?"

"Fine," he said and scrubbed both palms over his face. He'd just been hit in the head with a metaphorical two-by-four, but yeah. He was great. Shooting her a quick look, he said, "But you said you couldn't *get* pregnant. Because of the accident you told me about."

"I know, I know." She shook her head wildly enough to send her braid flapping back and forth. "Hey, I was as surprised as you look, believe me."

He found *that* hard to believe.

"I know what you're thinking," she said slowly, keeping her gaze fixed on him.

"Oh, I doubt that." Hell, even *he* didn't know what he was thinking.

"I brought all my medical stuff over so you could see that I didn't lie to you before. There really was almost zero chance of me getting pregnant."

"And yet . . ."

"Yeah." A short laugh shot from her throat and she dropped her arms to her middle and gave herself a hug.

"Guess your little guys are like commandos or something," she said, dropping her hands to her sides, then shoving them into the front pockets of her jeans. "The little buggers just stormed through and set up camp."

"My little guys." This was the most bizarre conversation he'd ever had.

"I didn't lie to you, Lucas," she said and pulled her hands out of her pockets before folding them at her waist. "If you'll just look at the records . . ."

"Don't have to," he said, still trying to think. Trying to figure out what the hell to say—to *do*. "I believe you."

"You believe me."

"Yeah." He looked at her and shrugged.

"Just like that?"

"You are *many* things, Michaela Marconi—but you're not a liar."

"Thanks." She blew out a breath and gave him a staggeringly wide smile. "It means a lot that you trust me on this."

"Of course I do."

"God, I'm glad to hear you say that," she said. "I was so worried you'd be all pissed off and crabby."

She bent over the bed and gathered up all the files, shoving loose papers into folders, stacking envelopes. "It's like a miracle or something, Lucas."

"Yeah," he murmured. "So I guess there really *is* something in the water."

She straightened up, and looked at him cautiously. "I know this is really new for you. I mean, I only found out an hour or so ago and I'm a little shaky with it myself, but I'm really excited, Lucas. Really. I'm gonna have a *baby*."

"Yeah." He walked to the edge of the bed and sat down. Looking up at her, Lucas could almost *see* exhilaration rippling off her like waves crashing against the shore. She practically glowed.

A baby.

He was going to be a father.

"I don't know what to say to you," he said.

She laughed shortly, and if it sounded a little strained, Lucas figured she had reason. "Look, you don't have to *say* anything. You don't have to *do* anything."

"What?" Her words pinged around inside him like steel balls ricocheting around the inside of an empty can.

"I'm telling you because you have a right to know—" she said. "Not because I expect anything from you." She pulled in a breath and kept going before he could say anything.

"I'm going to have this baby, Lucas." She covered her belly with one hand as if she could protect it from hearing anything it shouldn't. "Because for me, this is a one-in-a-million chance. This baby is alive inside me and she's—he's—*it's* going to stay that way."

Slowly, Lucas stood up and looked down at her. "Did I say anything at all about you getting rid of my child?"

"No," she acknowledged, "but just in case you were thinking it, you can forget about it."

For the first time, a flicker of anger sputtered to life inside him. Not surprising, really, since so much of his time around Mike was spent being mad. "And what have *you* decided is *my* part in all this?"

"No need to get pissy now," she said, planting both

hands on her hips and staring up at him through narrowed eyes. "I'm trying to be *nice* here."

"Doing a helluva job."

"Well, it's not easy being nice to a dumb ass."

"Most of the scientific community considers me a genius," he pointed out. "And the mother of my child calls me a dumb ass."

She sucked in air and then paused, holding it in and tapping the toe of one boot heavily against the floor. He was willing to bet she was counting to ten.

"Fine, you're not a dumb ass. But the point is, I'm the one who's pregnant and I'm the one who's going to call the shots. Starting with—" She walked to the other side of the bed, picked up her packed duffel bag and swung it around to drop onto the mattress.

"What're you doing?" He had a bad feeling about this.

"I'm moving out of your house," she said, as she stuffed her medical records into the open bag and then zipped it closed.

"What?" He grabbed her arm and turned her around to face him. "Why? Why now?"

"I'm pregnant now."

"So?"

"So, it's not . . ." She hissed a sigh, looked embarrassed, and then blurted, "We can't be living together, okay? I'm gonna be a mother. What kind of example is that for the baby?"

He laughed, loud and long, hearing his own voice echo in the cavernous room. Mike's eyes narrowed on him while the laughter rolled out around her, but she didn't try to shut him up.

"Finished?" she asked at last.

"Mike," he argued when he found his voice again, "the baby's the size of a rice grain at the moment."

She scowled at him and slapped one hand protectively against her still flat abdomen. "But she's—he's—there and her, his—damn it, *its*—mother is *not* going to be living in *sin*."

"Sin?" For the second time in ten minutes, she'd stunned him flat. "Thought you didn't go to church anymore."

"I don't," she admitted, scowling. "But trust me on this, when you least expect it, Catholic guilt comes roaring out of the shadows and slaps you back into line."

She meant it. She was leaving. He watched her finish zipping the bag, then fold the Velcro handle closed over the twin straps. She'd been here, in his house, for more than two weeks and now he couldn't imagine *not* having her here.

He was used to hearing her voice in the night. Watching her in the kitchen as she leaned over that first cup of coffee in the morning. He liked watching her at the lake's edge, tossing bread slices into the water for the ducks. He enjoyed hearing her talk about what she did all day and looked forward to having her curl up against him at night.

When had she become so important to him?

What the hell was he going to do without her?

"Don't go," he said softly, kneading her upper arm with his thumb.

"Hey, it's not like we won't see each other anymore," she said. "I'm not saying we can't have sex, we just can't be living together . . ."

Because the baby will know if they're living together, but won't know when they have sex? Her disjointed logic rattled him, but he didn't say so. He wasn't that stupid.

"I don't want you to leave, Mike. Especially now."

"I have to go," she said sadly, looking up at him. "Especially now. This . . . arrangement we have, it was never about us being a couple. You said so yourself. Remember?"

He closed his eyes against that memory and wished he could wipe it away. Things had changed since then. *He'd* changed since then.

"This was about neither one of us being alone." She lifted the duffel bag and slung it over one shoulder before he could stop her. "Well, you don't need me as a buffer against Justin anymore. And I'm not alone, either. I've got little Rocky."

"Rocky?"

She smiled. "I can't stay, Lucas. Not now. Not anymore."

Desperate to keep her there, he said, "You're moving back home? But your father's still at Grace's . . ."

If he could just convince her to stay, they could work this out. They could find a way. She had to give him time. Time to find the words.

That sensation of panic was rising within again, then just as it blossomed, it bled away, leaving behind an emptiness he hadn't expected. Hadn't been prepared for.

He had to fight for air. Mike. The woman who'd stomped all over his life in her clunky work boots, changing it forever, was now walking out of it again. And taking his child with her.

His child?

He couldn't really wrap his brain around that concept. It was too ephemeral. Too new.

But losing *Mike*.

That was different.

She'd become such a part of his life over the last few months, he couldn't imagine *not* having her around to drive him insane. Couldn't bear the thought of going back to the quiet, boring life he'd led before they'd met.

"Papa's with Grace," she said, "but it's okay. I'm not going *home* home." She lifted her chin and swung her long blond braid back over her shoulder. "I rented Stevie's old apartment. Over the Leaf and Bean. Doesn't have much of a roof right now, but it's close to coffee and it'll be good. Good for me. Good for little Anastasia—"

"Anastasia?"

"Good for *you*," she finished. "Spend more time with your brother. Enjoy him while you can."

"I can do that with you here," he pointed out.

"No you can't," she said and started past him. "Not anymore."

"Wait."

She stopped and Lucas came up behind her, sliding the duffel bag off her shoulder and taking it himself. "This is too heavy for you. I'll carry it."

"Okay," she said, giving him a smile despite the regret pooled in her eyes. "Thanks."

Lucas looked down at her and knew something was slipping away. Somehow, he'd lost his tenuous grip on the threads of his life and they were all unraveling.

He was losing his twin.

He was losing his child.

He was losing *Mike.*

"Don't ask me to stay again, okay?" Her eyes displayed every emotion she felt and he knew that despite her joy at being pregnant, she was as close to the ragged edge of misery as he was.

So he swallowed his own wants, his own needs, and nodded. "There is one thing, though. Bree and Justin are getting married tomorrow."

"Really?" She gave him a wide smile and it was breathtaking. Her whole face lit up. "That's great. I'm so glad for Bree. And for Justin."

"Will you come?" he asked. "Tomorrow. At two. It'll be just the four of us." He lifted one hand and reached to touch her cheek. But he stopped short and let his hand fall empty to his side.

She swallowed hard. "Sure. I'll be there."

"Thanks."

"You're welcome." Then she touched his face, gently, briefly, and whispered, "God, I hate us being so *polite.*"

Turning abruptly, she walked out, headed for the hall. Lucas stood alone in the sun-washed bedroom, fisted his hand around the duffel strap, and reluctantly followed.

Mike shivered as the minister took his place in front of Justin and Bree. Here on the back deck at Lucas's house, the wind was cold and the sky was gray. As if even nature were already mourning a marriage that would be too brief.

There were vases filled with chrysanthemums and a

string of white lights ringing the deck railing. Autumn leaves provided the music as they brushed together in the sighing wind.

Standing beside Lucas, Mike tried to keep her mind on the ceremony, but it wasn't easy. She'd been up half the night. First, trying to feel comfortable in a place that didn't—and would probably *never*—feel like home. The apartment over the shop was lovely, mostly wood and glass and a few braided rugs for warmth. It was furnished with a big, comfortable bed, a TV, some chairs, and it had a small kitchenette.

Mike had been unpacked in about five minutes, then she'd spent the next hour trying to figure out why she was there—and not with Lucas. Oh God, she'd wanted to come back here, to him. And knowing she couldn't—*shouldn't*—had made her head hurt and her stomach spin.

Then Papa had arrived and bad got worse.

He'd come by her new apartment, demanding to know what was going on. Why she was moving out on her own. Why Jo and Sam wouldn't tell him anything.

When she explained about the baby, he'd been torn between real pleasure for her sake and pure fatherly fury. He wanted to know when she was getting married, and when she'd told him she wasn't, that had really set him off. Watching his face turn bloodred, she'd worried for a while that he was going to have another heart attack.

But true to his nature, she thought, his anger went white-hot, then fizzled out just as quickly.

"Michaela, I worry for you." Papa looked into her eyes and shook his head slowly. *"You know about Jack.*

You know what a hard time Carol has had, raising him mostly alone."

"I won't be on my own, Papa. I'll have you. And Sam. And Jo."

"It is not the same as having the one you love beside you."

"I know, but—"

"Don't make my mistakes, Michaela," he warned.

"Papa, it's not that simple." She stepped away from him and wandered the gleaming wood floor of the apartment that felt too empty. Too new. Too unwelcoming.

Oh, she wished it were simple. Wished she could tell Lucas that she loved him, and be sure that he would say those three words back to her. But how could she? They hadn't made any promises to each other. There'd been no talk of a future.

So instead of being with the man she loved, she was here. In an apartment she didn't really want, preparing to be a single mother.

And since she'd have to be tough to pull that off, she thought she might as well start working on it now.

"You don't have to worry, Papa," she said again firmly, not sure if she was trying to convince him or herself.

He walked to her. "It's my job to worry. You'll see. That doesn't stop just because your child is grown. Your child will always be your child. And to see that child hurt or in pain is a hard thing."

Mike wrapped her arms around him and held on, finding comfort in the familiar strength of him. Papa patted her back and dropped a kiss on top of her head.

"You want me to talk to your Lucas?"

"*God, no, Papa,*" *she said, snuggling closer, content for the moment to feel a little less alone.* "*This is for me to figure out.*"

"*But you love him?*"

"*Oh yes. I love him. Enough to know that telling him now would be the most wrong thing I could do.*"

He leaned back and looked down into her eyes. "*How is loving wrong?*"

"*There's too much now,*" *she said.* "*Too much in his life. His twin brother is* dying. *He needs to take care of Justin. I can take care of myself.*"

Her father held her and sighed. "*Sometimes you can be too strong, Michaela. Sometimes it's better to lean a little. To hold and be held. To give the one you love a chance to be strong for you.*"

"I will," Bree said softly, and her voice brought Mike out of her memories and back to the house beside the lake.

A little disoriented, she drew in a long breath to steady herself. Then Lucas, standing beside her, took her hand and gave it a squeeze.

Mike's heart turned over in her chest, but she clung to the warmth of Lucas's touch as Justin promised to love Bree until *death* did them part.

20

Lucas opened the front door a week later and found Mike standing on his front porch. She was wearing a dark green sweatshirt over her T-shirt and her jeans were still clean—too early in the morning for her to have come from work.

Just seeing her again was a gift.

She'd only been to the house twice in the week since the wedding and both times she'd been there to pick up Bree and get her out of the house for an hour or two. Mike had come and gone so quickly during those brief visits, he'd had no chance at all to talk to her—and a part of him wondered if she'd arranged it that way purposely.

To avoid him. His hand tightened on the edge of the door, in an attempt to keep from reaching for her. Looking into her eyes, soft and open, was like falling into a cool lake on a hot day.

"Lucas?"

"Mike." God, he'd missed her. Missed being able to talk to her. Argue with her. Missed everything about her. "You here to take Bree out for coffee again?"

"No . . ."

"I phoned her. Asked her to come." Bridget's voice, soft and hurried, came from directly behind him.

Spinning around, he faced his brother's wife. Something cold and dark opened inside him as he registered the pain in her eyes. "What's going on, Bree?"

She wiped away a single stray tear that rolled along her stark white cheek. "I called Mike because she should be here. With us."

"What?" He cleared his throat, but it didn't help.

"It's time, Lucas," Bree said. "Justin will want his family near."

His family.

That's what they'd become, the four of them. Family. And since Mike had left, that family had been broken. He hadn't been able to touch her, hold her, and God, he'd missed that. Missed having her close. Missed turning around to find her blue eyes fixed on him.

Suddenly, something else Bree'd said hit him hard, like a punch to the stomach, exploding his breath.

"Time?" His throat closed up tight. He felt it shut down and wondered how he was still able to breathe. "Now? Already?" He swallowed hard enough to push a tangled knot of emotion down his throat. Glancing at the staircase and the guest room above, Lucas felt a clawing instinct to run. To just bolt out of the house and sprint into the trees. To somehow escape the helplessness that had him in its grip. How could he stand by and watch his brother die?

Why couldn't he do . . . *something*?

As if she could read his mind, Mike whispered,

"Sometimes the only thing we can do is be there."

"Not enough," he muttered, blindly reaching for her hand and holding on as he looked at her. "How can that be enough?" Then desperate, he shifted his gaze to Bree. "How do you know? How can you be sure?"

A tired, wistful smile brushed her lips, then faded. "I love him," she said simply, her voice a sad shadow, flavored by Irish music. "How could I *not* know?"

"You're wrong." He pushed the words past his throat, shaking his head, fighting the inevitable even as he knew he couldn't win.

"I'm not, no," she said sorrowfully. "Wish to heaven I were."

Tears pumped inside him, but he couldn't let them through. Couldn't let loose the howling grief that wanted to rattle the windows and rage at the sky. Couldn't do a damn thing but let Justin go.

"Ah, God . . ." Lucas's head dropped, banging into the door behind him. Eyes closed, he stood perfectly still for a moment, concentrating on the small ache in his head, because otherwise he'd have to focus on the enormous pain in his heart.

And he wasn't sure he'd survive it.

Mike stepped closer, laid her free hand on his forearm and left it there, as if she knew how much he needed that connection. That warmth, streaming in to ease the tremendous cold filtering through him. He pulled in a long breath, steadied himself and nodded, as if to reassure himself that they would get through this. Somehow.

"Come now," Bree said, stepping back and turning for the stairs. "Quickly."

"Lucas . . ." Mike whispered his name and then stopped, as if she didn't know what to say. But she didn't have to try. Because there was nothing she *could* say. Nothing any of them could say to stop the pain. To hold back time. To change the past.

"I'm so glad you're here." He squeezed her hand and held on. Pulling her inside, he swung the door closed and took off after Bridget, Mike keeping pace with him, their heels on the tiles clattering loudly in the still, silent house.

His heartbeat raced, his blood rushed, and the roaring in his ears was deafening. Fear chased him up the stairs, reaching for him with grasping, greedy fingers, and he didn't know how to fight it. Didn't know that he *could.*

When they reached the guest room, Bree was already inside, sitting beside Justin on the bed. She held one of his hands in hers, stroking his skin in long, smooth caresses.

Early morning light sifted into the room as gently as a promise. One of the windows was partially opened and a breeze ruffled the pale green sheers, making them dance lazily. Outside, the ducks on the lake quacked and squabbled, bringing life into the room where death hovered.

One look at Justin's face and Lucas knew the truth. He felt it, just as surely as Bree must have. She was right. When you loved someone, you just *knew.*

Mike's hand in his felt warm, strong. He held on tighter, using her to anchor himself.

The connection was *that* strong.

And he thanked God for it.

Moving to the bed, Lucas stood beside Bridget, laid one hand on her shoulder, wrapping his other arm around Mike's shoulder, unconsciously drawing her tightly into the circle they'd formed around Justin. Lucas watched, unable to look away, as his brother's chest moved in a faltering rhythm.

Each breath following the last just a little slower than the one before.

Seconds ticked past, marked by the heartbeats of those who watched and waited.

Justin opened his eyes, and for the first time in days, his dark eyes looked clear, almost overbright. As if he were already seeing something none of them could imagine and couldn't quite focus on the vision. He looked at each of them and managed a smile.

His voice, when it came, was hardly more than a breath.

"I don't know why I was so afraid of this." Another brief smile as he looked at his brother. "Thanks for . . ." He paused. "Hell. You know."

Lucas nodded, tightened his grip on both women, and blinked back the moisture clouding his eyes. He forced a smile that he feared was more of a grimace, but damned if he'd cry when the man dying was being so brave.

"Bree . . ." Justin looked up at her. Smiled. "I know. About the baby."

"Aw, love . . ." Her voice broke, and tears streamed down her face.

"I'm so glad," he whispered, still smiling as he closed his eyes and sighed his last breath.

As Bridget wept and Mike turned her face into his

shoulder, Lucas felt . . . *humbled.* He'd always thought that no matter what, everyone died alone. But it wasn't true.

The lucky ones died with family.

With love.

He bent his head to Mike's and quietly mourned his twin and all the tomorrows he had lost.

A few hours later, while Lucas was on the phone, making . . . arrangements for Justin's cremation, Mike spotted Bree, standing alone at the edge of the lake. The ever-present wind lifted the woman's long, red curls into a tangle around her, but she seemed oblivious. Staring out at the ducks on the lake, Bree might have been a statue, carved by an empathetic sculptor to represent sorrow.

Every curve and line of her body wept.

And Mike's tender heart fisted in her chest.

Slipping out the French doors, she quietly crossed the deck, and took the stairs to the grass below. She felt as though she were intruding, but she simply couldn't stay away. Bree was alone, now. Horribly alone, and the pain was so new, so fresh, that Mike couldn't turn her back.

"Bree?"

The woman slowly turned her head to look at her and smiled. Though her green eyes were filled with anguish and the shimmer of tears unshed, her smile was steady—surprising the hell out of Mike.

"Are you okay?" she asked, even knowing how stupid it sounded. People always asked that: *Are you okay with the way your world just ended?*

Idiot.

"I'm sorry," Mike said softly. "Ridiculous question."

But Bree reached out one hand to her, and when Mike took it, she said, "No it isn't. And I'm fine, really."

"I wish there was . . . *something* I could do," Mike said, waving one hand helplessly.

A long moment ticked past before Bree smiled again, even as a solitary tear trickled down her cheek. "There's no need for you to feel sorry for me, Mike."

"Bree . . ."

She shook her head, drew in a short breath and let it go again on a sigh as her gaze shifted back to the lake. The wind danced across the water, ruffling the reeds at the bank and rippling the surface until it looked as though each ripple moved into the next and the next and the next, moving into eternity.

"I've lost Justin," she said and her voice broke on the words.

Mike squeezed her hand a little tighter and let her own tears flow.

"But at least I *had* him," Bree added. "Some people live their whole lives never knowing what it is to really *love*. To feel it, as I did, bone deep inside me. To hold it in my heart, my soul. To be so filled with the light of it that no matter how dark things may get, the shadows will never reach me."

Mike's throat closed and her heart pounded in an achingly slow rhythm that seemed to echo over and over inside her. She felt the same way about Lucas. The difference was, for however briefly, Bree had known her love was returned.

And everything in Mike longed to feel that herself. To know that Lucas loved her as she did him. She didn't want him to want her just for the baby—the miracle of the child they'd created. She wanted the soul stirring, down to the bone love that Bree had found with Justin.

She'd never thought to find this chance at the Fairy Tale. And now that it was here, she wanted it *all*.

Bree spoke again and Mike focused on her. How could she not, as Bree stared intently into her eyes as if wanting to share the secrets of the universe.

And maybe she was.

"Justin gave me that kind of love. And I to him." Bree lifted her chin and tossed her windblown hair back from a face that was etched in sorrow, but proudly defiant at the same time. *"Nothing,"* she said, "not even death, can take that from me. I've no regrets save one—that Justin will never know his child."

She dropped one hand to her still flat abdomen and Mike could have sworn she felt the tiny child inside her stir in solidarity.

"Love is all there is, Mike," Bree said softly. " 'Tis the only thing that lasts . . . *forever.*"

Mike moved up beside her and the two women stared across the lake, as if trying to look into eternity.

"Tell me again why Sam isn't helping us finish this roof?" Mike demanded four days later.

Jo slammed her hammer against a roofing nail, driving it through the shingle with one neat stroke. "She's over at Mrs. Giuliani's painting the living room. The money fairy stopped by a couple weeks ago. Left enough money for the old lady to fix her house up before her son comes to visit."

"Busy fairy," Mike mused.

"Not lately," Jo said between hammer blows. "Been a couple weeks now since the fairy left anything. People are starting to worry she's stopped."

"She?"

"Or he." Jo shrugged. "Whoever."

Mike couldn't really care less about the money fairy's identity at the moment. She had other, bigger things on her mind. She stopped working, dangled her hammer from one hand, and looked at her sister. A full ten seconds passed before Jo felt her staring and glared back.

"What?"

"It's been four days."

"Since . . ."

"Since the funeral, Jo. God. Keep up."

Her sister scowled and shook her head. "Have I mentioned lately that you're crazy?"

"Four days and I haven't heard from him."

"Lucas?"

"No, Brad Pitt," Mike said snidely. "I'm just devastated."

"Hey, who wouldn't be?"

"Damn it, Jo, I'm worried about him. He's all alone at his place now that Bree's gone back to Ireland."

"So go see him."

"I can't."

Jo gave a dramatic sigh. "If you make me hit myself in the head with a hammer, I'm gonna be so pissed."

Mike blew out a breath and looked out over Chandler from her perch on Stevie's nearly completed roof. Even early on a weekday morning, things were hopping. Life went on, she knew that.

She just didn't know if *Lucas* knew that.

Sunlight poured down on them from a brilliantly blue winter sky with white clouds scuttling across its surface. From the street below came the muted hum of traffic and disjointed snatches of conversations. The cold ocean wind raced across the rooftops and Mike shivered.

"Well, how long should I wait?" she mumbled.

"For *what*?"

"God," Mike muttered and briefly considered pitching Jo off the roof. But then she'd have to finish the job herself and she was already tired. Little Horatio was really sucking her energy. "Don't you listen to me at all?"

Jo snorted. "Hard *not* to listen. You talk all the damn time."

"Damn it, Jo, this is serious." Mike turned and plopped onto her butt, as at home on a roof as she would have been in her living room. Actually, more so, since her living room was now in Stevie's old apartment and that place still didn't feel like home. "I don't know the etiquette on this."

"*Etiquette?*" Jo laughed and sat down herself. "Since when are *you* concerned with etiquette?"

"Since now, basically." Mike studied the hammer she held and twisted it in her hands so that the sunlight caught the old metal and glinted into her eyes. "I mean, Lucas just lost his brother. How long am I supposed to wait before telling him I love him?"

"You are *so* asking the wrong person," Jo admitted, then added, "And why are you suddenly doubting yourself? You've always had enough self-confidence for three healthy people."

"I'm not doubting *me*," she snapped, irritated that Jo just wasn't getting what had her so twisted up inside. "I'm doubting what to *do*."

"Don't know why," Jo said. "If you want him, go get him, like you have every other thing you've ever wanted. Hunt him down like a dog and drag him home."

Mike shook her head and kept her gaze locked on the glinting sunlight. "This is different. It's fragile, sort of. He just lost his twin brother. I mean, how'm I supposed to say, 'Wake up, time to live again'? How can I tell him that I care without scaring him off?"

"Okay." Jo sighed. "I get that you love him. Why not just say so?"

Glancing at her sister, Mike took a long moment before answering. She'd been thinking about this a lot over the last several days. She'd considered her options from every direction and still hadn't come up with a plan. Which was damn frustrating for a woman who *always* knew what to do and when to do it.

"It's not enough to hunt him down and drag him home," she finally said. "I want him to *love* me. You know?"

Jo nodded. "Yeah. I can see that."

"No one's ever been there for Lucas. I want him to know *I* will be. He's lost everyone he's ever loved. His parents, a fiancée—who was an idiot, in my opinion—and now Justin. How do I convince him he won't lose me? How do I make him believe that I want *him*—not just because we made little Sophia together—"

"Sophia?"

Mike ignored the interruption. "—but because I love him more than I ever thought I'd love anybody." She looked at Jo. "How do I do that?"

Blowing out a breath, her older sister hooked her hammer to the worn leather belt she wore around her waist and jerked her thumb at the ladder, peeking over the roof's edge. "Okay, we need a coffee break."

"What? That's not what I need. I need *help* here." Mike stuck her own hammer into a belt loop. "Sisterly help. Understanding. *Sympathy,* damn it."

"I'll give you sympathy, you annoying little shit. I'll give you coffee. As to the rest, I just don't know." Jo stopped and stared at her. "When it comes to love, I know *zip*. And frankly," she added with a knowing look at Mike, "judging by what it's doing to *you*, I don't want to know. From the outside, love looks like it sucks the big one."

"You're wrong," Mike said, her voice going low and dreamy, despite the frustration swarming inside her. "It's great."

"Oh yeah. I'm convinced."

"It's just . . . *confusing.*"

"Not just coffee, then. Coffee and a muffin. Good for clearing away confusion," Jo said, stalking toward the ladder, leaning back with the slope of the roof.

Mike laughed shortly. "Since when is a muffin brain food?"

Jo looked back at her and shrugged. "Since we need it to be. Come on, Mike. Coffee and sympathy, on me."

It wasn't a solution, Mike told herself as she moved to follow her older sister. But it was the best offer she'd had all morning.

Lucas wandered through his empty house and idly wondered if it had *always* been this big—or if it just *felt* bigger now that he was alone?

His running shoes made almost no sound on the tiles as he walked from the great room, headed for the back deck. He pushed the sliding door open and, instantly, a rush of icy wind raced past him, as if it had been sitting on the deck, waiting for a chance to get inside the house.

The trees were at their most colorful—brilliant splashes of orange, yellow, and deep crimson. On the lake, the ducks he'd come to think of as belonging here made slow, lazy circles on the water.

Lucas glanced at the Adirondack chair where his brother had spent so many hours and his heart ached. Ached for all they'd lost. All they'd missed.

Ached for Justin himself—for the life he wouldn't lead, for the love he wouldn't have, for the child he wouldn't know.

But along with the pain came something else. A kind of admiration he hadn't really expected. Closing his hands over the iron railing at the edge of the deck, Lucas focused blindly on those damn ducks and recognized a simple truth.

Being given a death sentence hadn't stopped Justin from finding love, creating life, sucking every last drop of joy out of every minute left to him. He'd lived—and died—the way he wanted to.

And he'd left with no regrets.

How many people could say that?

In dying, Justin had shown Lucas how to live.

Tipping his head back, Lucas stared up at the wind-blown sky overhead and spoke softly. "Not sure if I'm looking in the right direction . . ." He paused to smile at a joke that Justin could have appreciated. "But I want you to know that I'll miss you. And I'll look after your child. Make sure Bree and the baby are safe."

From deep inside the house, the sound of the door-bell rang out and Lucas scowled as he glanced over his shoulder at the interruption. A second later, though, the scowl disappeared.

Life.

A stupid doorbell was a reminder that life went on—in spite of everything. When it rang again, he forgot about philosophy and stalked back through the house to answer the summons.

He yanked open the door in time to see a van, with the words DONOVAN IRON WORKS stenciled on the side, pulling out of his driveway. A large, flat card-board box had been left on his porch and Lucas bent to pick it up.

Carrying the heavy package into the living room, he set it down on the apothecary table and pulled up the cardboard flaps. Inside was a fireplace screen. Black, curving iron was backed with gleaming black metal net and on the front of the screen: "A *parrot*."

Lucas laughed out loud, snatched up the screen and carried it to the fireplace. Setting it in front of the now cold hearth, he stepped back, stared at the stupid parrot, and felt the last of the pain drain away.

Still laughing, he shouted, "God, I *love* that woman."

In the Leaf and Bean, the late-morning crowd was mostly regulars. A few tourists were sprinkled in to keep things interesting, but in the winter months, Stevie's was a place for people in Chandler to gather and gossip.

Mike and Jo had a corner table all to themselves and they'd each already plowed through two blueberry muffins and two lattes. She wasn't any closer to an answer, but she felt better somehow just stuffing herself, with her sister for company.

When the front door flew open and Lucas charged inside, Mike almost spewed a mouthful of latte right into Jo's face.

His gaze darted around the inside of the shop until he found Mike. Then, keeping that gaze fixed on her, he stalked across the crowded floor, weaving in and out of the tables and chairs, ignoring the stunned faces of the people watching him.

Mike kept her gaze locked on his. She'd never seen Rocket Man so charged up. Worry sneaked up her spine, but was quickly swallowed by an instinctive surge of defiance. If he had a problem with her, then she was ready to take him on.

He stopped at their table and nodded at her sister. "Jo. Good to see you."

"Yeah," she said, "you look real happy about it."

He ignored that and focused on Mike. She was all he

could see. All he'd *wanted* to see for months. How stupid of him to not have admitted it sooner. How stupid of him to waste even a *moment* of what they could have together. "Had to see you," he finally said. "Figured you'd be in your apartment. But here works."

"What's going on, Lucas?" This was so not how she'd imagined seeing him again.

She'd pictured him sitting alone in his house, miserable, lonely. Hell, she'd *counted* on him being miserable and lonely without her. She'd thought that when she finally went to see him, he'd be so glad to find her on his doorstep that he'd sweep her into his arms, kiss her senseless, and *beg* her to marry him.

Okay, so it was a sappy dream.

No one had to know she'd indulged in it, did they?

"You bought me a *parrot*," Lucas blurted.

"A parrot?" Jo echoed, looking from Lucas to Mike and back again.

"On the fire screen," he said, still ignoring Jo. "It came today. There's a parrot on it."

"Oh, crap," Mike muttered and stood up. The screen she'd ordered from Donovan's. She hadn't even thought about it in weeks. Had planned to cancel it after he'd gotten so pissy about the parrot drawer pulls. "Sorry about that, I forgot to cancel the order and—"

"You bought me a *parrot*," he repeated, and reached for her, grabbing her shoulders with both hands and hanging on.

"Yeah," she said softly, as if reassuring a crazy person, which she was pretty sure he was. "That's been established, and like I said, I'm so—"

"Don't be sorry," he interrupted. "I *like* it. It's hideous and tacky and nothing like what I wanted—and it's perfect."

"Huh?" Brilliant, Mike, *brilliant.*

Someone in the store snorted out a burst of laughter and someone else hushed them. The Leaf and Bean went as still and quiet as it had ever been and Mike felt dozens of pairs of eyes focused on them.

Didn't matter a damn.

All she saw was Lucas.

"The parrot thing—that's just *you*, Mike," he said, laughing, shaking his head in wonder. "You shaking up my house, my world, my *life.* That's why the parrot is perfect. It's so you. And *you're* perfect."

"God, don't tell her that," Jo muttered.

"For me," Lucas qualified quickly. "You're perfect for *me.* And I'm perfect for you."

"Lucas . . ."

He kept talking, faster now, as though she was going to argue with him. "We could stay apart, Mike. Be alone. You and I, we've done alone a long time. And we were good at it. It's not enough, though, Mike. Not for me, not for you. And *together*, we're *great.*"

Mike swallowed hard and focused solely on the emotions churning across the surface of his eyes. But they changed so quickly, she couldn't identify them. She'd have felt a lot better if she'd known what was in his mind.

"I can't live without that," he said quietly, lowering his voice so that only she could hear him now. "Can't live without *you.*"

"Lucas . . ." Tears blurred her vision and she blinked them back frantically, not wanting to miss a moment of this.

"I need you, Mike. I *love* you." He pulled her closer, until she had to tip her head back to keep their gazes locked. "Without you, nothing is right. The house is empty, *I'm* empty."

"Lucas, I love you, I just—"

"I want to marry you, Mike. I want you to drive me nuts every day and I want to hold you every night. I want us to build a life together. I need you in my life, Mike. Without you, there's *nothing*."

"Oh God . . ."

"I want *you*. I want our baby." He bent, brushed a kiss onto her forehead, then straightened up and grinned at her. "I want *surprises*."

Everything in her went warm and liquid. Her knees wobbled and she was grateful for the tight hold he had on her. This was all she'd ever wanted. Someone to love her for *her*.

"Rocket Man," she whispered, reaching up to cup his face between her palms. "I *do* love you."

He grinned. "Thank *God*."

"And yes, I'll marry you."

Behind them, someone applauded.

Jo muttered, "Hallelujah. Now we can get some work done."

Lucas laughed.

"And I promise *plenty* of surprises," she said, going up on her toes to link her arms behind his neck.

Wrapping his arms around her, he lifted her off her feet and laughed even louder. "Bring 'em on, Michaela.

I'm a changed man. With you beside me, I can take anything you can dish out."

"Oh yeah?" she challenged, laughing with him as the crowd got to their feet to cheer. "Here's one for you . . . how do you feel about *twins*?"

Lucas's eyes went wide, he staggered slightly, then found his balance again, just by looking into Mike's shining, laughter-filled eyes.

"Twins?" he managed to croak.

"Surprise!"

Don't miss:

Turn My World Upside Down
Jo's Story

By Maureen Child

Return to Chandler, California, and the wonderful romances of the Marconi sisters. This time, it's Jo's turn...

Coming in August 2005
from St. Martin's Paperbacks

Coming soon from
Maureen Child and Silhouette Desire

❧

Society Page Seduction

in March 2005

and The Three Way Wager trilogy
starring the Reilly triplets—

❧

The Tempting Mrs. Reilly

May 2005

❧

Whatever Reilly Wants

June 2005

❧

The Last Reilly Standing

July 2005

MC 09/04